VEIL RISING

Tales of a Teenage Saint Volume 1

BY

Joshua M Moore

ISBN: 978-1736066126

First and foremost, I'd like to thank my hetero-life-mate, Caleb. Without him, this book never happens.

Also, I'd like to thank my wife and kids, for their conditional support.

Also also, I'd like to thank many other people who inspired and supported me in this. If I had to list you all, the book would be twice as long.

Greater love hath no man than this,

that a man lay down his life for his friends.

~John 15:13

CHAPTER 1

BOY MEETS GIRL (AND VICE VERSA)

Theodore Roosevelt Advanced Learning Academy looked more like a fortress than a high school. Considering what some of the students were, that might have been intentional. The entire compound was surrounded by ten foot high granite walls, and as I walked through the wrought-iron gates, I stood for a moment to take it all in. At least a hundred students walked down a tree-lined path to a large central building, which was three stories tall with two wings on either side. It looked like it belonged in an anime. There was a mural on the main building featuring Teddy Roosevelt in the woods with a standing bear behind him. He was pointing slightly to the side in a heroic pose. I could almost hear him say, "Bully, my boys, tally-ho, and onward."

I covered a yawn. The morning had not been kind to me, nor had the previous night. Moving into a new house the day before school started would have to go down in the "don't" column of things to do. My smartwatch buzzed and I checked the message my mother sent me.

If you don't get these clothes out of bags and into drawers by tomorrow you are going to wear uniforms for a week.

I grimaced at the thought. One of the only good things about our recent move was I no longer had to wear a white polo shirt and blue slacks every day. The downside was that I apparently had abused my freedom by wearing a shirt that I hoped was clean but still smelled like the odor-reducing garbage bag it had been stored in. Pouting Scott was not a neat packer, and Sleepy Scott was not a neat dresser. I took some time to try and straighten out the many creases on my "Zombie Rednecks 2: The South Shall Rise Again" shirt.

As I stood looking around, trying to find anything remotely resembling registration, I felt a tap on my shoulder. I looked back to see a girl who I hoped was about my age. She was pretty. Very pretty. Strawberry blonde hair, blue eyes, a cute, little turned-up nose, and a round face. She had small freckles that skipped elegantly from cheek to cheek across the bridge of her nose.

"You look lost," she said. "New?"

Her smile stunned me for a moment. Some ineffable quality about her tugged at my chest in the best way. I suddenly felt like I should have heeded one of my mother's many warnings against wearing one of my joke shirts and camouflage pants. When she'd told me she wanted people to like me, I'd laughed it off. "It might already be too late for that," I'd told her. Looking at this girl as we sized each other up, I hoped I was wrong. "Yeah. I just moved to town last week. I almost got lost getting here." If I was trying not to sound nervous, I was failing horribly.

"Welcome to TRALA." She giggled and adjusted her backpack. Her blue hoodie hugged her curves. I used the design on it as an excuse for my eyes to linger. It read 'TRALA' above a picture of the twenty-sixth president in a cowboy hat, lifting a club and riding a mean-looking bear. Underneath it was the word 'Bears.'

"Trala?" I asked stupidly. "What's that?"

She smiled and pointed to each letter, "Teddy Roosevelt Advanced Learning Academy."

She giggled again, and my stomach flipped. I could not take in how cute she was, nor could I believe she was talking to me. Was there something wrong with her? "Does anybody call it that?" I slowly moved my eyes back to her face.

"Only all the time."

"Okay, but… why?" I scratched the back of my head. "You could just as easily call it 'Roosevelt,' or even "Roosevelt Academy' or something and not sound so… silly?"

She shrugged. "You should hear the chants. Those jerks from Blomgren call us 'Tralosers.'" She held her hand out. "I'm Riley."

I shook it. It was cool and soft, and I liked the way it felt in mine. I lost track of how long I was holding it. Even though I was almost seventeen, had been playing varsity-level rugby for a year, and my mom swore up and down I was handsome, I didn't have a lot of face time with girls. Let alone pretty girls. Not to mention this one was so far out of my league she was playing a different sport.

I cleared my throat. "Scott." I realized that I was shaking her hand for entirely too long and pulled it back awkwardly. "Do you know where we get our schedules?" I tried desperately to change the subject.

She nodded and brushed her hair away from her face. "Of course, they're on the app."

She grabbed the phone from my hand. She was so close I could smell her vanilla-scented shampoo. The invisible fist in my gut clenched again.

"What year are you?" she asked, looking up.

Our eyes met and my head spun. "Um, Junior. Eleventh grade. However you say it here," I said. It was getting hard to think. I needed to focus. I almost tripped on a boy in black-framed glasses tying his shoes.

"Me, too," she said. "Where are you from? Up north?"

"Uh, sorta, I grew up in Utah." Was Utah north of here?

She tapped on the screen and downloaded the TRALA EDU app. "Oh, are you from Salt Lake City?"

"Everyone always assumes that," I said. "There's more than one city in Utah, you know. Not everyone lives in the same town." By the look on her face, I assumed she was about to apologize. "I mean, I *am*, but I hate how everyone assumes that. People seem to think two things if they hear you are from the 'Beehive State.' One, you are from Salt Lake, and two, you are a Mormon. I am only one of those things."

She hit me lightly on the arm and smiled, letting me know she wasn't upset, which was a huge relief. She gave me back my phone and watched me enter my information from over my shoulder, hugging my left arm. I suddenly noticed every molecule in my face vibrating. It occurred to me I would walk to a million wrong classes if she would just keep holding onto my arm like that. I was doomed, and I liked it.

*   *   *

From the teacher's lounge, my dad watched students mill about in the entryway and quad. He took a sip of his coffee and sniffed. He held no perceptible expression on his face, and his eyes were, as always, hidden behind the mirrored lenses of his wraparound sunglasses. His friend of twenty years stepped next to him. Tony's head reached the top of my dad's shoulders.

"He down there?" Tony Garcia asked while stirring a mug of his own.

"Yup. White shirt, camo pants." He gestured with the "World's Okayest Dad" tumbler I'd gotten him for Father's Day two years prior.

"Next to the girl in the blue sweater?"

"That's the one."

Tony smirked. "Nice."

My dad walked to the sink to dump the rest of his drink. "You'd think with the budget this place has, they wouldn't buy such garbage coffee."

"Be glad you got it." Tony took a sip and winced. "Back in Douglastown-"

"The Fathers didn't let you drink coffee, so you had to use instant coffee like dip." My dad looked up. "I remember."

"Them Catholics are a crazy breed."

"Said the Jesuit."

Tony laughed and returned his attention to me. "He's definitely got more game than you."

"Who's 'at?" A newcomer asked. He was about average height with short brown hair and a bright orange motorcycle jacket.

"Scott's son. Nabbed a piece before first bell," Tony replied

My dad grunted as he washed his mug.

The other teacher looked out of the window, scanning the crowd.

"White shirt, camo pants, next to blue sweater blonde," my dad said.

The new teacher clicked his tongue. "Might could be she's juss bein' friendly." He walked away from the window to the coffee machine. "That's how she is."

"You know her?" my dad asked, turning on the sink and rinsing his tumbler.

"Not err'one's as brand new as y'all. That there's Riley McKinsey." He shot a grin at my dad as he shot his head up. "'Fore you ask, yeah, same McKinsey."

My dad put down his cup. "Like hell." He took a step toward the door.

Duke Lee held out his hand and caught hold of my dad's red leather jacket. "She ain't her dad, ya know. She's a sweet girl."

"She could be cotton candy given human form, for all I care." He tugged his sleeve free, but he didn't continue towards the door.

"Duke's right, bud."

"You don't know her any more than I do, Tony."

Tony shrugged and took another sip. "What's to know? She's a hot girl."

"She's sixteen," Duke reminded him.

"Oh, right, let's all pretend she's hideous until she can vote. Pull your head out, Duke. You know, for most of human history--"

"I don't like it," my dad interrupted.

"Oh, let's all pretend Tony's a pervert 'cause he knows that at sixteen… oh, you meant about McKinsey. That's fine. You don't even like me, and I'm your best friend." He turned to the window again.

Duke joined him. "So y'all are really retirin'?"

My dad shrugged as Tony smirked. "Don't really have a lot of choice. Tony One's been wanting to settle down, and with the situation being what it is…" He took another sip and shuddered.

"Akchully, y'all might wanna get on down there after all."

My dad turned slowly to regard him.

"See that big fella? That's Jim Morgenstern. He don't like it much when boys talk to Riley."

My dad turned back to watch.

"No reaction to that one, huh?"

Antonio smiled. "If there's one thing little Scotty knows, it's fighting."

"I specifically told him not to start any fights," my dad replied. "Though, I might have been unclear about fighting back."

CHAPTER 2

GOOD VIBRATIONS

I stood next to Riley and read my list of classes. It was mostly standard, Math, English, History, and so on, but Individual Advancement was new to me. The schedule just had room numbers and subjects listed, but not who the teachers were. I frowned at the number of honors classes. They meant more work, and I hated work. My mother obviously had some say in my schedule. She was determined to get me into a good college and, as she often told me, four-point-five GPAs don't earn themselves.

"Get anything good?" Riley asked as she scrolled through her own schedule.

I didn't look up. "They're classes, so no," I replied. Her laugh made me smile. "What the heck is 'Individual Advancement?'"

"Hey, there he is," a voice familiar to me said. I looked up to see Tony, my older cousin. His straight, brown hair had blond streaks and was as messy as usual. He approached with a smile. His eyes were a mismatch, one blue and one hazel, and they stood out brightly because of his dark skin. He was a little shorter than I was, even though he was older by about a year.

"Yo, Tony. Long time," I joked. I had seen Tony the day before when he helped us move. "What's Individual Advancement?" My eyes shifted when a boy taller than me by quite a bit walked up behind him. He had a ragged mop of brown hair, a square jaw, and it looked like he was working his way towards not having a neck. He yelled something at a freshman as he ran away. When his gaze fell on me, he glared daggers. Riley shifted nervously beside me. I instinctively stepped in front of her. This seemed to bother the giant.

"It's different for everyone, but they teach you a bunch of..." Tony drifted off when his giant friend stepped between us. "James, I wouldn't..."

I looked up at James, who was about a head taller than I was, musclebound, and audibly growling. Standing as close to me as he was, I could also tell he likely hadn't showered this week. "Good morning," I said as calmly as I could. "Can I help you?"

His only reply to my question was to look between me and Riley and huff. I knew from the stories Tony told of his best friend I was not dealing with a genius. He poked me with a sausage-thick finger. I staggered back a step, my chest aching where the finger had jabbed me. I instantly decided I didn't like this guy.

"James, is it?" I asked, trying my best to keep Angry Scott at bay. I stared as bravely as I could into his eyes. "I'm new here, so I'm not rightly certain how things are done, but tell me--"

"Keep walkin', meat," he growled.

The order cemented my feet. There was a stubborn voice in my head that wanted to do the opposite of what I was told at all times. It was immature, sure, but so was I. "Listen, my dad specifically told me not to start any fights my first day."

His snarl told me there was no avoiding violence. His muscles tensed and he squared up his shoulders.

I rolled my shoulders back to loosen them. "But my dad's not here."

He moved to push me. I sidestepped and punched his arm, doing nothing. I dodged his fist and blocked his next punch. He was so strong that all I managed was to deflect the left hook slightly, getting walloped in the back of the head instead of the face. Dazed, but not daring to yield, I unleashed a flurry into his chest and stepped back to gain distance. He followed, wrapped me in a big hug, and squeezed. I hit him with hands, elbows, and even a knee to the groin, but his grip just tightened. My ribs felt like they might crumble, and I was going to have to exhale eventually. With the force being exerted, I knew getting air back in wasn't an option.

"James, STOP!" Riley shouted, her voice higher-pitched and less controlled than I'd heard it before. I recognized panic. It was not a good sign. The giant didn't let go, but his grip weakened slightly. I took the opportunity to shove my hands down under his arms, push them out as much as possible, and slide down. I got caught on my backpack, but my feet were on the ground. It was something.

I kicked the side of his knee with all the force I could muster. It was just enough to stagger him for a moment. I kicked the opposite side of the same knee with my other foot. He let go with one arm to break his fall, taking me with him. I rolled opposite his controlling arm before we hit the ground and was first to my feet. He was turned around and still bent over as he tried to stand. With two quick steps, I jumped on his back and put him in a rear-naked chokehold, right arm around the front of his massive neck and my hand hooked into my left elbow.

I applied leverage quickly, squeezing with all my might, and pushing his head forward with my left hand. There was a burning in my lungs, and I remembered I was supposed to breathe. All my focus was on bringing this guy down. The world felt like it faded away and it was just the two of us fighting in a spotlight. I didn't even notice that a crowd was forming.

Amazingly, he stood up with me attached like I was a backpack with the world's worst strap design. He tried pulling at my arms, but the lock was in too tight and he couldn't get a grip. He resorted to slamming me against the wall of lockers a few times. I didn't dare let go. He started losing strength, but I kept the hold. He went on one knee, but I didn't dare let go. *Go to sleep!* I thought, as if willing it made the process faster. My arms were burning with the effort of squeezing his solid neck. All I heard was the rush of blood in my ears and his choked grunts.

"I said knock it off," bellowed a voice dripping with authority. It took a moment for the tunnel vision to wear off, and in a rush, the rest of the world joined us again.

I let go and took as many steps back as I could before crouching in a defensive stance while I took my bearings, in case he decided the fight wasn't over. As the adrenalin haze lifted, I became aware of a large crowd making way for a tall blond man in a tan suit.

"What in Zeus' *hairy* butthole are you two playing at?" He stormed toward the two of us. "This is the *first day*, Sunshine," he yelled at James. He reminded me of a younger version of the Drill Instructor from Full Metal Jacket. He turned his gaze to me and my arms fell to my side. I could feel his judgment. "And you must be the *fabulous* Mr. O'Connor," he sneered, staring down at me. "Your dad might be hot shit, but to me, you're just some punk kid starting fights in my hallway. Let's go."

"What?" I protested. "He started it!"

"Oh, you learn that one in Kindergarten, kid?"

"But he--" I began again.

"Mr. Keith," a new man interrupted. He had a deep, soft voice. "If I recall, Master Morgenstern has a history of this behavior. Master O'Connor was likely defending himself." The new teacher was a short man with a long white beard. He seemed genuinely disinterested in the whole affair. He didn't look up from his book as he walked past.

"True," Mr. Keith admitted, calming down quickly. "He's a bit aggro." He looked back at me. "Fly right, O'Connor. Famous parents don't count for much here." He turned and walked away, grabbing the back of James' shirt and tugging him along as he went.

"Bro, are you okay?" Tony asked. "Do you need to see the nurse or something?"

"How can a nice guy like you be friends with a guy like that?" I asked with a groan.

He shrugged and looked down the hallway. "Opposites attract, I guess." He shrugged again.

"Oh," I said with an epiphany. "I didn't know you were..." I trailed off.

"What? Friends?"

"No," I struggled. "You know…" I held out a hand and wobbled it from side to side. "Not that there's anything wrong with that."

"He's not gay," said a short kid who appeared beside me. He stood less than shoulder high, maybe to my armpit. He looked like he should be in one of those magazines that teenage girls read. His hair was just tousled enough that I suspected it took a great deal of time to achieve. His hazel-green eyes sparkled with mischief. "Dense as custard, but not gay."

"Woah, you thought I was gay?" Tony asked, surprised. He paused. "Not that there's anything wrong with that."

"No," I replied quickly. "But I just realized we never talked about…" I drifted off and looked at the smaller kid, who was standing right next to me. He was examining me like I was a museum exhibit. "Can I help you with something?"

"Well, can you fix lockers? Cause you broke mine," he said coolly, pointing at the dented sheet of metal.

"*I* didn't break it," I said and pointed down the hall. "That guy did. You wouldn't blame the baseball bat for your busted mailbox."

"My *box* is not the issue," he said with a troublesome grin. The way he said it made me suspect he was making an innuendo.

"Urchin, don't be gross," Riley said. She handed me my phone and brushed something off my shoulder. Her hand lingered on my deltoid. I glanced at her and she removed it, brushing some hair behind her ear, which was slightly flushed.

"I'm not gross, I'm just written that way," he replied. He gave me a wink and walked off without grabbing anything from his locker. The mental overload was starting to wear away my patience.

"Ok, pause," I said. "Who was *that* guy?" I pointed at Urchin's back, then turned to Tony. "Why are giants trying to kill me?" I turned back to Riley. "Did the whole world just wake up this morning and choose violence?"

Riley and Tony looked at each other, but the bell rang before they could speak.

Tony looked at his empty wrist where a watch should be and shrugged. "Another time, Cuz. I've got IA, and that's *way* across campus." He took off in a sprint and almost knocked a girl down in his rush. I closed my eyes and took a deep breath.

"Come on," Riley said. "We both have history in A207. We can walk and talk." She grabbed my arm again and we started walking. "The cute boy is Urchin. Nobody really knows a lot about him. I think he's a Sinner, 'cause he's able to figure a lot out about you after only talking to you or watching you for a little bit."

"Wait, what? How does sinning make him good at reading people?" My brain was still in fight mode, and I wasn't really processing her words properly.

"Not 'sin' like the bible," she explained. "I assumed 'cause Mr. Keith knew your dad that you were in the know."

"In the know about what?"

She didn't answer right away.

I changed the subject, but not to a better one. "Does that James guy have a crush on you, or does he hate you?"

"Both," she said eventually. She sighed and shook her head, taking a hairband from her hoodie pocket to put her wavy hair in a ponytail. "We dated a while a few years ago. He was nicer then. A lot nicer." She sighed again, this time more dramatically. "When he hit his growth spurt, he really changed. He got jealous of anybody that looked at me. I couldn't take it, so I broke up with him." She smiled grimly. "He did not take it well."

"So now if he can't have you, no one else can?" I mused.

"I don't know *why* he does it," she answered. "I just know that any boy I like gets beaten up." She gave an apologetic look. "Sorry." There was a long silence between us.

"So... you like me?" I asked. I don't know how much I blushed, but it felt like my face was on fire.

Her ears turned as red as strawberries. "That's what you got out of that?!" she retorted, tucking a stray hair behind her ear. My stomach flipped again. "Not that some lumbering hulk is going to pummel you?" She turned her face so I couldn't see it.

"Hey." I used my deepest voice, which is not as suave as I would have liked it to be. I stopped her and put my hand on her shoulder, my heart beating as fast as when I was fighting the behemoth. "I've been in *a lot* of fights, seriously, tons, but I've never had a girl *like* me before."

She looked up and smiled. "Thanks."

We looked into each other's eyes, and I felt like I was falling.

"Are you two done playing footsie?" A mocking voice interrupted the moment. I turned to address the rude speaker and saw a middle-aged man wearing a black button-up shirt and jeans. He had olive skin and black, curly hair. I recognized him as my "uncle" Tony. One of three male role models I'd had for my whole life, Tony was the guy who taught me that a sense of humor could be as good a suit of emotional armor as tough-guy bravado.

"Tony Two?" I asked incredulously. "What are *you* doing here?" He looked at the name on the door we were standing outside. "**MR. GARCIA**," it said in etched letters.

"I suppose I'm here to tell you how one society rose above the rest, subjugated their neighbors, created a vast empire, and then imploded," he replied dryly.

."So..." I said with a frown.

"Get in the room, Romeo. You too, Belle."

"Those are different stories, Mr. Garcia," she pointed out.

He sighed and pointed into the room.

"Did you call our history teacher 'Tony Two?'" Riley whispered. We had found chairs next to each other near the window. Antonio Garcia was explaining what was going to be expected in the course, typical first-day fare. I nodded absently, half listening to the lecture.

"Why?" she asked.

"My dad used to be a cop," I began. "And Tony was one of the guys that helped him out on... a big case. They became friends. I've never called him anything else. Except 'Uncle Tony,' but that didn't last long."

"Okay, but why 'two?'" she pressed.

I leaned closer to whisper. "The other guy who helped him was *also* named Tony. So he called them Tony One and Tony Two." I smiled. "He calls my cousin Tony Three," I added. "For me, they are, respectively: Uncle Tony, Tony Two, and just Tony."

"Because if you don't pay attention, you *will* fall behind, isn't that right, Romeo?" Tony Two asked from the front of the room. He stood in front of the whiteboard, glaring at me.

"Couldn't agree more," I replied sheepishly. When he turned his attention to the rest of the class, Riley looked like she was going to ask more questions, but I put a hand up to hold her off. "After class?" I offered.

She nodded reluctantly and looked at her syllabus again.

Riley and I also had the same class for second period, so we walked together.

"So like, he just helped a cop and he got adopted?" she asked as if we had been holding a conversation the whole time. "And how does a civ help the police that much? My dad's a cop and he hates it when civilians get involved."

"Well…" I began;. I stalled as I tried to remember. "It's a really long story. Filled with explosions and plot twists." The answer didn't seem to satisfy her, but we had arrived at our next class, Algebra II. Mr. Keith sat on his desk as students filed in. With one look from him, I decided sitting in the back was the most prudent idea.

Third Period was listed as my Individual Advancement period, and Riley had Chemistry, so I gave my farewells and made my way across campus. I walked to a small, mirrored glass building. Several students were entering and others were leaving, including the short boy from earlier, Urchin. I followed the flow of bodies to a set of elevators. I watched as the students tapped their student ID cards on a digital display and then walked to a line. I tapped mine and was told to go to number five. When it was my turn, I entered the elevator alone. Instead of buttons, there was a place to insert my ID card. Once I did, the elevator began to drop quickly.

The door opened to a large room with blue mats on the floor and walls. On one wall was a long rack of wooden and plastic weapons. In the middle of the room was a giant of a man. He wore a crocodile skin jacket and boots, and his brown hair was tied back in a ponytail. I sighed. "Is there anybody I know that's not a teacher here?" I asked sarcastically. Anthony Grace laughed.

"Hey, mon petit," he said in his gravel-like bayou drawl. "Makin' friends?" He gave a playful smile.

"That wasn't my fault," I exclaimed, slipping out of my backpack. "Just some big jerk looking to beat up on the new kid."

"Relax, bon ami," he laughed. "It's just a joke."

"It wasn't very funny," I stubbornly said.

He cracked his neck. "Allons, we only have an hour, and if you gonna fight stronger fellas, you gonna need to learn leverage."

*　　*　　*

The bell for lunch rang, and I finally collapsed.

"C'est bon. We gonna work on that tomorrow," Tony said. His breathing was even and he was hardly sweating. He pulled me up and handed me my shirt and backpack, both of which had been discarded during the lesson. He walked me to the elevator. "Get some lunch."

I nodded my consent and put my shirt on while we waited at the door. The elevator dinged, and I slipped my shoes back on.

"'Member the best way to wrassle a werewolf?" he asked when the door opened.

"Don't," I remembered. I stepped in and waved as the door closed. When I exited, I saw other students leaving the elevator lobby towards lunch.

"You would not believe the course load this year," a short boy said as I sat down at the table. "All AP classes," He had well-groomed black hair, light brown skin, and designer glasses. "Thanks, Dad, I'm going to need that six-point-oh GPA to get a job in *your* company." He noticed me arrive. "Who's the new guy, and why is he here?" The question wasn't addressed to me.

"Is there something in the water here that turns people into jackasses?" I asked in reply.

He smirked.

"This is Scott," one of Riley's friends, a red-head, said in an attempt at civility. "Mac's new toy." She said it in a teasing voice.

I rolled my eyes and tried to focus on eating. Only the teenage need to be around the pretty girl that liked me could make me suffer such abuse.

"Mac," the boy said sternly. "Are we sure that's a good idea? Do we want to bring that kind of trouble around? Jimmy is gonna break our table again and scare the new kid away."

"Doubt it," I replied, opening a chocolate milk carton. I casually took a sip without looking at him.

"Then you've never met James," he replied with a smirk. The redheaded girl laughed.

"Bix, you need to get around more," the ginger girl replied. "They've met. What's more, Scott here almost won the fight."

I looked at Riley, who was eating her salad with grace and poise, as though her friends weren't talking about her like she wasn't there. *Almost?* I indignantly thought as I took a bite. It was a fair assessment. One didn't *win* a fight with James as much as *survived*, but at the time, my pride was a sensitive thing.

"Wait, he what? How?" the new boy, apparently called Bix, asked, dumbfounded.

"That's a question for him," she replied.

I felt both of their gazes and turned to face them. "What?" I asked, pausing finally from devouring my burger. Trying to grapple giants was hungry work.

"How did you fight James and not *die*?" Bix asked incredulously.

I considered giving a full description, but this rude little boy didn't deserve the effort. "Expertly," I replied with a shrug, and took another bite.

"That's not an answer," he replied.

"It's not a *good* answer."

"Fine, be mysterious," he said defiantly. "Just know that I have ways of finding things out." Then, as if someone flipped a switch, the subject changed back to classes. He turned to a tall boy next to him. "This workload is going to take like, an hour a day..."

"Sorry about my friends," Riley said.

"I can handle it," I replied. I glanced quickly at the conglomeration. It was definitely a change from the group of nerdy jocks I was used to hanging around.

"Anyway, that's Myra." She pointed at the redhead. "Her sister Kyra is off somewhere; they're identical, though, so you'll know if you see her. The boys at the end are Travis and Bixby. Bixby is the short one."

I looked at the end of the table, past Bixby. The tall boy at the end was wearing a pair of silver sunglasses. He nodded at me when he noticed I was looking.

"Well, I guess that's 'meeting the friends' out of the way," I muttered quietly as I chewed.

English was my next adventure. The teacher was not at the door to greet us. Just a sign that said, "You know what to do, pick a seat and shut up." The nameplate revealed my worst fear. **MR. O'CONNOR.** They say you can learn a lot about a teacher by how they decorated their room. It might not be a hard rule, but in this case, they weren't far from wrong.

There were no inspirational posters, just charts with quotes from various American authors, a lot of them were by Mark Twain, and a sixteen-year-old picture of my mom holding a baby and a toddler. I sat near the back and looked at my watch. I still had plenty of time before the bell rang, so I began reading a book about everyone's favorite drow. As I mused about the dark elf's plans to defeat the orc army, I became aware I was being stared at. I looked up to see the same smart-mouthed boy from the morning, Urchin. He was smiling like he knew something I didn't. "Can I help you?" I asked for what felt like the millionth time that day.

"You offering anything specific?" he replied quickly.

"What?" I asked, confused.

"So," he ignored my question and sat down backward on the desk in front of me. "Big man on campus. You got a lot going for you so far. Hot girl, you already found the biggest guy in the yard and made him your--"

"He found me," I interrupted. "Look, are you still mad about your locker?"

"Nah, I'm over it," he shrugged. "You just have this 'protagonist' vibe about you. Fan favorites rarely die, so I figured I'd ingratiate myself." He held out his hand and, after a moment, I warily shook it. "They call me Urchin. Do you have a name besides 'that kid from this morning?' Or did your parents hate you, too?"

"Scott," I replied slowly.

"So, what brings a saint like you to TRALA? Are you a Cuss or a Sinner?"

"You what?" I asked. The breakneck speed his thoughts operated on was too much for me.

"So, you know how hip kids always come up with nicknames or shorten words to sound cooler than they really are?" He began.

"I guess."

"So we call Custodians 'Cusses,' and Supernatural Entities 'Sinners,'" he explained.

"Oh," I said. "That. I'm a Cuss, at least, that's what my parents say." "Both of *them* are. Well, my mom used to be before going back to work as a trucker..." A thought occurred to me. "Why am I telling you *any* of this?"

"I have a trustworthy face."

"That can't be it," I said. "And I thought we weren't supposed to talk about that. Confidentiality and all that." According to the official school rules, a person's paranormal status was supposed to be secret. Altruistically, this was to stop bullying and to practice *not* talking about paranormal activity to the outside world.

He laughed. "Oh right, those rules that nobody follows. Anyway--"

"Alright, settle down. Get off that desk!" A tall man in a red leather trench coat walked in and slammed some books down. "My name is Mister O'Connor, as I hope you might have guessed. If not, this might be the wrong class for you. This is Honors English. I hope you like writing essays as much as you like passing notes, Miss Perry." He suddenly turned to look at a blonde girl typing on her phone. She slipped the phone into her backpack and seemed to shrink.

"I am not here to hold your hand," he went on. "I am here to teach, and you are here to learn." He walked up to a laptop on a podium and pressed a few buttons. A projector turned on and a book list appeared, followed by a syllabus. "I did not print copies for you. Get to writing." He sat down and observed the class. His mirrored sunglasses that he never seemed to take off made it impossible to tell where he was looking, which was probably how he liked it. The rest of the class silently copied the information from the syllabus for the rest of the period, with a few minutes being spent listening to my dad tell us his great expectations for us.

When the bell rang, I stood up, along with the rest of the class, and tried to sneak out unseen. I was unsuccessful in my attempt. "Junior, a word," my dad said without looking up. I closed my eyes and sighed. Nothing good ever happened when he called me Junior.

"Yes, Sir?" I said. The last of the students filed out, leaving us alone in the room before the next class shuffled in.

"I hear you have a new girlfriend," he said mirthlessly, sitting behind his table. "Riley McKinsey?"

I smiled at the mention of her.

He did not. His book closed with a clap. "End it."

CHAPTER 3

THESE DAYS

He might as well have hit me with a brick. It felt like something inside shattered. "What? No way," I said, ignoring his hand coming up to stop me. "I like her, and she likes me. Do you know how often that's happened?" Even if he hadn't raised me and been up to date with most details of my life, my tone would have told him that such things didn't ever happen.

"Boy, I've told you once, I don't want to do it again."

"This is so unfair," I replied and shot him an accusing look. "Don't you trust me?"

"Of course I trust you. Now you need to trust me."

"Why?" I asked.

His eyebrow rose.

I spotted my mistake and corrected it. "Why can't I have a girlfriend?" I rarely tried to argue with him since it was almost universally futile. But at this moment, I couldn't think of anything more important than trying to be close to Riley.

"I don't care if you get a girlfriend," he paused, then lowered his voice. "Just not the daughter of the Police Chief," he said with finality.

"I don't care about that, why wouldn't he--"

He held up his hand again. His next class was coming in. "I've said my piece. I expect you to respect it. I know what's what more than you do." There was a pause, and I could see my warped glowering countenance reflected on his sunglasses. His face was calm.

"I'm going to be late for my next class," I finally said. I turned and walked away, dejected. I barely paid attention to Professor Mogrim, the chemistry teacher, as he droned on. My thoughts kept circling, revolving around how unjust the whole thing was.

The coaches in PE did little more than sort us up, give us gym clothes, and assign lockers. I sat to the side as the other boys joked with each other. Their words were a buzz in my ear until I heard her name.

"Riley Mac? She's dummy thicc this year."

While it was crass, I couldn't honestly disagree with the statement; she did indeed have all the right curves in all the right places. My eyes shot up to find the speaker. He was among a group of football players. They were in their practice jerseys and pads.

The one talking was taller than the others, and he had his long, brown hair pulled back in a wet ponytail. "I mean, she was hot before, but dayum."

My eyes narrowed in anger.

"Don't let Sunshine hear you say that, bro," said another boy, this one with short black hair and brown skin. "He'd sack you into graduation."

The first boy laughed it off. "I ain't worried about it." He tossed his helmet onto the bench and began taking off his jersey. "He ain't here. Got sent packing for fighting some freshman. Plus, that Sinner won't last much longer. If he attacks any more Cusses, he's off the team, and you know being a star tackle is the only reason he's still here and not the lockup. Once he's gone, it's open season." He started making obscene gestures, making his cronies laugh.

I stood and put my new gym clothes in my backpack, doing my best to ignore it.

"Hey, you," the rude boy yelled.

I turned quickly, ready to punch him in the face. His attention was on Urchin, though, who was opening a nearby locker. I took a calming breath and zipped up my backpack.

Urchin turned and gave a bored look. "Listen, Lexie, I'm going to ask you to fast forward to the part where you tell me why you need to make me smell your B.O." I saw him shift his weight slightly. It was hardly more than moving his foot back half an inch and a bend of the knees, but years of studying various martial arts had told me to be on the lookout for such things. I doubted this football player had the same advantage. I set my backpack down and watched with interest.

"My *name* is Topher, Sinner. And I heard you were hitting on my girl." He cracked his knuckles threateningly.

"Statistically likely," Urchin replied matter-of-factly with a smile. He paused for a moment and turned to one of the other boys. "See, statistics is where you--"

"Now I'm gonna pound you," Topher interrupted.

"Pound me?" Urchin laughed. "Are you even trying? That's like, Stephen King bully bad. Listen--"

Topher interrupted with a swing but only hit air. Urchin's movement was so subtle and quick I hardly noticed it. He moved his back foot an inch or so and leaned back, letting the fist barely miss him. Topher swung again with his other fist, this time Urchin stepped in, turned, and grabbed his arm at the wrist and elbow. He made another small movement and Topher hit the floor hard. Two of his friends joined in, and I felt like that was my queue. I wouldn't interfere with a fair fight, but I felt honor-bound to stop a beat-down.

I rushed in and tackled the one on the right. I slammed him into the wall. His pads protected him, though. He brought an elbow down into my back and I responded with a punch that landed square on his cup. I hurt my hand, but it shook him enough that I could push him back and land an elbow to his face. He went down. Another set of hands grabbed my shoulders. I grasped one of them and spun with a kick to the leg, which would have sent him to the floor if I hadn't been holding on. I kneed him in the face and let go. He was out of the fight as well. I looked around and stood in a boxing stance. The rest of them were on the ground.

"Awe, you *do* care," Urchin said from the bench. He was looking through Topher's wallet. He looked up at me and smirked at my judgmental look. "Annoyance tax," he explained.

"Theft." I corrected him.

"Tomayto/tomahto." He shrugged and tossed the wallet to the floor, then pulled a phone from his pocket. "By the way, you dropped this." He tossed it to me.

"This was in my backpack," I said. "It was zipped up."

"Weird," he responded with another shrug. He stood and walked away, hands in his pockets. A question was forming in my mind when I was distracted by a bleep from my phone. I checked it and saw I had fourteen notifications on Sploosh, the latest in social media apps. I opened the app and read that ten were new friend requests and I had four new messages from Riley. I only recognized a few names and added them to my pool, which was the Sploosh version of a friend list, and looked at the messages.

Hey you Are you free after school today? Say yes We are going to all hang out. We'll walk from school its not far Are you there? I'll wait by the flagpole

It was a moment I hadn't thought to dread. I had to think of a way to break it off without seeming like a jerk. Nothing came to mind. I was not very practiced at tact, and I had never been in a relationship before, let alone ended one.

Something came up, I replied. I'll tell you about it tomorrow. I stared at the screen as a bubble showed me she had seen the message.

oh ok is everything ok?

My frown deepened. I hadn't foreseen her asking follow-up questions. As I left the locker room, I pocketed my phone and let out a loud sigh.

"Well, that's not a good sound." I looked up to see my cousin approaching by himself. I scanned for his giant friend. He must have noticed, because he chuckled. "He's home for the day. Suspended before first period. A new personal best." I took a moment to regard him. Like me, he preferred the tee shirt and cargo pants look. He wore a grey, single strap backpack. His face was rarely without a smile. His dark complexion made most people question the validity of the "cousin" claim, which was fair. We weren't actually biologically related. Tony had been adopted by a close family friend around the time I was born. When both your parents are only children, their friends become your aunts and uncles, and their kids become your cousins. At least, that was the case with us.

"You got time now to explain what his major malfunction is?" I asked.

He laughed and ran his fingers through his straight hair. "Only if you're paying. Pop is on assignment, so it's been PB&J for the last couple of days."

I nodded in understanding. His father contracted for the organization that also ran the school. Our parents' work was impossible to predict, and we never knew when they would leave or get back. That was the main reason my mom quit. If I was honest, I'd considered Tony to be more like a big brother than a cousin because we spent so much time at each other's houses. The last few years since we had moved away from each other had been tough on both of us.

"I know a great place.," he said. "Come on."

The place he knew was a diner a few blocks away from the school. It had massive windows and chrome walls. The front window had a painted display that read **WELCOME BACK BEARS**. Above the windows, the chrome continued and was broken up by a sign that read *Archie's Place* in unlit neon letters. It looked pretty full on the outside. All of the window tables were full of students from TRALA. Inside, the restaurant was filled with teenagers from stem to stern and smelled like baking pizza and grilled onions. There was a bar on one side, and on the other was a checkered dance floor with a lit jukebox playing a Chuck Berry song. In between was a counter that flowed into the bar.

A middle-aged man in a white soda jerk hat and a name tag that labeled him as Archie smiled as Tony and I approached. "Hey! Tony! How ya been?" he asked in a kind voice.

"Been good, Arch," Tony replied. He put his hand on my shoulder. "This is my cousin Scott. He's new in town."

"Glad to meet ya, Scotty," the jovial man said.

I tried not to grimace at my least favorite name.

"Stayin' outta trouble?"

I looked away, not necessarily to ignore him, but rather to avoid the question. A group left, and the table was claimed before it could be wiped down.

After we paid for the pizza, a "Carnivore pie," we found a standing table just off the dance floor.

Tony looked at his phone and frowned.

"What's up?" I asked, trying to be heard over the Tom Jones song that had just come on.

Tony rubbed his eyes. "James says he wants me to come over. He needs help with something or other."

"Like tying his shoes?" I asked, causing Tony to chuckle. "What is his deal anyway? I know you told me he was grumpy, but..." I gestured at my chest, which was still sore.

"He's gotten worse since Riley broke his heart," he replied and took a sip of soda pop.

"Wasn't that years ago?" I asked.

"A couple," he replied.

"She said she broke up with him because he was being a jerk," I said.

He shrugged and played with his straw. "Chicken and the egg, I guess. He changed about the time they split. He wasn't *that* bad before." He looked up and noticed me staring hard at the table. "What?"

I didn't answer at first. "My dad said I need to keep away from her."

Tony stuck out his bottom lip and raised his eyebrows. "Maybe it's for the best," he said with a tilt of his head. "Look how James turned out."

"Yeah, I'm not buying it."

Tony could only shrug his shoulders in response before our conversation was interrupted by a woman wearing a traditional diner waitress outfit carrying our food. I smiled my thanks and grabbed a slice before it had a chance to cool. I blew on it once and foolishly took a bite.

*　*　*

"You didn't!" My mother's voice made my dad jerk the phone from his ear. He slowly put his flip phone back. "You can't just make these unilateral decisions."

"I'm his dad. I know better than he does."

"No one's doubting that, hon."

"So why am I in trouble?"

She sighed. "You didn't ask me. You remember that conversation we had when you caught him looking at--"

"I remember, Dix, but this is--"

"Yeah, fine, blood feud. He's my son, too. Or did you forget that time I pushed him out?" She pulled out a pot.

"It's laser etched into my brain." He sighed and rubbed his nose. "But I-"

25

"Scott, he might have your name, but he is not *you*. You might have always been Mister Toe-the-line, but, well…"

"Yeah, I get it. Look, I'm sorry."

"Did I just faint?"

He laughed once through his nose. "I should have talked to you first. We'll have a talk when I get home."

She turned on the sink and began filling the pot with water. "He'll be home after he's done with Tony Three. I hope."

"You hope?"

"Yeah, Scott, hope. You told him to break it off with the first girl to show an interest in him. I've run away for a lot less." She sighed and turned off the water.

"I'm sure it'll be fine."

"O'Connor, one of these days, you're going to have to learn how to pick your battles. Charging in headlong and then standing your ground is going to get you hurt."

"It might already be too late for that," he replied. "I'll see you when I get home."

"Love you, too."

He closed the phone and returned his attention to the report in front of him. The door opened and Mister Keith filled the threshold. My dad looked up. "Bandit."

"Slayer," Keith replied curtly. He walked fully into the room and reached for a mug. "Surprised to see you aren't tucked away in your own corner."

"Wi-Fi's garbage. Which, you'd think we could afford some half-decent routers."

"Geeks set up some block so the kids aren't streaming or whatever. I heard you let loose on one of my players."

"The fat kid who wouldn't shut up? He told me I was interrupting his conversation."

Keith snorted. "Speaking of kids who don't like to shut up, I met your boy." He sat on top of one of the desks, with his feet on the seat in front of him.

My dad raised an eyebrow. "I saw that. What did you think?"

Keith thought about it. "I think I got a spot on the team for him."

It was my father's turn to laugh. "Good luck with that, Howie. He hates football."

"I'm very persuasive."

My dad smirked and shook his head as he reopened his laptop. Keith poured something from a flask into his mug and took a sip. "You mind if I ask you somethin'?"

"I got a feeling me minding won't stop you."

"What are ya doin' here?"

"I teach here now."

"You know what I mean. You had your family all settled down in Utah, and all of a sudden, out of nowhere, you take the job here. What's goin' on?"

My father closed the laptop again. "Kel."

"Not this again."

"The Tonys and I came across... something in Vegas. A week later, we tracked down some deadheads in my neighborhood. Frank decided it would be safer for Scott here."

"So even when you're out of town, he's got a bunch of backup," Keith said, following the reasoning. "I mean, he's got a point. Kel'd have to be crazy to come here."

"Good thing he's not crazy," My dad retorted sarcastically.

*   *   *

Once my mouth stopped burning and the pizza had run out, we sat reminiscing about the good old days, filling each other in on the last four years. "So then I said, 'that wasn't my dog'." Tony finished his story and we both laughed. He wiped a tear from his eye and looked at his watch. "Oh, man. I gotta get going. I left my pills at home and I have to swing by The Manor." I raised an eyebrow in question. "Morgenstern Manor. It's a big, big house on the far side of town." He picked off the last bits of meat from the empty tray.

"Okay, I think you should go home first. You never know when symptoms could hit. You don't want to pass out in the middle of the street again, do you?"

Tony shook his head. "It won't take long, and it's on the way to my house."

"If you're sure, the least I can do is walk with you."

"Great. More time to chat."

It took us half an hour to reach Morgenstern Manor. Surrounded by black wrought iron gates with an elegant lawn leading to the marble house, there was no confusing it for anything other than a mansion. I whistled.

"I know, right? I'm going to head in. See you tomorrow?" he asked.

I didn't respond because, at that moment, I saw three feminine figures leaving the house: a beautiful girl in a blue hoodie and a pair of identical ginger girls. I recognized Myra by her hair, which hung past her shoulders and was intricately braided. I assumed the other was Kyra. Her hair was newly buzzed on the side of her head, making her look like a Viking. Riley stopped ten feet from the gate when she noticed me.

"Scott? What are you doing here?" she asked in a surprised tone.

"Me?" I replied. "What are *you* doing here? Isn't this James' house?"

"More than one person can live in a house, you know," replied Kyra in a harsh tone. "She was visiting *us*."

"Kyra, it's fine. I'm not mad, just surprised," Riley interjected.

Tony looked from me to her and spoke up. "Hey, didn't your dad--"

"Thanks, Tony!" I said to interrupt him. "Glad you're safe. Go play with your friend now." He looked a little hurt, which softened me. "I'll handle it, bro," I whispered.

He put a smile back on and held out his fist. I bumped it and embraced him in a hug. He waved at the girls, who returned the gesture, and then he opened the gate and walked past. He didn't notice Myra's gaze linger on him. I rubbed the back of my neck. "So anyway…" What was there to say? What could I say? I had hoped for a few more hours to think of what to tell her, and hanging out with Tony had all but taken my mind off the subject.

"Scott? Is something wrong?" Riley asked with something like concern in her voice.

I looked at the twins, then at her, being careful not to make eye contact. "No. Well… It doesn't… It can wait." I stuck my thumbs under my backpack straps to give my hands something to do. This was a lot harder than I thought it would be. That brick to the gut feeling was worse than ever. "I gotta get home, bye." I turned and started walking. Riley and the twins were whispering something that I couldn't understand. I pulled out my phone to navigate back home.

"Scott, wait!" I turned around to see Riley running to catch up.

That's a sight I could watch forever, I thought to myself as she approached. I quickly chastised myself.

"What's wrong?" she asked. "Don't say 'nothing,' either, 'cause your face is like its own lie detector."

This was it. The dreaded moment. I wouldn't be able to put it off anymore. "I uh," I cleared my throat. "I can't see you anymore." I looked at my shoes as I fought back the strange sensation of tears welling up. I didn't see if she did the same. I couldn't fathom why I was having such a strong emotional reaction. All said, I barely knew her, but I felt like I was losing a lifelong companion.

"Why not?" she asked. She raised my chin to make eye contact. Hers were definitely moist. "I thought we had a connection."

Something about her eyes made me do a somersault in my brain. "We did. We do." I pulled away and looked at the darkening night sky. "It's my dad. He says I can't date you. 'Cause your dad is the police chief. I don't know." I threw my hands up and turned my back on her. She stood silently for a moment.

"So we can't date?" she asked. "That's what he said?"

"Essentially."

"Did he say anything about being friends?" she suggested. I turned around with a quizzical look. "I mean, obviously, I'd rather have a boyfriend. But I could settle for a friend." She smiled.

I thought about it. I knew the spirit of what my dad had told me. I also understood the letter. I wasn't ever one to *break* the rules, but I did love a loophole. I also knew that I could only describe what I felt for the girl in front of me as sheer, head over heels, love at first sight. "I think that might work. But you have to promise not to fall for me again. No matter how handsome or manly I may be," I joked.

"And I'll try not to seduce you with my feminine wiles," she laughed.

It might already be too late for that, I thought.

*   *   *

James let out another growl as he watched me from the window.

Tony opened the door to the spacious room. "What's up, bud?" He joined the large youth at the window and stared out. "You should just let that go, my guy."

James grunted in reply.

Tony rolled his eyes. "You don't really have to worry about him, you know."

James turned to his much shorter friend. "Huh? Why's that?" His speaking voice sounded a lot like his growling voice.

Tony walked away from the window and sat in a gigantic bean bag chair. "His dad told him to stay away from her."

James turned back to the shades and parted them, watching as I walked away, Riley hurrying after me. "Will he listen?"

"Who, Scott?" Tony laughed. "Unless he's changed his entire personality, yeah. When his dad puts his foot down, Scott's a good boy." He paused and squinted. "Pretend I said that a nicer way."

James turned to look at Tony. "He better."

Tony laughed again. "You understand that he's not one of the mooks from a cushy family, right? His dad is the *Slayer*, chief among Custodians. He's had tutors for academics *and* fighting since he stopped pooping in diapers. Even *my* dad isn't as hard core as his. Plus, he already took you down once."

James narrowed his eyes. Anybody but Tony would have wilted, but my cousin knew the big man wouldn't try to hurt his only friend. "He got lucky."

"Sure."

"I would'a had him if Coach hadn't stopped us."

"Sure, sure."

"You don't believe me?" James' anger roused again.

Tony sighed, the smile leaving his lips. "James, you're my best friend, but Scott's like a brother to me. I don't care who'd win in a fight--"

"Me."

"Okay, fine. Again, I don't care. I don't want you to fight him." He spoke with a tone of authority. It wasn't a voice James was used to hearing.

"But Riley..."

"...Broke your heart *years* ago. It's time to get over it, move on. Let *her* move on, man." Tony sat up and shrugged. "She's not coming back. Acting like the world's biggest jerk isn't going to change that. Besides, after what happened, what she did to you, I'm constantly shocked you'd *want* her back." James crossed his arms and sat on his four poster bed. "Now, what was it you wanted my help with?"

"I can't pass this part of the game," James muttered, pointing to his game screen.

"Are you kidding me? You said it was an emergency."

"It is. I need to rescue the princess."

"James, just play another game." Tony stood and walked toward the door.

James watched him.

Tony looked back and sighed. "I forgot my pills at home." The overly large boy continued to stare, expressionless. Tony ran his fingers through his brown and blonde hair and sighed. "Fine, I'll help you, but just for a couple minutes. It's already almost sunset."

*   *   *

I'd decided to be a gentleman and walk her home. At least, that was the rationalization I gave myself. When we were halfway to her house, a black and white police car pulled up next to us. I waved politely to the police officer inside. "Hi, Chet," Riley said as she approached the open window. Chet gave me a look of skepticism. "Chet, this is Scott." I waved again to no response.

His attention turned to her. "Evening, Riley. The chief wanted me to make sure you got home okay. He's working late tonight."

"Thank you, but Scott is a perfect gentleman," she replied.

"All the same, if I go back to your dad and tell him you didn't want a ride 'cause you were walking with a boy…"

"Fine," she said with a sigh. She turned around to hug me. I put my hand up to shake hers. She laughed and shook my hand. "You're a funny guy, Scott O'Connor."

Yeah, I'm a real clown, I thought as she got into the back of the car. After the car turned the corner, I sighed. *Don't even think about it*, I warned myself. A lone howl pierced the night. It was time to get home.

I was a few blocks away from home when I glanced at my map program and saw that I could avoid being late for dinner if I cut through a few alleyways. I looked down the backstreet. It was dark and foreboding. I looked at the clock again. If I was late for dinner, my mother would have my hide. I decided to cut through the alley.

Moving as silently and swiftly as possible, I was halfway through when I heard the whimpering. It sounded like it was coming from behind a dumpster just ahead. I slipped my backpack off and held it in one hand as I slowly crept up and looked around it. Two men were hovering over a woman. She looked from one to the other. I took as deep a breath as I could this close to a garbage heap. Getting a good look at her, she looked middle-aged, I guessed she was a secretary by her clothes. Her leg was bleeding and jutting at an unnatural angle and I saw terror in her eyes.

She noticed me and cried for help. I winced. I had hoped to sneak up on one of them and take him out before the other could react. One-on-one was better odds than facing down two grown men together, even if they were as skinny as this pair. The two men turned to look at me, their eyes bright in the night.

"Guys," I began. I took a step backward. "We can all walk away from this and no one needs to be hurt." I backed up to the wall and felt around for any object that might be of use.

"Foolish boy," one of them said. His voice sounded more like a snake sliding over sand than a man. "If you do not resist, then it will hardly hurt at all."

"Ah," I said, my groping hand grabbed onto a round wooden object. "There's the rub." The silent one hurled himself at me with a hiss. I brought the broken pool cue up instinctively as he flew, and he impaled himself on it. There was a sickening squelch and thud. I struggled to hold onto the stick, and I felt his cold blood ooze onto my hand. One look at the length of wood now buried into his chest told me that he was doomed. His mouth contorted in anger and pain, revealing a row of sharp teeth. He staggered back, taking the cue, now slick with blood, with him as he fell. Dead.

The other vampire spent no time in mourning, and jumped at my distraction. I barely had time to block his overhand strike, which I hardly saw out of the corner of my eye. The force of it nearly broke my arm and forced me down. Ignoring the cut on my forearm, I jumped toward my improvised weapon, but he grappled my leg and I simply dropped. I turned, arms up in defense, and lifted my legs to keep him at bay. He glared at me. One look into his eyes and I was paralyzed by fear. He slowly approached. I couldn't hear anything but the rushing of blood in my ears. He reached down and clutched me around the neck, choking me.

I felt myself being lifted but I couldn't fight back. Those eyes stopped me. As everything began to fade to black, I heard a voice from a billion miles away say, "It is not yet your time," and suddenly, I was free of the spell.

I felt myself get knocked over and a loud, angry growl rang out in the alley. I looked up and saw a creature covered in fur attacking the vampire. It looked like someone had stuck the head of a German shepherd onto a burly man, wrapped him in fur, and given him sharp claws. The serpentine voice cried out in pain as the dog man bit into his arm and threw him at least ten feet. Sudden realization hit me like an egg timer going off, and the blood rushing back into my brain came up with one word: Werewolf. I gasped and tried to stumble to my feet. It noticed me.

The werewolf approached slowly, malice in its eyes. Foam dripped from its massive sharp teeth. I held my hand up inexplicably; maybe I thought it might be satisfied with just eating my arm. I looked up at it. "Puppy?" I said in a timid voice. It growled, then turned and bounded off into the night, chasing the vampire that had used the momentary lapse in combat to flee. With the danger gone, I turned to help the fallen woman, but she had disappeared as well, leaving me alone with the rats and roaches. I collapsed from the toll of the day, wondering if anything else could go wrong. Shaking that dangerous thought, I picked myself up and ran home before I could find out.

CHAPTER 4

<u>New World Man</u>

I floated through space, watching idly as my hands elongated and turned to birds. I watched them fly through the forest I suddenly found myself in. I reached out to touch one of the trees with my once-a-bird hand, but it was no longer within reach. I chased after it, reaching a clearing where I saw Riley in her iconic hoodie. She was smiling, which made the whole earth move under my feet, though I stood still. She turned away but was still somehow facing me; her face now sad. She and the world vanished. Leaving me alone except for a giant. His eyes on fire, his skin a translucent blue that flashed with lightning strikes. He had too many wings and shining armor made of gold and bronze. He stared down at me and opened his mouth. "Be not afraid," he said with all the voices of the world in all the languages of the world. I opened my mouth to speak, and I began beeping the same way my alarm clock did.

"M'up," I mumbled as I woke up drenched in sweat. Bleary-eyed, I slapped my alarm clock and rubbed my eyes. I had been having different flavors of the same dream for almost a week. It was the Monday after the incident, and a full six days had passed. I opened the mini-fridge next to my bed and grabbed an energy drink.

When I told my parents I had fought a vampire, they had mixed reactions. Despite my insistence that I wasn't, in fact, actively trying to get killed, they berated me for taking needless risks. My mom treated my wounds, telling me again and again that she knew this would happen. Once my dad was sure I was okay, he headed out the door. The atmosphere at school had changed for a few days as well. Everyone was talking about the vampire attack.

"I heard it was a student here." I had overheard a freshman girl say.

"Well, you know it wasn't a boy, or he'd be bragging about how he fought off an army," her friend giggled in reply.

I simply kept my head down. Determined to follow my father's orders but still stay close to Riley, I made sure we didn't spend any time alone or sit next to each other. Instead, I had been next to either Bixby or Travis, the golden-skinned senior who wore shades all day.

I lazily got ready for the day. I brushed my teeth, trying not to think about the razor-sharp maw that almost ended me. Until the werewolf showed up. It was smaller than I had imagined a lycanthrope to be, but that didn't take much away from how terrifying the thing was. Still, something about its eyes… I ate my breakfast in silence. I looked at the clock on the wall and headed to school. There was no one to see me off this morning. Mom was off on a run somewhere in Oregon.

I arrived at TRALA still distracted, which is why I didn't notice the boy until I walked right into him. I instinctively became combative. "Yo!" I exclaimed. "Walkways are for walking." I brushed off my wrinkled anime shirt and looked down at him. "Slower traffic to the right, man."

"Sorry," he said. "I'm still new." He was a boy most would call attractive. Brushed back blonde hair, bright blue eyes, set jaw. He had a bit of the All American vibe to him. I shook my head.

"Sorry I snapped. Bad week." I held out my hand.

"It's Monday," he observed as he took it and pulled himself up. He brushed himself off and held out a hand of his own. "Garryowen Bradley," he said.

I shook his hand. "Oh, we're doing full-full names? Scott Richard O'Connor the Third," I replied.

"No, my name is Garryowen. One word. Like the song," he said as he looked around. "Do you know where A Hall is?"

"That'd be the one with the A on it," I retorted. "Come on, I'm headed that way myself."

I escorted Gary to what ended up being Mr. Keith's class and wished him luck. Then I settled in to learn about ancient Sumatrans. By the time IA came around, I was beginning to feel like I might have a "typical" day. The doors opened earlier than they usually did and in the opposite direction, causing me to stumble since the wall I was leaning on was no longer there. This was clearly a different room than the one I had been training in. I looked around and saw two other students already in attendance. A slender haughty woman in a long, green dress beckoned me to sit. The board behind her read "*Introduction to Homo Vampiris.*" I took a new notepad out of my bag.

I heard a vaguely familiar voice say, "Vampires are homo?" Which drew a scandalized look from the teacher.

"Unamusing as always, Mr. Beck. Take a seat," she said as soon as she recovered. Topher did so, sitting at the desk next to mine. Out of the corner of my eye, I saw him recognize me. His mouth opened, but he was interrupted. "Now that we are all here, we can begin." She waved her hand, and the board cleared. The words were replaced by new ones that read, "*Characteristics, Powers, Weaknesses.*"

"At most times, it is impossible to tell a vampire from a human with the senses available to normal humans. However, there are several distinctions. Vampires smell of iron. This is due to the way their bodies break down hemoglobin."

I raised my hand, but she continued. "At night, their eyes shine in the same way a cat's do. Obviously, they have elongated and sharpened canine teeth. Some homo vampiris have been known to file their teeth further, but this is rare, as a mouth full of sharp teeth not only hinders speech but also reduces their ability to remain incognito."

I raised my hand again.

"Mr. O'Connor, this is a lecture, not a discussion. If you have questions, I suggest you visit the library." She looked at the rest of the class. "Moving on to their powers..." She waved a hand, and words appeared on the board following her speech. "Enhanced strength, speed, thickened skin, and mental hypnosis. Never look a vampire in the eyes without protection." She waved her hand again and words formed under "*Weaknesses.*"

"Vampires are averse to silver and a number of woods. The *exact* reason is unclear, but the working hypothesis is that they are simply... allergic. They are not immune to their own hypnosis, thus they avoid mirrors and mirrored surfaces. Additionally, they are averse to sunlight and other bright lights. An unprotected vampire may receive a *nasty* sunburn in as little as a few seconds. Modern homo vampiris often wear strong sunscreen and cologne." She telepathically wiped the board again. "Now, onto their history..."

As we waited for the elevator, the thin teacher moved to her office, and Topher leaned in. "So I hear you're one and done with McKinsey."

I tightened the straps on my backpack, trying to ignore him.

"So, does that mean you hit it?" His mocking laugh made violent thoughts spring up in my brain.

"Look, I'm not your friend, and I don't want to *be* your friend," I replied through my teeth.

"Hey bro, relax," he replied. "I mean, I didn't snitch on you about attacking out of nowhere. No hard feelings, right?"

"The only reason you didn't say anything is because you tried a six on one attack on a kid half your size. And he probably didn't need my help," I said, facing the elevator. The door opened before he replied, and I stepped in with the other three.

"That Urchin kid is not who you want as a friend. He'll steal your wallet and your girl."

"Well, my wallet is perpetually empty, and I don't have a girl." I looked at him humorlessly. "Remember?"

* * *

Riley sat her backpack down and smiled at her teammate. "Hi, Katie."

"Oh, hey, Riley." Katie Hansen looked up from her book. "How was your weekend?"

"Boring. How about you?"

Katie bit her lip. It was a slightly dangerous habit for a vampire to have. "We had company over so I was serving them."

"Friends?"

"More like family." The curly haired girl gently placed a worn bookmark in the book she had been reading and closed it. "Why didn't you go out with your boyfriend?"

Riley blushed and tucked her hair behind her ear. "He's not my boyfriend."

"Does *he* know that?" Katie smiled, not able to resist poking.

"He made it pretty clear." Riley glanced at her and narrowed her eyes. "Why do you ask?"

Katie smiled. "He watches you. He can't keep his eyes off you."

"I'm sure he looks at a lot of girls."

Katie shook her head, an action that made her hair bounce from side to side. "He notices them. But he only has eyes for you."

Riley blushed and stared at the blank notebook in front of her.

Someone sat in the desk next to her. "Are you okay?" Gary asked her.

She looked up and smiled. "Yeah, I'm great." She furrowed her eyebrows. "I don't recognize you."

"It would be kind of weird if you did, this is my first day." He stuck his hand out. "I'm Garryowen, but my friends call me Gary."

She shook his hand. "What do your enemies call you?"

"Gary, or they would, if I had any enemies." He frowned, letting go of her hand. "I hope I don't, anyway."

She gave him a friendly smile. "Welcome to TRALA."

He tilted his head, then raised his eyebrows. "Thank you."

"So where are you from?"

He clicked his tongue. "Most recently, L.A., but before that? Germany, Japan, New Zealand for a minute…"

She smiled. "Marines?"

He shook his head. "Army."

"Ooh, rough. My dad was Navy."

"I'll try not to hold that against you," he joked.

Duke Lee, the English teacher, and BOSS wheelman, walked in and tossed his orange jacket onto his desk. "All right, youngins, simmer down. Hansen, get rid of that smut."

Katie looked up from her book, mortified. "It's just Shakespeare's sonnets."

"And?"

She looked around for support. "It's literature."

"It's a smutty book."

The boy who sat behind Katie adjusted his black framed glasses. "It's romantic, but I'm pretty sure it's not smut."

Duke didn't break eye contact with him. "'But since she pricked thee out for women's pleasure, Mine be thy love and thy love's use their treasure.' I wonder what that pervy hack coulda meant by that? An' besides which, it's not even romantical." He turned around and popped the top off of a marker, writing, "If you write her a sonnet, you love her. If you write three-hundred sonnets, you love sonnets." He underlined it twice and re capped the marker. "Shakespeare was just writing 'I wanna git wit you, gurl' a thousand times like a frumpy collared Ed Sheeran." He faced the class. "Any more comments, criticisms, or violent disagreements?" He didn't wait for an answer. "No? Good."

* * *

My dad sat down on the leather couch in the teacher's lounge. He let out a long sigh.

"You've been a teacher a week and you're already done with it, huh?" Howard Keith asked.

"Something like that."

"Still haven't found them?" Keith shook his head. "You boys in Team Seven were never all that great at 'S' part of S and D."

"Thanks, Keith, that's just the advice I needed."

"What did Frank say?" He bit into his peanut butter and banana sandwich.

"Apparently, there are more pressing matters than a handful of vamps."

The door opened and teachers began to pour into the room. Tony Two was among them. He walked up behind my dad and patted his shoulder. "School food sucks, let's go grab something."

"I'm not hungry."

"Oh, then come with me while I get food."

My dad sighed and stood.

As soon as the doors to the red Jaguar closed, Tony Two broke his silence. "I'm calling BS."

"I had a big breakfast, alright?"

"Not about that, you mope. Since when is Frank too busy to take your calls? That dude loves you like a son. Something's going on, I can smell it." He banged the steering wheel and sighed.

"Well, you aren't wrong. But between taking care of the boy and this teaching nonsense…" He let the sentence hang.

"That and the fact that your idea of investigation is to kick down every door until you get it right or you make enough noise." Tony turned on the car and backed out of his spot.

My dad sat in silence for a while as they drove away. "You know, there is someone that's a lot better at this than we are."

"Yeah, but Dixie's retired."

"I'm not talking about her." He held up two fingers.

Tony tilted his head. "You thinking Two Dogs?"

"Why not? He's not *technically* BOSS. He's got a vested interest. Even *you* can't deny he's one of the best."

"Don't get me wrong, I love the guy, but he's so paranoid."

"Paranoid people are rarely shot in the back."

Tony laughed. "Yeah, they see it coming. Fine, give him a call. You want chicken or burgers?"

"Something with bacon. I'm starving." My dad pulled out his purple flip phone and dialed.

*　*　*

"That guy is a grade-A prime certified dick," Bixby said after I had told the group about my encounter with Topher.

"He's got a point about Urchin," Kyra said. "That kid is off. I wonder what his Sin is."

"Lust or greed," I replied. She gave me an unamused stare. "Put me down for teleportation. He always seems to show up out of nowhere." I looked around. "Also, maybe don't use his name, in case it summons him." That got a snort of amusement from her and a laugh from the others.

I looked around the busy room. Riley hadn't shown up yet. I knew she wasn't absent unless something happened since second period. I finally spotted her exiting the food line, and I waved her over. She hesitated for a second, then the new boy, Gary, followed her with a tray of his own. Suddenly a battle waged in my chest.

"Down boy," Travis said, giving me a reassuring pat.

"Hey, guys. I want you to meet Garryowen," Riley said. "He just moved here from L.A."

I forced the raging beast inside my chest back into his cage. "Oh yeah, we met this morning," I said with a fake smile.

Travis and the twins offered greetings of their own.

"By all the laws of magic forbidden! Another stray, Mac?" asked Bixby. "You know these tables don't expand, right?"

Gary acknowledged each of us in turn. He smiled brightly. "It's a pleasure to meet you all." He and Riley sat down opposite each other.

"So," began Bixby. "Los Angeles, huh? Do you know the Carmichaels?"

Gary shook his head. "We just moved there over the summer," he said after swallowing a slice of meatloaf.

"Why'd you get transferred here so soon?" Bixby asked. It was a fair question. Custodians rarely moved their families more than once a year to avoid situations like these.

"We didn't transfer." He paused and poked his mashed potatoes with a somber look. "We moved so I could go here. A guy showed up out of the blue and started playing up this school. Said I'd been awarded a scholarship. Came with a subsidized apartment, so it beat the alternative." He shrugged.

The rest of us exchanged knowing glances. Something Gary must have noticed.

"What?" he asked.

"So," Travis said. "You're a Sinner."

"Well, we've all fallen short of the glory--"

"Not that kind of sinner," I interrupted. I looked at Travis. "Start from the start."

"Well," Travis began. "The short version is that magic and fairytale monsters exist, and you are one of them."

"You're joshing me," Gary said.

"Not yet. Look, everyone in this school is either a Sinner, formally known as a Supernatural Entity, or their parents are Custodians, or they've been the victims of monsters. Sinners come from a wide variety of origins, and not all of them can pass as human. But all of them have abilities well beyond human limits. Take Bixby here," he gestured. "He's what we call a polymath. A super genius. Think 'the Doctor' with one heart." He ignored Gary's furrowed brow. "Custodians, conversely, are tasked with maintaining normalcy and keeping the secret. They work as everything from personal assistants to exterminators, like Scott's dad, when he's not pretending to teach."

"We can infer that you are a Sinner," Bixby cut in. "Because if you were a Cuss, you would already have known that. They'll probably explain in I.A."

"Right," Gary said slowly. "Assuming this isn't hazing, which is illegal by the way, you think I've got some superpower?"

"Either that or you're a monster," Kyra answered.

"He doesn't look like a monster," Myra mused.

"Look, Gary," I said, interrupting what looked to be the start of a long dialog about someone at the table as if he weren't sitting right there. Having been the subject of these many times, I wanted to save Gary the same strife. "We aren't going to spill your secret," I told him, then I looked at Travis. "And we aren't going to pry." I fixed Gary with a significant look. "What you should do is make people assume you're a Cuss."

"That's what most Sinners do until they are outed," Riley confirmed. "Even then, some keep denying it without proof. Life here is harder for Sinners, whatever the founders intended. It's human nature to push the outliers to the fringes." She was staring at her vegetable medley, her voice somber.

"That's right," said Myra, placing her hand on top of Gary's. "Your status is sealed when you are here. Only the staff know. They are all trusted members of BOSS, and you can bet they won't let anyone know who's not supposed to."

"While I appreciate the advice, I honestly don't know what you are talking about except for BOSS. But I don't know what this has to do with single soldiers," Gary replied.

"Brotherly Order of the Silver Sword," Travis said. "It's the organization that runs this place, among other things."

"Look," Gary sighed. "I'm just a regular Army brat. Nothing special."

"He's telling the truth," Myra informed us. "He's never awakened."

Gary pulled his hand away.

"If he's not awakened and his parents aren't Cusses, why is he here?" Kyra asked. "Why now?"

The bell to end lunch rang out.

"A mystery to be sure," Travis mused.

Topher's policy of not snitching had apparently changed over lunch. I was listening to a conversation two girls were having about a cute new boy in their class when the same small boy I'd almost tripped over on the first day ran up to me with a note in his hand. Without a word, he held it out. I cautiously took it and read. I rolled my eyes as I saw Coach Keith had summoned me.

As I approached the field, he was talking to Gary. "Yeah, check with Coach Zamora. He'll run you through the paces."

The handsome boy jogged over to a squat coach wearing shorts that were much too short. Mr. Keith noticed me walking toward him. "I see you got my note," he said. I held it up.

"I hear you picked a fight with my quarterback."

"Nope," I answered evenly. "I just did what I could to stop a beatdown."

"Relax, Sport. I'm not going to give you detention. Yet."

I narrowed my eyes, wondering what his game was. "Martinez said you had a good tackle. I have a spot on the team for a good tackle."

"I don't play football," I replied. "I play rugby."

"They're almost the same game," he said.

I scoffed, wounded that anyone would think that.

"I'll make you a deal. You practice with us just once, and I'll consider all your transgressions forgiven. I'll even consider assigning your class less homework this week."

"Fine," I said. "But I don't have any…"

He picked up a set of pads and a helmet before I could continue and tossed them to me.

CHAPTER 5

<u>Bad Company</u>

By the time I had reached the flagpole after school, Riley was standing alone and looking at her phone. I waited until a group of bikers with ultra-loud tailpipes rode past before speaking. "Hey," I looked around. "Where's the rest of the clique?" The plan had been for all of us to meet up and walk to Archie's together, as usual.

"They got tired of waiting, so they went ahead to save a table." She stuffed her phone into her pocket. "I decided to stay behind for you."

"Sorry about that," I apologized. "I got held up by 'Coach' Keith." I made finger quotes around his title. "He tried to get me to join the football team."

"Ooh, you should," she said as we began walking. "You'd look cute in those tight pants." My ears burned and goosebumps ran up my neck. I briefly reconsidered my position. But I'd already flatly refused.

"I'll tell you what I told him," I told her. "I play rugby." There was a part of my brain, a large part, that was bitter towards gridiron football for leading America away from the clearly superior game.

"What's the difference?" she asked.

"Well, for one," I scoffed. "Rugby is played by men." My sardonic comment drew a sharp look from her. "As opposed to boys," I said in a panic. "Women play rugby, too. Another key difference." I was on the back foot again. It was strange that ordinarily, I wouldn't have bothered defending my stance. For the first time that I could remember, it mattered to me what someone thought. The notion was terrifying in its own right because she was just a friend. A friend that made me weak every time she smiled at me. A friend I didn't trust myself to be alone with.

She looked unimpressed at my feeble attempt to backtrack but seemed willing to overlook my insensitive comment. "Well, it's not like I know the rules anyway," she said dismissively.

Her phone buzzed, and she pursed her lips as she checked the message and sent a reply. She was quiet for a minute. I wasn't sure how to restart the conversation. I simply watched out of the corner of my eye as she slid the phone into her back pocket. She had her strawberry blonde hair in a braid today. My stomach did its usual flip when she moved to tuck the stragglers behind her ear. We turned a corner and the mob of freshly released students lessened.

"So," I began, partly to avoid thinking. "You get a lot of homework, too?"

"Mmhmm," she said, clearly distracted. *Probably with the same thoughts you are*, I thought to myself. There was a rumble in the distance; it was those bikes again. They'd been thundering around since the weekend began. We were only about a block away from Archie's. The rumbling grew as the band of bikers approached from ahead and passed us. I hardly took notice until they stopped just behind us. *Trouble*, a voice in my head told me. I moved to trail at her heels. I was looking at her Q.P.D. backpack, but all of my attention was focused on the men behind me.

"Hey, you," a man's voice shouted from behind us. "Wait up!"

"Keep walking," I told Riley.

"I said, wait up!" The voice was closer now. I turned and took my hand out of my pockets. He was a little taller than me, wearing a leather jacket over a white tee shirt. His face was rugged and he had three parallel scars running down the right side. He was wearing aviator shades, so I couldn't tell where he was looking, but I got a feeling it wasn't at me. "You kids go to that freak school, don't ya?" he asked in a gruff voice.

"We go to *a* school," I replied.

He smiled at me and rubbed his leather-gloved hand on his shaved and tattooed head.

"Yeah, you do," he said. His menacing smile showed several missing teeth. "I recognize little Missy's sweater," he growled. One of his friends sidled up next to him, with three more on the way.

I took a few steps back. "You know what they do in that school of theirs?" he asked his friend as he followed me. "They teach freaks how to pretend to be human." His friend laughed mirthlessly at that. "And they try to make fine, upstanding freak lovers out of pure-blooded humans." I took another step back and bumped into Riley, whose eyes were wide in terror. "Like this pretty little thing here," he said, gesturing at her. "Seems a shame to me." He smiled again, pure malice rolling off him.

The adrenalin was coursing through my whole body. My hands began to shake.

"Listen," I said shakily. "You need to back off."

He laughed at the tremor in my voice. He pushed me. I shoved back. Before his surprise wore off, I launched a punch to his throat that missed and hit his neck instead. "Go!" I shouted at Riley, who was just standing there, dumbfounded.

I blocked a punch aimed for my head and countered with a body blow. "Hurry! Get help!"

Finally, she turned and ran. One of the bikers tried to follow her, and I spun away from the leader, who was trying to wrap me in a bear hug. I took two steps and tackled him around the legs. He fell over, but so did I. Before I could recover, I received a steel-toed boot to the stomach and a blow to the head that made lights flash in my eyes. I forced myself up, but two strong arms grabbed me and pulled me off the ground. I thrashed around and punched at the arms holding me while kicking straight out before I hit the wall. I managed to soften my landing with my outstretched arms but couldn't turn around before another of the thugs wrapped his arms around me. He spun me around with my arms pinned behind me. I struggled to get out but received several blows to the stomach and ribs, sapping my energy. There were too many of them. *At least she got away*, I thought as my vision narrowed. I struggled for breath as they took a break from beating on me.

"You got more balls than brains, kid," the leader was saying from about a mile away. "I can respect that." I blurrily saw him pull something shiny out of his pocket. "Too bad you so-called 'Custodians' are fighting for the wrong team." He ran his knife down my chest and stopped over my heart. "I was going to send a message to The Chief, but The Slayer's kid will do just as well."

"Dou talk too mush," I mumbled through my bleeding mouth. I could just barely see my reflection in his now bent aviators. I was a bloody mess.

"I'll work on that," he said. He pulled back the knife and disappeared in a blur of white and black.

"Huh?" I wondered aloud. I was released and heard shouts through the ringing in my ears. Three new figures had joined the fray. My right eye was swollen shut, and it was getting hard to see through my blurry left eye. Two darker figures and a giant were plowing through the surprised gang.

"Grab Scott and let's go," said a familiar voice that I couldn't quite place. The entire world was spinning. The biggest of the three picked me up easily into a fireman's carry. Then I was rushing down the street sideways and backward, which did nothing to calm my dizziness.

Darkness took me.

*　*　*

Once again, I was standing in an infinite plane of light. I floated along, weightless, formless, clueless. "It is not yet your time," a voice from everywhere said.

So you keep saying, what is that supposed to even mean? I thought out loud.

"All things shall be revealed. In time," the voice replied. Instantaneously, the beryl skinned giant was in front of me. His flaming eyes flashed, and the world was dark again.

"He's suffered a concussion, fractured his right orbital socket, and has three cracked ribs," a female voice was saying. I opened my eyes. Well, *eye.* I was on a hard bed in a white room. Everything ached. "So he won't be going anywhere tonight."

"Will there be any lasting complications?" I heard my mother's voice ask.

"Hard to say at this point," the other woman, who was wearing a white coat, said. "TBI often has unforeseen consequences. I recommend scheduling an MRI tomorrow morning." My parents looked at each other and nodded their consent. The doctor left, and my parents noticed I was awake.

"Scott!" my mother cried.

"M'up," I replied stupidly. My voice was hard to find, and my lips were the wrong shape.

"Scott, sweetie, are you okay?" she asked, holding my hand with tears in her eyes.

I nodded.

"Good, honey," she said. "Now tell me who did this so I can kill them." Her voice went from gentle to hard instantly. My dad put his hand on her shoulder and smiled at me.

"Listen, son," he whispered to me. "The cops are on their way to question you. Assume you were filmed, but remember, you were in fear for your life."

"Scott!" My mother said to him. "He's barely awake. Make them give him a minute."

"I'm fine," I lied.

"Sure you are, honey."

"Dix, remember that I used to do this for a living. They're going to want to know who did this, but Leo, being who he is, they're going to ask if he started it."

"They looked like they were going to attack Riley. I couldn't do *nothing.*" The sudden change in his face made me instantly regret my words.

"You were walking with Riley McKinsey?" he asked, anger rising in his voice. He forced himself to be calm after my mom shot him a withering look. "I overlooked the fact that you still ate lunch with her group because I thought I could trust your judgment. I guess I was wrong."

"I didn't know it was going to be *just* us," I replied. My bruised brain clouded my judgement too much to mount a decent defense.

"That's enough, sweetheart," my mother interjected. "Just let it be for now." I couldn't tell if she was talking to my dad or to me.

The detective who came in to interview me was a short athletic man with brown skin and slicked-back, black hair. I put down my jello dinner when he arrived. My parents stood to shake his hand. He introduced himself as Detective Lopez. I began telling him what happened, but halfway through, a tall, handsome man with short bleach blonde hair walked in. He was wearing a blue suit with many pins and a badge that identified him as Leon McKinsey, Chief of Police. My parents stood again, much less politely this time.

"Ah, here's the young man himself," he said in a jovial tone.

I tried to smile, but my split lip made the action painful.

He addressed my parents next. "Hello, Scott, Joanna."

They didn't respond.

He took his hat off. "Apologies for the intrusion. Detective, have you taken his statement?"

"Just about, Sir."

"Good, good," he said absently. "You can finish in a bit. I'd like to have a word with young Mr. O'Connor." Detective Lopez packed up his notebook and left without a word. I tried to look friendly to the Chief. Neither of my parents did. "If you don't mind," he said, addressing them. "I'd like to speak to him alone."

"Oh, why didn't you say so," my dad said and looked at my mother. "He wants to be alone with our son."

"Well, it would be rude not to leave them to it," she responded quickly.

They both sat back down on the couch next to my hospital bed with crossed arms.

Chief McKinsey pursed his lips. "Very well." He looked at me. "My daughter says you saved her life, at great personal cost."

"I didn't really think about it much," I said honestly.

"Nevertheless, I want you to know how grateful I am." He reached out his hand. My father shifted behind me as I gripped it firmly. He paused, then nodded and walked out of the room.

"That was weird," I said when he was gone. My father stood up and straightened his signature red leather duster. "Why did he want to be alone just to say that?" I asked the room.

"He said that *because* you weren't alone," my father replied as he walked to the glass door. He looked down the hall and back past me to my mother, who subtly nodded. "Back soon," he promised me.

As he left, my Uncles Tony showed up. "Was that Leo?" Tony Two asked. "That looked like Leo."

"That was him," my mother said, pulling out a tablet. "He wanted a private word with Little Scott."

I hated that name more than Scotty. I would have preferred Junior, but she refused to call me that. Even better would have been an original name. Both Tonys sucked in air in unison.

"Bold," said Tony One musingly.

"Dumb," Tony Two matter-of-factly retorted.

"Hi," I interjected. "Does someone want to fill me in?"

They both looked at my mother, who scowled at them.

"'Cause it seems like I'm missing some pretty crucial information."

"He's old enough," Tony One said, then he shrugged his massive shoulders. He patted my arm. "He's tough enough, anyway."

Her glare softened as she looked at me. I looked back at her. Her eyes were still wet. I've heard that mothers always see their children as the babies they held in their arms. I could be older than she was with every medal they could give strapped to my chest and have twenty-seven children of my own, and I knew she would always see me bald and screaming for milk. In later years, I would learn how true that was. I suddenly felt very guilty for putting her through this worry.

With a defeated sigh, she looked back at the tablet, swiping up. My Uncles took this as positive consent and began. "You 'member how we all met?" Tony One asked me.

"The bus investigation," I replied. It was a long story, and I'd heard it many times. It began with an exploding bus and led to my father getting kicked off the force and discovering the paranormal world that BOSS tried to keep hidden.

"The cop that sold him out," he stated. He pointed his thumb at the door behind him.

My jaw dropped, causing pain to shoot across my face. "No way."

"He was trying to stop us from finding out about the Sindicate meet in Vegas," Tony Two confirmed. "Your old man brought evidence against him to the brass, but the Captain was already on the take. I tried to warn him, but he wanted to do things by the book."

"That sounds like him," I said. There were few things he loved more than law and order, and all of them were in the room with us, save maybe for my cousin.

"Well, then the Chief got promoted up the chain when Kel blew up the station." He shrugged and popped a breath mint into his mouth. "The Slayer's never quite gotten over it," he said, referencing my dad's "work" name.

"It didn't help that he also sent us on those suicide missions," Tony One said. "Memba the shadow portal?"

"Oh, yeah," Tony Two said with a smile. "What a perfect bastard."

"Wait," I said. I held up my hands in a halting motion. "So he sold you guys out, and then he was your director? So he *did* work for BOSS?"

"'Did' being the imperative word," said Tony Two. He leaned back in his chair.

"How did he end up the Chief all the way up here?" I asked.

Tony One sat down on a folding chair that creaked worryingly under his muscular frame. Tony Two stopped smiling and looked at the chair with a concerned expression.

"It helps to smooth things over in a hot town," his tone was distracted, and he spoke slowly. "When you have friends in high places…"

Tony One glared at him.

"Don't look at me like that," the smaller man told his friend. "It's not my fault they didn't have behemoths in mind when the lowest bidder cranked that thing out."

"Fine," the big man retorted. "I'll stand up." That was when the chair gave in.

The next morning, I laid uncomfortably in the world's most expensive echo chamber. "Please try not to move," the tech told me for the twelfth time. I was trying to think of how I could be more uncomfortable. *You could be back in a biker's arms*, I answered myself.

The previous night had been miserable. I couldn't sleep on my side. The bed was hard, and leaving it was a nonstarter because someone had stolen my underwear. It wasn't until the morning when my mother brought me a fresh pair that I felt brave enough to use the bathroom. Then I was wheeled to the MRI room, placed on a plastic plank, and shoved into a machine that would haunt a more claustrophobic person's nightmares. Still, my ribs felt better and my headache was gone. As I laid there, staring at the chamber's dark beige roof, listening to the arrhythmic ticking, I heard the door open. "Morning Doctor," Dave, the imaging tech, said.

"Good morning, David," my doctor responded. "How's our patient today?"

"I'm bored," I replied from the chamber.

"Please try not to move," Dave repeated for the thirteenth time.

"That's… interesting," Dr. Nguyen said, ignoring us both.

"What's that?" Dave asked.

"Well, his charts say he should have a concussion, but look. It's a perfectly healthy brain. No swelling, no sign of damage at all. But last night, the C.T. showed definite signs of T.B.I."

"Does that mean I can get out of this thing?" I asked.

"Please try not to move," Dave said for the fourteenth time.

"It's remarkable," Dr. Nguyen told my parents. "Children often recover from injury more rapidly than adults, but this is…" She let the sentence hang there. Scott and Joanna O'Connor gave each other a knowing look that I ignored.

"I've always been a fast healer," I explained. "Does this mean I can go home now?" I was hoping to avoid sleeping on the remote-controlled bed from hell again. The hope died when she shook her head.

"We don't like to send head injuries home without a couple of nights' observation," she explained kindly. "But I'm going to allow your friends to visit you."

The thought didn't cheer me up as much as she thought it would. I didn't want them to see me in this state. "Great," I lied. "Next best thing."

The first to show up was (predictably) Tony. Despite my earlier skepticism, it cheered me up to see him. "So then we come tearing around the corner, right?" he was saying, his hands moving like a banking plane. "And we see these Hunters holding you up. Well, James is like 'Only I get to kill him,' and BAM!" he punched his palm. "He clobbers the guy holding the knife. Trav and I start swinging away, James picks you up, and we bolt before they even know what happened." He held his hands out, palms up. "And that's the true story of how we saved your life." He finished with a smile.

I returned it."All the same," I joked. "Owing a life debt to James… maybe you should have left me."

As we recovered from our laughing fit and Tony wiped his eyes, there was a knock on the door. It was Travis and Bixby. I waved them in. "Thanks for saving my life," I said to the golden-skinned senior.

"Everybody gets one," he replied.

"Trav told me the whole thing," Bixby said. "Can't believe those Hunters tried to off a Cuss." He shook his head.

"I didn't even realize they were Hunters at first," I said. "I just thought they were super-racist, kinda-rapey bikers. How'd you find out?"

Travis took a seat on the couch next to Bixby. "I recognized their patches," he said. "Van Hellsings." He pulled his foot up to his knee. "Vampire hunters. Must have been looking for the Sindicate hideout. That's the tea with the interns."

"Sindicate? What's that? Some sort of Vampire Mafia?" Bixby asked jokingly. His smile disappeared when he saw our expressions. "Oh?"

"I thought my family took them out years ago," I said.

Travis shrugged. "I guess they're under new management."

I laid against the back of my bed, which was almost fully in the upright position, and looked up at the hospital lights. "Still doesn't explain what they are doing here in Quentin."

"They're probably here for the same reason as us," Travis responded. "Eldrium."

I looked at him quizzically. "What's that?" I'd never even heard of it before.

"Eldrium is a rare ore with several 'magical' properties," Bixby recited. "Mostly used as focus gems for spellcasters, but many supernatural life forms are drawn to it instinctively. Recently, a process was discovered that can convert it into clean energy. That's why the town has grown so much in the last few years. It used to be a sleepy little logging town, famous only for being a music festival venue. Now the mines are open. Mining brings business, the business brings people, and exposed eldrium is bringing creatures who feed on people."

"Wow. Thanks for the expo dump, Encyclopedia Brown," Urchin said.

Tony was the only one of us not to jump in surprise.

"Knock or something first, dude!" I scolded Urchin.

He knocked on the open door without breaking eye contact.

"Come in," I said flatly. "There's plenty of room."

"I'll take up very little space," he said. "I'm mostly here to endear myself."

"To whom?" I asked.

"You, the audience, but mostly to the girls who are on their way," he said as he moved to the far corner. "Chicks dig loyalty."

"The girls are coming?" I asked idiotically.

"No, they hate heroic acts of derring-do," he said sarcastically.

"Did you not think they were coming?" Bixby laughed.

"The thing is, I'm not really dressed," I admitted. "I don't suppose you brought an extra change of clothes?" I asked Tony.

Before he could answer, three girls stepped into the room.

I self-consciously made sure the blanket was covering my waist. "Uh, hi," I said. Riley blinked back tears.

"Um, thanks fo--" I was cut off as she closed the distance between us and locked her lips with mine.

CHAPTER 6

Falling for the First Time

In a fortnight filled with ups and downs, (mostly downs,) this was the zenith. It was the best thing that had ever happened to me. Sure, I was in a hospital bed with no real pants on. Sure, all of our friends were watching, but I wouldn't have traded that moment for anything. My senses flooded with the softness of her lips and the scent of her hair, and I was totally at peace. Either after a couple moments or a couple days, maybe somewhere in between, she pulled gently away. She looked me in the eyes again.

I gave her a dopey smile. "I should almost die more often," I said.

She smiled.

"Oh, is that all you have to do," Urchin quipped.

"I think…" Travis said as he stood. "…we should clear the floor for now."

Riley thanked him and they filed out, Urchin muttering about missing the good part. I shifted uncomfortably in my torture bed, and Riley sat down, looking at her hands.

"So," I began after the door was closed and Tony had dragged Urchin away from the window.

"So," she replied. "I'm sorry, I just…" She took out a tissue and dabbed her eyes. "You could have died."

"Yeah, I almost did," I said. *Not helping.* I thought. I fought off the part of my mind that was solely focused on kissing her again. I liked that part. Genesis 2:24 was beginning to make more sense.

"Promise me," she eventually said. "That you won't do it again."

I raised an eyebrow. "What, almost die?"

She smiled ruefully. "Sacrifice yourself for me."

I stared at her for several long moments. She couldn't be serious, could she? She was essentially asking me to change a core part of myself. I'd inherited a good brain and sarcastic wit from my mom, and my dad had given me height and a tendency towards self-sacrifice. "I really want to, but I can't." I shrugged.

She looked disappointed, but there was nothing I could do about that short of betraying my nature. "I can't control these situations. I don't know why trouble has it out for me. My life used to be…"

"Peaceful?" she offered.

"Boring, I guess," I replied as I swallowed, confused by the strange rush of loud emotions. Hormones coursed through my brain, making everything even more confusing. I was fighting with myself. Intellectually, I knew these feelings were forbidden. I understood now why my father was so opposed to the idea. But Riley wasn't her father any more than I was mine.

"It's all my fault," she said.

"Personally, I blame the bikers," I replied.

She didn't immediately respond but stared at her fingers as I watched her, trying to read her mind.

"You got beaten because you were trying to save me," she said at last.

"I got *beaten* because I tried to take on five grown men at the same time," I replied,."I don't regret it."

She raised her eyes to meet mine.

"I'd do the same thing again," I offered. "And again and again. Even if I knew no help was on the way." Tears were forming in her eyes. "Twice on a Sunday."

"Why?" she demanded, her voice raised.

"Because I like you," My tongue stuck on the 'L' as I barely stopped myself from saying the word I couldn't take back. I was becoming tired of hiding my feelings. A determination swept over me, and I decided then and there to say something unconscionable. "And I want to be with you."

She tried to hide her smile. "I thought you couldn't--"

"My dad said I would get hurt," I interrupted. "And I did." I touched my lip lightly and smiled. "And it was worth it. If it's a mistake, it's a mistake I *want* to make." I put out my hand. "If you want to make it with me…"

She reached out and held my proffered hand.

We looked into each other's eyes and kissed again.

*   *   *

Tony Two sipped merrily on his cherry soda while his best friend scowled next to him. Tony didn't begrudge my dad for his foul mood. Having your son sent to the Emergency Room will do that to a man. Still, I survived and wouldn't have any lasting damage.

A dark haired man in a fedora and sunglasses slid into the opposite end of the booth. "This needs to be quick. My… family thinks I'm going out for milk."

Tony smirked at the comment, but the other two men found no humor in the choice of words.

"Anders, you called us," my dad replied evenly.

"What the hell are the Van Hellsings doing in your town? Does BOSS not care about order anymore?"

My dad growled. "It was *my* son they attacked, Hansen, so watch where you throw those accusations."

Anders sighed. "Sorry, I forgot, but you can see why I'm a little nervous." He took a deep breath.

Tony Two slid the glass mug a few inches away from himself. "They'll leave when they find the vamps they think are running around. Our source tells us there's more hunters coming soon." What little color Anders had in his face vanished. "Now, your family's probably safe from them, but the sooner they find what they're looking for, the sooner they leave."

My dad leaned forward and pulled off his sunglasses. "Out with it. I know you're hiding something."

"Several of them." Anders quickly admitted. He looked around nervously. "It's an entire coven. They've been hiding in my basement for weeks."

"You told us your coven had been wiped out, your Nosferatu destroyed." My dad continued to stare into Anders' eyes. The vampire couldn't look away from him. "So who's in your basement?"

"The Sindicate."

"Told you," Tony said.

My dad didn't look away from the man across from him. "I told *you*."

Anders licked his lips. "I need--"

"You need to tell us what you know if you want anything like help," my dad said, interrupting him.

Anders Hansen nodded. "Okay. I'll do what I can. Just promise me you make sure my daughter Katie doesn't get caught up in this. Not with the hunters, and not with Kel."

"Andy, we're going to do everything we can for you. Trust me on that." Tony held his arms out wide. "I'd hate for anything to happen to my favorite student."

*   *   *

"They what?" James pounded his fist into the table.

"James Matthew," his mother scolded.

"Sorry," he muttered. He glared at Myra.

She didn't look up from cutting her butternut squash. "Don't look at me like that, I'm just the messenger."

"I'mma kill him," he growled.

"You most certainly will not," Margaret Morgenstern replied sternly. "You will leave those two alone. Lord knows they'll have enough trouble with their fathers," she muttered to herself.

"Shouldn'ta saved his stupid life," James growled into his mashed potatoes.

Tony patted his shoulder. "But you did. Bud, you gotta let it go."

"You told me he wouldn't kiss her," James accused.

"I *said* his dad told him not to." Tony picked up his knife again. "I guess I just don't know him that well anymore."

"Surprising no one," Kyra retorted.

"Huh?" He cocked his head to the side.

"Think about it, Tony. Mee and I spend more time with him than you do."

Tony poked at his steak. "Well, yeah, cause... he's spending all his time with Riley."

"Have you tried calling him?" Myra asked.

"He hasn't called me either, you know." Tony's tone was defensive.

Myra put her salad fork down and clasped her hands in front of her. "We're not accusing you of anything. I'm just saying that friendships take time. He's told us countless stories of all the time you spent together. As it is, you spend all of *your* time with the guy that tried to break his ribs without ever having said a complete sentence to him. What's he to think?"

Tony looked up at his gigantic best friend. "What do you say, big guy?"

"I'd rather eat my own face than hang out with that guy." James ripped a chunk out of his steak.

"James, use your utensils like a gentleman," his mother scolded.

After dinner, Tony sat on the floor of James' room, deep in thought. He put down his controller and sighed.

James frowned and paused the game. "What?"

"I'm gonna head home." Tony grabbed his bag and stood.

"You said you were crashing here tonight."

"Yeah, but I'm just not feeling it."

James frowned and his face scrunched up, as close to being deep in thought as he had ever been. "You're mad at me?"

"I'm not mad, I just…" He slid his pack onto his shoulder. "You aren't just my best friend, you're my only friend."

"Good."

"See? That's the problem. You're so jealous all the time. If I stopped hanging out with you for even a couple hours, you'd throw a fit."

"Cause yer my friend."

"Yeah, friend. Not pet." He looked at James, who was frowning. "Look, I'm going to try and hang out with other people more. If you have a problem with that, let me know."

"I have a problem with that," James replied right away.

"Then *we* have a problem."

"I don't want to stop being friends." James' voice was stoic.

"Neither do I."

James sat quietly for a moment, controller still in hand. "Myra says sometimes we have to let people have space so they like us more." He looked at his hands. "If you have to have space, I'll give you space."

"Thank you."

"But I'm going to complain the whole time."

*　*　*

It was Thursday before I was allowed to go back to school. I still hadn't told my parents about what happened with Riley. That was a problem for Future Scott. He was wiser, anyway. As I walked through the gates, I could hear whispers over the music in my bone conduction headphones. Rumors about my knight-in-shining-armor act had spread. The whispers ranged from awe to incredulity.

"There's no way he took on a gang of Hunters," a boy with black-rimmed glasses was saying. "Look at his face. It's not even bruised up." This was true. By the time I was discharged, I barely hurt at all. The next morning, my ribs weren't even sore.

"Hey," Riley said.

I snapped my eyes up. How long had she been there? "Hey," I greeted her, pulling my headphones down to my neck and pausing my music. I held my hands at my side and smiled. "So," I said, unsure what else to say. I'd never been in a relationship before. The next steps were in the dark for me.

"So," she agreed.

"Fun fact about me: I'm awful at starting conversations," I said, making her laugh.

She took a step closer and put her hand in mine, our fingers interlaced. An electric charge ran up my spine.

"That's fine," she said. "Nobody's perfect." I had just opened my mouth to respond when the twins joined us. They both looked like they had spent a great deal of time on their hair. Being a guy whose hair hadn't been longer than an inch in ten years, I wasn't the best judge of that. Myra had a princess braid, Kyra had shaved the other side of her head and had some sort of braided mohawk.

She looked at our hands. "It's official then.".

I smiled and shrugged. Riley giggled and looked down, placing her free hand on the other side of mine. "Good thing James isn't here today."

"Shame," I said ironically. "What happened to him?"

"He threw Topher Beck through a window yesterday," Myra said. "Poor thing."

Kyra rolled her eyes, then squinted behind me, an incredulous expression on her face. "Is that man wearing two pairs of parachute pants?"

We all turned and saw a short man with a shaved head and a well-groomed red beard. He was walking toward the main building, my jaw dropped. I understood her confusion. He wore a pair of pluderhosen, old German pants usually found in sword treatises. They were baggy, black, and tied off just below the knee. There was what looked like another pair of pants, this one red, pouring out of the slits that ran up and down the outer layer. He was carrying a long athletic bag over his shoulder. "That's Ryan Ramirez," I said in awe.

"Who's that?" Kyra asked. "Besides a guy with weird fashion."

I looked pointedly at her hair. She cracked her knuckles, and I took a step back. "He's last year's world longsword champion," I explained.

The girls gave me confused looks.

"He's one of the foremost scholars on Joachim Meyer." Still nothing. "He's one of the best sword fighters in the world. I have, like, three of his books." The bell rang. "What's he doing here?" I wondered aloud.

"Will someone, anyone, tell me why Rome fell?" Tony Two asked the class.

I raised my hand.

He glared at me. "I swear to God, Claudio, if you say it slipped on Greece..." He let the threat hang.

My hand lowered. Half the class laughed.

"Great," he said, annoyed. "Now I have to teach. Thanks for nothing." He started writing on the whiteboard.

"Were you really going to say that?" Riley whispered incredulously.

"He taught me that joke when I was five," I replied. "It was my favorite for... years, really."

"But it's so... *lame*," she said.

"So am I," I joked, and I started writing down notes about trusting too much in foreign labor and having an overgrown government. "Besides, are you telling me that you didn't have a lame joke you loved at five?"

"Not really," she said. She wasn't smiling anymore. "I was very sick when I was young. The doctors told my parents I wouldn't see my next birthday. Leukemia." She shrugged at my concerned look. "Obviously, I got better. By the time I was six, I was healthy enough to go to school," she said. "It *did* mean I started school a year late." She seemed to realize something. "I guess that makes me the older woman. My birthday is in a couple of weeks, and I'll be sixteen."

"Older by a month. Really robbing the cradle there," I replied as I absent-mindedly copied notes. She turned her head to the side. "I uh," I softly cleared my throat. "I had to repeat the second grade," I admitted. "We moved about five times that year. I was so upset about it I refused to do any work. I sure showed *me*."

"Well, that just proves it," she said with a smile as she picked up her pencil. "It was meant to be."

I smiled, too.

My next two classes went by with normal tedium, if such a thing as normal even existed. Mr. Keith reiterated that he had an open spot on the football team. I replied that since their first game was tomorrow and that the game was still football, I would once again have to pass. The real surprise came when I swiped for Individual Advancement. I assumed I'd be continuing the refresher course in vampire lore. Likely, they had reached the section that explained how vampirism was considered an STD, but I was back in the workout room I had started the year in. Instead of a hulking alligator wrestler, I saw one of my childhood heroes. He was practicing a drill with a broadsword in the mirror. I watched him for a moment, the elevator dinging behind me.

"I'll be with you in a moment," he said in a smooth voice. He finished the drill and hung his sword on a wooden rack that held dozens. He mopped the sweat off of his shiny head and smiled politely. "You must be Scott's son. You look just like he did at that age."

My jaw dropped. "You know my dad? My dad knows you?"

He nodded. "High school fencing team. Though he was more fond of kendo." He clapped his hands together. "So. I'm told you have some talent with swordplay."

It took a lot of effort to lift my jaw from the floor. I nodded. "A little. I've been learning from my dad for years."

"Outstanding," he replied as he reached the weapon rack and picked up two swords. He tossed me one and put on a fencing mask. "Let's see where you're at."

Half an hour later, we both sat on a bench. He was breathing harder than I was, which I took as an ever so small victory. I sat with my gambeson open, pounding water and letting the fans cool my soaked shirt.

"So," he began, opening his own padded jacket. "What do you think you did well? What were you having success at? Then we can talk about where you struggled."

I smiled. One of the best HEMA fencers in the world was giving me a lesson. I promised myself to thank my dad when I saw him. "Well, Mr. Ramirez..."

"Please, call me Ryan." He reached out to shake my hand. I almost fainted. I definitely needed to remember to thank my dad.

"What's a HEMA?" Myra asked later when I told the group about my new instructor.

"Historical European Martial Arts," Bixby said, answering for me. "Fancy term for sword fighting."

I let the oversimplification pass.

"What I want to know is why?" he asked. "Why swords are suddenly on the docket. If anything, it makes sense to teach you to learn how to fight multiple people." He held his palms up. "I mean, how often do you walk around with a sword?"

I shrugged and took a bite of my cheese-less bean and cheese burrito. I hadn't thought of that. I didn't tell them that when my dad went on missions, his long coat often hid a sword.

At home, my mother was working on dinner. "Where is Scott?" she asked absently. "Dinner is ready in five, with or without him."

I looked up from my algebra homework to see the sun less than an inch above the horizon. I straightened my arms up with a groan. I'd been working since I got home. My hospital stay did not relieve me of my workload, and I'd been assigned three days' worth of work. We didn't have long to wait, though. A few minutes later, his black van pulled into the driveway. I closed my books and stretched again, ready to hug him whether or not he wanted it.

As soon as the door opened, I rushed. "Dad! Thanks so--" My hug and sentence were both interrupted by his rough push. "What?" I asked.

"You know what," he snarled. A chill went down my spine. "I told you, didn't I?" He started pacing. "I told you to stay away. We said we didn't want you to get hurt. Even your mother backed me up on this, remember?"

My mother exited the kitchen with a casserole dish in her hands. "What happened?" she asked coldly.

My stomach dropped, and I sat back down in the chair. My neck buzzed with guilt.

"He was walking around with McKinsey's daughter," my dad said. "Even though last time he did that, he wound up in the ER. Tony Two told me they were holding hands in his class. He's not even trying to be sneaky about it."

"Scotty, is that true?" she asked. She was calm, and her tone had no accusation in it.

I looked up at her while blinking back the tears that were stubbornly trying to push through. Her face was emotionless. I nodded, and she sighed. She walked back into the kitchen.

"I said 'end it,' and I expected that to sink in." His voice was calmer now, though no less frightening. "I overlooked you going on an end-run around me with a loophole," he said. "I thought 'Nah, he's smart enough to know where the line is. You raised him right.' But I guess I was wrong." He took a deep breath. "I'm telling you now. End it. For good. No friendship, no phone calls, nothing."

"No," I said. I was as shocked as he was.

"That wasn't one of the options." He crossed his arms.

"I don't care," I replied. "You just won't let this stupid feud with Leon go. Don't take it out on her, we aren't part of your--"

"You are not Romeo, and she is not Juliet," he interrupted. "This is about--"

"This is about you controlling my life!" I shouted. We were both so stunned that there were several seconds of silence. I realized I was standing up. Thunder rumbled in the background. He suddenly looked drained and sat down with a groan.

"We talked about this," he reminded me. "The whole family, together. I don't want you getting hurt or--"

"I got hurt anyway," I said. "So what's the difference if I do it with her?"

"You sure are stupid for such a smart kid," he said. "You were with her when you got hurt."

"I--" I took a deep breath. "I think--" He sighed, but I kept going. I needed to be honest with someone. "I think I'm in love with her," I finished.

"Ugh," he rolled his eyes so hard his head moved. I wondered how many times he'd rolled his eyes so far in the conversation. "You are not in love, you're sixteen."

"I'm almost seventeen," I replied.

"That's not better."

"I feel what I feel." I held my chin up proudly.

"You feel what the cocktail of hormones you're jacked up on tells you to feel," he replied.

"Scott," my mother said from the doorway. We both turned. She was looking at me. "Go to your room."

"But--"

"Now," she said firmly.

With an exasperated moan, I stomped down the hall.

"He's not twelve anymore," I heard her say before I slammed the door. Once I did, their pending argument was too muffled to understand. I sat down and pulled my phone out of my pocket.

<u>Hey you.</u> <u>I like you.</u>

I looked at Riley's message. The tears fought their way back. I blinked them away and tossed my phone across the room, then rolled over. *I was this close to a perfect day*, I thought as I drifted off to sleep.

*　*　*

"I know he's not a kid anymore, Okay? I get it." My dad began pacing the living room.

My mom crossed her arms. "Do you, Scott? 'Cause the way you're just laying down ultimatums..."

"Dixie, he's walking into a situation that's guaranteed to get him hurt. McKinsey--"

"Drop this Hatfields and McCoys horse crap for a minute and think about how your teenage son-"

My dad punched the wall and left his fist there. "I know."

She blinked. "I'm sorry, what?"

62

"You're right." He sighed and hung his head.

My mother looked at her watch, then felt for a fever. "Did you just admit to being wrong?"

"No. I think getting in bed with McKinsey is a mistake."

"They're just kissing." She shot a glance at my closed door. "They'd *better* be just kissing."

"Not what I meant." He sighed and sat down. "Why can't he just be a good kid?"

She kneeled and held his hands. "He *is* a good kid. He's just… didn't you have a girl you had a massive crush on in high school?"

He looked at her. "You can't possibly expect me to answer that."

She smiled. "Good boy. Fine, I guess I need to remind you he's not just *your* son. You know more about my history than anyone else. I told you what happened when my daddy told me I couldn't go out with Johnny Grant."

He nodded. "Okay, you win. This ain't the hill I wanna die on."

"Thank you."

"But don't expect me to like it." He took off his glasses, revealing his bright blue eyes. "Why can't he just be my little buddy again?"

"Kids grow up. It sucks, but it sure beats the alternative."

CHAPTER 7

Moth Into Flame

The end of September was approaching fast, and my life was falling into a pattern. I'd been waking up earlier so I could shower in the morning, getting to school early to get an extra five minutes with Riley, and then school. My lessons with Ryan continued. I'd thought I was good before, and for my age group, I was, but this last half of a month had seen drastic improvements in areas I didn't know were flawed. After school, the clique would walk to Archies for some cheese fries and/or a pizza.

"So anyway, the party is on the third at one," Riley said. We were all walking together. My arm was around her shoulder, and she was holding my draped hand. "My place, of course. Oh, and bring a swimsuit," she finished.

"Oh, really?" Kyra quipped. "You want us to bring swimsuits to a pool party? Pure madness."

"She only picked a pool party because she wants to see a certain someone without a shirt," Myra teased.

My face burned and Riley's ears turned scarlet.

A new sign was up, advertising the return of "Pizza Tuesdays," which confirmed what we would be splitting. Bixby ordered while the rest of us grabbed our table.

"So, is your dad going to let you go?" Travis asked me.

"We have an... understanding," I said, the smile no longer on my face. The morning after the big blowup, he'd knocked on my door. I hadn't expected that, since he was almost always gone by the time I woke up. He told me he'd take me to school. His tone was odd. It wasn't as sad as when we had to put Nina, our old German shepherd, down, but it was just as defeated. He asked if I planned to fight him on this. I told him I would.

"You're almost a man," he'd said. "And getting to the point that you have to make your own mistakes. And that's what this is: *your* mistake." He looked at the road the whole time. "That means when this thing blows up, I won't help you clean the mess."

Bixby showed up and mussed Travis' golden blonde hair, shaking me from my memory. The conversation turned to an episode of a popular TV show that they watched and I didn't, which was probably why I noticed the rough-looking man in his early twenties sitting down at the bar. He was looking around like he was expecting someone.

"Right, Scott?" One of the twins, most likely Myra, asked.

"I guess," I replied distractedly. When the guy answered his phone, I excused myself from the table and walked toward the bathroom.

"Yeah, I'm here," he said into his phone. "Archie's. Third and Lee. What? No, he didn't. Kermit's? Like the frog? Ok, where is it?" He took out a pen and notepad and wrote down an address. He had a patch on his left sleeve that said 'Zombie Response Team'. He looked up and made eye contact with me. I put my head down and continued to the bathroom. "Be right there," he said as I walked past.

I was standing at the urinal when he opened the door. He took the one next to me. Apparently, he had never heard of the code. "You're that kid that took on the Van Hellsings," he said as he stared at the wall.

"That's a polite way to say 'almost got killed by,'" I responded.

"That's balls, kid," he said. "I can vibe with that."

"Gee, mister, thanks," I replied sarcastically.

"Hey, I'm not on their side or anything. But your little town is seriously messed up."

I finished my business and flushed. "So messed up that roving Hunter biker gangs start trying to assault innocent girls?" I demanded.

"Look," he said as he flushed. "I already said what they did was wrong, but your chief is--"

But I didn't find out what the chief was, because Travis walked in and went to the sink. He looked at us in the mirror.

"Pizza's here, bud," he said as he turned on the water. I washed my hands and walked back to the table with Travis, and the Hunter walked out and into an old muscle car.

"Actually, I'm not feeling good," I said. "Can you let the others know?"

He looked at me for a long time, his expression unreadable, his silver sunglasses causing me to stare at my reflection. He nodded. "Be careful."

I nodded in return.

Kermit's Bar and Grill was a gastropub at the edge of town with an old-timey saloon-style facade. It also had about twenty bikes in front of it. My phone rang as I approached. It was Riley. "Hey, you," I said.

"Are you okay? Trav said you didn't feel good." Even through the phone, I could hear the concern in her voice.

"Just an upset stomach," I lied. "And I have a bunch of homework." I was distracted by trying to get in. I decided approaching from the front was going to be a bad idea. Several of the bikes had a familiar logo.

"How are you going to do it?" she asked.

"What do you mean?" I asked. There was an opening that probably led to the back alley.

"You forgot your backpack," she said.

I winced at the realization. "I guess I feel worse than I thought," I offered.

"I'll give it to Tony and ask him to drop it off for you."

"Thanks, you're the best. I like you."

"Like you, too." She giggled, and I pressed the "end call" button.

While no one was looking, not that there were many people in this part of town anyway, I slipped into the alley and found a locked mesh security door. I didn't have to wait long for an idea, as I saw movement and hid. A kid, probably from Blomgren, opened the door and kicked down the doorstop. He wore a white apron and headphones and was entirely distracted by his music. He walked two full trash bags to the dumpsters on the far side of the alley. Without a second thought, I slipped in and found myself in a hallway leading out to the main bar area. I snuck down the hall and slipped into a closet. I left the door slightly open.

"I don't need to hear it from your lot, Bruce," one of the Hunters said. "You brought the heat down before anything could get done."

"Hey!" A voice I recognized said. "We were trying to send a message."

"Oh, you sent a message, all right," the first voice snapped. "You told the chief of police that we wanted to molest his daughter. Great. Now we have BOSS *and* Q.P.D. breathing down our necks. It's a wonder that we can walk down the street without being picked up."

"I ain't sorry," the guy named Bruce said. "My only regret was putting that Sinner lover in the hospital and not the morgue." A worrying number of cheers answered him. "I just wish I got that Sin-loving traitor girl, too."

"Sounds like you got more than one regret, Bruce," I heard the man from Archie's say.

"Shut up, kid."

"Shut up *everybody*," the first voice said. "Look, we know where they sleep. We can get them--" I didn't hear what he said next because my phone rang. I panicked and answered it.

"Riley, now isn't a good time," I whispered loudly.

Only distorted noises responded. I could hear faint voices that sounded underwater. It seemed fitting somehow that I'd be given away by a butt dial. I hung up the phone and listened, but no one was talking. The door opened to reveal three large figures. "This isn't the bathroom," I said before they yanked me out.

"Let me finish the job," Bruce, the leader of the Van Hellsings said as he pulled out a knife.

"Shut up, Bruce," the young man from Archie's retorted, drawing a murderous look in his direction.

"We don't kill kids here," said the man who owned the first voice. He looked a lot like an older version of the young man. "Especially if they aren't Sinners." He thought for a moment and looked at me. "You aren't a Sinner, are ya?"

"We all fall short of the glory of--"

"Shut up," he interjected. "What are you doing here, little spy?"

"Do not worry," said a smooth, wise voice from the back of the room. "He is no threat to us." The whole room full of rough-looking guys, and a couple of rough-looking women, turned to address a middle-aged Navajo man who was sitting in the corner of the room.

"Two Dogs?" I asked in surprise. There, in the room packed with Hunters, sat Timothy "Two Dogs" Acothley. I couldn't for the life of me think why Tony's dad was here.

"You know this kid, Two Dogs?" the Hunter asked.

Timothy nodded calmly. "I do. He is The Slayer's son, and he's the one who was attacked."

"This kid?" Bruce asked rudely while still gripping my shirt. "He killed a vamp? He's harmless."

"Did you find him easy to kill? Or did you fail at such, even with help?" Two Dogs asked.

Bruce considered this.

"Either way, he will not interfere with our plan," Two Dogs concluded.

"I don't even know what the plan is," I said.

"Let him go," the first speaker said. "Cisco, take him out back."

The younger man broke Bruce's grip and pulled me along by the shoulder. "You aren't very smart, kid," he said as we walked down the hall. "Either that or you're too smart for your own good."

"I've been getting that a lot lately," I replied.

He turned the handle and pushed me into the door to swing it open. He let go and I stumbled forward a step. I turned to look at him.

His gaze softened a little. "Look, kid, keep your head down for the next few days."

"What were you going to say about McKinsey?" I asked.

"If all goes according to plan, you'll find out for yourself soon enough." He closed the door and locked it.

*   *   *

"You sure this is the place?" Cisco asked. "Looks like your typical Americana."

The three men stood at the tree line, away from the yellow glow of the street lights.

"Two Dogs never steered us wrong before, don't see why he'd start now," Alex replied.

"Well, what are we waiting for?" Bruce asked impatiently.

"For the signal, Bruce, were you not paying attention?"

"Knock it off, both of you," Cisco's dad replied. He put the binoculars up to his eyes. "There's definitely a party in there." He looked at his watch. It was less than an hour until first light.

"I have confirmation that our informants are clear of danger." Two Dog's voice made the three men jump.

"I hate it when you do that," Bruce complained.

"Perhaps if you stopped talking, you might start listening."

Cisco snorted with laughter.

His father slapped his chest. "Focus up, son."

Two Dogs placed a hand on Alex's shoulder. "Remember, any children must be spared."

Bruce rolled his eyes. "You and your moral bullcrap. If there's kids in there, they already been bit. And I don't leave vamps alive."

"Then leave." Two Dogs looked the man in the eyes. Bruce seemed to shrink under the gaze and turned away.

"Yeah, Bruce, no one invited you," Cisco replied.

"This is Two Dog's party." Alex looked at the Van Hellsings leader. "You know the rules."

The bald biker muttered a string of curses under his breath, but didn't put up any more arguments. Cisco spoke again. "My question is why? Why is there a coven here, of all places? Isn't this town supposed to be a BOSS stronghold or something?"

"If you showed up to the meeting on time, you'd know that," Alex growled.

Cisco was about to respond when Two Dogs spoke up. "These are not just random vampires, these are Sindecate agents. According to the most recent rumors, Kel has placed himself at their head."

Cisco rolled his eyes. "What, so now we're doing BOSS's dirty work, just cause they're too busy playing bureaucrat?"

"We're here because if we don't take care of this, people are gonna get hurt," Alex replied. A mote of light flashed from the trees behind the house. "Alright boys, that's the signal."

* * *

"What were all those sirens about?" I asked Riley as we walked to class on Thursday. She gave me a curious look.

"Sirens?" she asked.

"On Trilogy and Mill Creek," I explained. "There were maybe ten cop cars there. The whole block was taped off."

"I don't know," she said. "I know my dad got called in early this morning. Just after dawn."

"Huh," I said "Dawn…" I could hear the little egg timer ticking in the back of my mind. Puzzle pieces were being fit together somewhere in my head. *Hunters came into town. Why? When? After I was attacked by a vampire.* "He was the one who was attacked." *The plan. Dawn…* The egg timer dinged.

"Vampires!" I shouted. The whole hall turned to look at me. I tried to shrink into my neck. A girl with curly black hair scowled at me.

"What about vampires?" Riley asked.

"Yeah," said Mr. Garcia, standing in front of his room. "What about them?"

"Uhhh," I said, afraid to explain my theory. "I think a coven of vampires was hit by Hunters this morning," I whispered.

His face changed instantly. "How did you hear about that?" he demanded.

"I saw the crime scene and put two and two together," I said. I told him a heavily edited version of what I had overheard at Kermit's.

"That's not two and two," he finally said. "That's the Pythagorean theorem." He rubbed his eyes. "You have Scott's talent for staying out of trouble," he muttered.

"I thought you weren't feeling well," Riley said seriously as she took notes.

"Huh?" I asked.

She continued to write. "You left Archie's because you weren't feeling well. You left your backpack. Remember?"

I felt an all too familiar sinking feeling.

"Oh, that." I searched my brain for an explanation. Nothing came.

"Fun fact about me: I don't like being lied to," she said.

I opened my mouth several times, but nothing came out. I stared at her, but she refused to so much as glance at me.

"And the only exception is what, Scott?" Tony Two asked from the front of the room.

"The Mongolians," I said, deflated. The Mongolians were always the exception.

Lunch came and went without Riley talking to me. I didn't get a chance to talk to her after school, because she'd left for Archie's early.

"You really stepped in it," Travis said.

"That bad?" I asked nervously.

"A bit worse," he confirmed.

At Archie's, the cold shoulder routine continued. Normally, this would have frustrated me to anger, but all I felt was remorse. I'd do anything to get her to forgive me. I decided I'd give it one last shot. As we all stood outside the diner, saying our goodbyes, I tapped her on the shoulder.

The look she gave me was pure ice.

"Hey…"

She crossed her arms. "Yes, I'm still mad at you. You lied to me, and what's more, you lied to go risk your life again. And after you told me you weren't looking for trouble. Another lie."

"I don't have an excuse," I said. "I just hope you can forgive me and trust me when I say it won't happen again."

"You can promise you won't go looking for trouble?" she asked incredulously.

"No," I replied quickly. "I only make promises I intend to keep." She didn't appear impressed. "But, I can promise never to lie to you ever, ever again." She looked me in the eye. I didn't dare look away.

"You could be lying to me now," she said skeptically.

"No, I couldn't," I told her.

It took her an agonizing minute to finally reply.

"Fine," she said, "but I demand penance."

CHAPTER 8

Fire It Up

Riley's house was backed into the forest. The house itself was a large wooden building about three stories tall. Whoever designed it must have loved the forest because the whole property seemed to be growing out of it. Tony and I stood our bikes outside the gate and waited for a response from the intercom.

"Swank," Tony said. "There's gotta be twenty cars in there."

I frowned at this observation. For some reason, I thought this was going to be a small affair. Thinking about it, it made sense. Riley was a very popular girl. It helped that she was nice to just about everyone. She was forgiving, too, though apparently her forgiveness was conditional. The intercom buzzed, and the gates rolled open.

"I wonder if they have a bat cave." Tony mused as we rode our bikes up the drive.

Riley was waiting for us on the front porch. She wore a blue and green tartan mini-kilt and a matching bikini top and my face felt suddenly hot. "Come on in," she said.

The inside was just as stunning as the outside. I let out a low whistle.

"Great, huh?" she said as she led us out back. "It's based on the California Craftsmen style." She gestured around. "This is the great hall, the kitchen is there, the guest bathroom is there, and upstairs are the bedrooms and study." She opened a sliding glass door and revealed a huge backyard with a good-sized pool. It looked like half the school was back there. I smelled carnitas and grilled onions and corn and other delicious scents I couldn't immediately identify. It didn't take me long to spot the taco man. Tony saw him, too. His eyes grew to the size of saucers and he made his way over without saying a farewell.

"Thanks for having us over," I said as I pulled a small gift-wrapped box out of my pocket. "I got this for you."

She ripped it open right away and pulled out a pair of open-ear headphones.

"I remembered you liked mine, and these are the same model," I said. "But I found a pair that were the same color--"

"As my hoodie," she finished for me as she wrapped me in a tight embrace. Warm feelings washed over me and I returned the hug. "Now," she said, pulling away. "Did you bring the other half of my gift?"

I frowned. "I hoped you were joking."

"I was not." She crossed her arms.

"Okay," I sighed. "Well, as you can see, I'll need to change."

She pointed at the guest bathroom.

"I'll be out in a bit." It was larger than I expected. The room itself was bigger than my whole living room. It had a bath on one side of the room and a shower in the other, or at least I assumed it was a shower. I didn't see the showerhead. In one corner there was a small steam room and next to it were changing stalls. I locked the door and got ready.

"Look out!" Riley yelled. "Hot stuff coming through." She gave a "woo" and started clapping. A chorus of cheers and jeers rang out. I raised a hand and waved. A nervous smile came across my face and I approached Riley. I was wearing my rugby uniform. It had been tight when I'd worn it to play last year, but now it barely fit.

"I just need a pitch to not feel ridiculous," I said as I tugged at the bottom of my shorts, willing them to magically become longer. They didn't even reach halfway down my thighs.

"You look good." She smiled mischievously.

"*You* look good." I returned the smile and kissed her.

Kyra made a disgusted face. She was one of the only people not dressed in swimwear, wearing a sleeveless shirt and yoga pants instead. "Get a room," she said.

"I have a room," Riley replied.

"I have tacos," Tony chimed in, grinning from ear to ear. I looked with jealousy at his plate. He sighed and handed me one. "That's two you owe me, Junior." He gracefully hopped up on a planter wall.

I surveyed the scene as I bit into the taco. *Of course he'd give me the chicken*, I thought.

"Why isn't anyone swimming?" I asked no one in particular. There were maybe fifty people in bathing suits and not a single one even looked wet.

"Thank you!" Kyra exclaimed as she shot a look at her sister, who was wearing a gold, intricate two-piece swimsuit that looked like it might fall apart if it got submerged.

Myra didn't move as she laid sunbathing on a pool lounger. "It's a pool party, not a swimming party," she explained, as if this were obvious. "What are you complaining about, anyway? You didn't even come ready to swim."

"Oh, bet?" Kyra replied. She quickly took her shirt off, revealing a red, white, and blue TRALA water polo top. Myra tipped her sunglasses down, looking nonplussed. Kyra looked at me. "You wanna race?"

I looked down at my rugby uniform. "I might pants myself," I told her, gesturing at my short shorts. She made a clucking chicken sound. I re-tied the drawstring on my shorts. "Fine, one lap," I said as I took off my shirt.

One lap turned into fifteen. Kyra's determination to notch a win was so fierce that I don't think she would have given up if Tony hadn't cannon balled into the pool from the roof of the guest house. Kyra huffed as more people started entering the water, giving her a wide berth. "How did you learn to swim so fast in the desert?" she demanded.

"Well," I replied, as out of breath as she was. "If you pay attention to the first two words of 'Salt Lake City' you'll find--"

She splashed me in the face and waded away. I felt a leg touch my shoulder and turned to see Riley sitting at the edge of the pool.

"You should have let her win," she warned.

"I would have, if she was faster," I joked, standing up and wiping water off of my face. She offered her cheek to me and I kissed it. "Happy Birthday," I whispered. A pop party anthem began and several people gave cheers and started dancing on the grass. I rested my head on my elbow, which was relaxing on the edge of the pool, and took an opportunity to appreciate the pulchritudinous girl next to me as she slowly kicked her legs in the water. "You think Kyra'll forgive me?" I asked.

"For winning? Never," she smiled. "But eventually she'll stop thinking about it. She likes you."

I raised an eyebrow in disbelief.

"Not like that," she said with a splash. "You're a good friend."

"You're gosh darn right," I said.

"You say the funniest things," she giggled.

"O.C., You aren't trying to take my job, are you?" said Urchin as he hopped into the pool next to me.

I leaned back and looked at him blankly. "You have a job?"

"Comic relief, remember?" he said and winked at someone behind me.

"What are you talking about?" Riley asked. "And how did you get in here?"

"I figured my invitation got lost in the mail because a nice girl like you would *never* deny a dying boy his dearest wish," he held his arms out wide. "A party with all of the prettiest girls in school wearing next to nothing."

"You're disgusting," Kyra said. I hadn't noticed her joining us again. "We're going to need to clean the pool now."

"Great, I've always wanted to be the pool boy," he replied. He waggled his eyebrows suggestively at her.

"Dude." I groaned. "There are ladies present."

"I know. Remember why I'm here? Try to keep up."

"I'm going to defenestrate you," Kyra warned, matching my sentiment.

"Any excuse to hold me," he replied with a sly grin. He was moving before she even swung.

It amazed me how quickly he maneuvered, even in the water. Two other things also occurred to me as Kyra was frustratedly swinging at him. He could have thrown her as easily as he tossed jocks, and after dodging a flurry, I saw him sigh and wince. Then she made contact with his face. He had moved before the fist hit him, telling me he saw it coming and allowed himself to be hit on his own terms. I decided not to share my observation with Kyra. She'd likely take that as less of a victory and might try to hit him harder. Urchin was annoying but didn't deserve that. Cheers went up as he sank below the water.

*　*　*

Outside of town, two cars sat in the dirt lot of a roadside diner that faced a valley. "Can't beat the scenery," Cisco commented after taking a sip of coffee and gazing out the window.

"It is quite beautiful," Two Dogs agreed.

Alex joined them in the booth and wiped his wet hands on his jeans. "Whenever you ladies are done navel gazing, we have some business to attend to."

"I have not forgotten our deal."

"I don't doubt it, Tim, but..." He trailed off as he noticed a familiar black van with a red stripe running through it. "The hell is *he* doing here?"

"I invited him." Two Dogs sniffed the coffee in front of him, but didn't take a sip. Opting to drink from the canteen in his hand.

"Who is it?" Cisco asked.

The doors swung open and three men stepped out. One wore a red leather duster.

My dad and the Tonys made their way to the entrance, and Alex narrowed his eyes at the Navajo man across the table. "Is this some kind of trap?"

Two Dogs regarded him. "Yes, but not the kind you are thinking of. They can help us."

"Like hell. It was bad enough working with the Van Hellsings, but BOSS?"

"Wow, real nice." Tony Two looked at his companions. "Hear that guys, we rank somewhere below horse molesters. Good to see you too, Warfield."

Alex stood, not willing to remain seated against the threat of Tactical Team Seven. "I said what I said. What do you want, O'Connor?"

"I just want to talk, Warfield. That's it."

"Last time we talked, I ended up getting tossed through a window."

"In Tony One's defense, you insulted one of his favorite people," Tony Two retorted.

My dad held his hands up to shoulder height. "I'm not here to judge or serve papers or anything. Actually, I'm here because I need someone I can trust."

"Trust?"

"Whatever your other faults, you never lied to me, and I know somewhere under all that engine grease is a good man."

Alex seemed stunned. Whatever he was expecting, it hadn't been a compliment. He narrowed his eyes. "Why are you tryin' to butter me up, Scott?"

My dad motioned for him to sit. The Tonys each grabbed a chair. Alex slowly sat, weary of any treachery. In the position he was in, standing wouldn't have done him any more good than sitting. My dad slid into the booth next to Timothy Acothley. "I saw your handiwork."

"That was--"

"Two Dogs, I know. I'm his informant."

"One of them, yes," Two Dogs interrupted.

"One of his informants." He shot a glance at his friend.

"Yeah, I guessed that when I found out it was your son who got attacked."

Scott O'Connor sighed. "Two Dogs filled me in on most of it, and the less I know, the better."

"What, is the Slayer afraid of more paperwork?" Cisco chimed in.

"Hey, kid, remember that time I asked for your input? Me neither." My dad turned back to Alex.

"You wanna maybe skip to the part where you tell me what you need?" Alex asked.

"I need someone to keep an eye on my son, among other things."

"Other things?"

"Yeah, I have a feeling the Sindecate's about to make some moves, and I have a hunch that some of those moves are gonna be here."

"So you want me to babysit your kid? That's rich."

"Honestly, he can take care of himself, much as I hate to admit it. But I don't think he's ready to be swimming with sharks."

"What kind of sharks are we talking?"

My dad leaned in and whispered. "Kel."

Alex clenched his jaw. "That's a big ask, Scott."

"I know."

"Why don't you ask Two Dogs, or Dixie?"

"It has to be someone without BOSS ties."

"That rules me out, then." He leaned back.

My dad tilted his head toward the window.

Alex turned and looked at his son. "You've gotta be kidding me."

"It's a paying gig, Warfield. No paperwork, and it's not like he'll run out of things to do."

Tony One nodded. "Thas' true, cher. The ley lines round these parts give off major juju."

Alex inched away from the big man, remembering the last time they had interacted. He let out a long breath from his nose as he weighed his options. "You'd owe us."

"Goes without saying," my dad agreed. He turned to Cisco. "Well, kid?"

"You're asking *me* now?"

"You ain't twelve anymore."

Cisco looked out of the window and shrugged. "Fine, but I got some conditions." He turned in his seat. "Pay me up front. I don't want to sleep in my car." He held his hand up and began counting on his fingers. "I'm not doing any paperwork. And stop calling me kid. It's condescending."

My dad smiled. "Sure thing, Sport."

*　*　*

Riley's party lasted well into the night. It was sundown before I knew it. Only about half the guests were gone. When I told Riley I needed to call my mom, she sent me to her room. I found my backpack and sent my mother a message. <u>Dear Mother. I have not been eaten by monsters yet. Signed, your son.</u>

A moment later, she responded. <u>That's nice dear, let me know if that changes.</u>

"The party's outside, hon," a woman stated from the doorway. She was shorter than me and I could tell right away where Riley got her looks. Her hair was bottle blonde, and her eyes were a dark green.

"Oh, sorry," I said and held up my phone. "I had to check in with my mom."

She smiled and gave me a once over. "You must be Scott the Hero." She leaned against the door frame.

"Um, just Scott," I said. I nervously waited for her to move from the door.

"Anyone who saves my daughter is a hero in my book," she replied.

"Thanks, I guess."

"Are you enjoying the party?"

"Yeah, the tacos were a nice touch," I replied.

She laughed. "Well, I should let you get back to my daughter. It was nice to meet you, Just Scott." She left the threshold. I exhaled. *I guess that's 'Meeting the parents' out of the way,* I thought.

As I made my way back, a blue light behind a slightly-open door caught my eye. I tried to warn myself against investigating, but Curious Scott won out. I approached as silently as I could.

"Yes, that's what I'm telling you," Chief McKinsey said, unseen. I figured this must be his study. I started to sneak away when he said something that caught my attention. "Kel, at midnight on the ninth." I froze. "Kel" was a four-letter word in my family. He had betrayed BOSS shortly after I was born, and for some reason, he took pleasure in finding ways to attack us. He'd blown up my first house. I had to hear more. "No, I don't know why, maybe to check on the eldrium mine. Just make sure he's taken care of." He hung up his phone sharply and sighed. "Freaking morons." I heard his chair creak, and I hurried back down the hall.

I was still distracted as I walked outside. "What took you so long?" Riley asked, separating from the group she was talking with and handing me a drink. I instinctively sniffed it. Root Beer. I took a sip.

"Honestly?" I asked.

Her smile disappeared.

"I was eavesdropping on your dad," I sighed.

She rolled her eyes so hard her head moved.

"I overheard him talking about Kel." She shook her head and shrugged with her arms, indicating the name wasn't familiar.

"He's… a real bad guy who inexplicably wants to kill my dad," I explained.

"I've met your dad," she said plainly. "It's very explicable."

"Fair enough," I admitted with a shrug. "It's probably nothing, I think he was talking to my dad, anyway. Called him a moron when he hung up."

"And you aren't running off to do any Derring-Do?"

"No." I smiled grimly. "You couldn't *pay* me to take on Kel. He's crazy."

She draped her arms around me and pulled our bodies together. I brushed her damp hair away from her face and stared into her blue eyes. My stomach flipped the same way it always did when she smiled at me like that. I hoped my dad was wrong; I wanted this to be what love felt like.

CHAPTER 9

<u>Those Nights</u>

I said my goodbyes to Riley for what Tony deemed an agonizingly long time, and by the time we finally left, it was well and truly dark. We were the last to leave, save for the few girls staying behind for a slumber party. Visions of pillow fights danced in my head. *I could destroy them all in a pillow fight,* I thought. *Then I would be king of pillow mountain. Together with my queen.*

"You and your Minnesota goodbyes," Tony said, and I snapped out of my daydream, or whatever the nighttime version of that was. "Honestly."

"Yeah, 'cause it was so much brighter when you finished with whichever girl you ended with. Number Five, I think her name was."

"Don't blame me for who I am," he said. "I love intensely and often." He tilted his head and stopped pedaling.

"Slut," I replied, and he slowed down.

"Shut up," he said in a loud whisper. I frowned and hit my brakes.

"Hey, sorry if--" I began, but he shushed me into silence and stopped riding. He was looking at the tree line. This section of town was as far from the city center as it could be. We had about half a mile's ride to Tony's house, but there were no streetlights on the road we had taken. There were houses in between us and our destination, but very few of them. If you lived in the outer part of Quentin, you didn't do it because you enjoyed being close to your neighbors. The crescent moon didn't help visibility. Suddenly, I heard it ,too. The crunch of pine needles.

"Flashlight?" I whispered to my cousin. He leaned over his handlebars, intent, and focused like a predator watching prey. He nodded slightly, and I pulled a penlight out of a side pocket of my backpack. With a quick thought, I grabbed the folding knife that was next to it. The wind blew softly on our backs and the leaves rustled again. I handed the light to Tony. He pointed it at a spot and twisted the light. It didn't illuminate much, but six pairs of eyes shone red. "Racoons?" I hoped.

Tony shook his head. "I think we should ride. Very fast. Now." He palmed the light and started pedaling. I followed close behind. I couldn't hear anything behind me over the rush of wind and the clinking of bike chains. I saw Tony cross the road in the dim light from one of the houses as we rode past.

"Crap," I exclaimed as I felt my back tire slip. I looked back and saw a small, dark shape against the road. It was running after me. From my quick glance, I saw it had large bat-like ears attached to the side of a big, round head. It was on all fours and definitely not a raccoon. I clicked into the highest gear and pedaled faster than I ever had before. It couldn't be far. We'd already passed three houses. Tony's would be on the right. I saw the tiny point of red light that represented him in our dark flight swerve in that direction. I followed and heard a small growl pass behind me. I heard the skid of tires on dirt and Tony came into sight. He was trying to get the door to his backyard open.

"Behind me!" he shouted over the sudden noise of giant dogs barking. I skidded to a stop behind him and ditched my bike, pulling the folding knife out of my pocket. Tony opened the door and four grey and brown blurs escaped the doorway. Tony's massive dogs ran out and grabbed the creature that was right in front of us. It gave a small squeal that was drowned out by snarling as they quickly ripped the thing apart. Tony and I scrambled inside with our bikes. Once past the gate, Tony let out a short whistle, and the dogs rushed back to the yard. The gate closed. I looked at the four animals. Each one was about waist high on me, one was a bit taller than the others. They all stared intently at me.

"Puppy?" I asked before five hundred pounds of attack dog pounced. Within seconds, they covered my face in slobber. "Who's a good boy?" I said, giving ear scratches. "Yes you are! And you!" I didn't have to bend over to pet them, which was the best part of large dogs. The downside was that each of them was almost as heavy as I was, so it was a struggle to not get knocked over as they all fought and pushed to be the one with their paws on my shoulders. "Okay, down," I said. They ignored my command and continued, intent on licking my face off.

Tony clicked his tongue twice, and they all sat down in a row. He was standing on a beam of the wooden fence, looking for the things that had chased us. "There's still five out there," he said. "I'll have to bring the dogs in."

I joined him on the fence. It was impossible to see very far. "Don't you guys have like, a flashlight worth a darn?" I asked in frustration.

He looked at me like I'd invented a cure for hiccups. Then he disappeared. I kept looking intently at the creatures' red eyes reflected in the tiny amount of light. Tony returned quickly with a flashlight about as long as his arm.

"This should do," he said and flipped the switch. The difference was night and day. Almost literally. Suddenly, the grass was green again and we could see a quarter-mile out. The creatures shrieked.

"What the hell?" Tony and I both exclaimed at the same time. They looked like someone had mated garden gnomes with naked cats and a chimp. They weren't tall, maybe a few feet at maximum, with pinkish-gray skin that hung loosely on their stocky frames. Giant eyes took up half their oversized faces. Large, triangular ears stuck out on either side of their head and I could see jagged sharp teeth. As the light bathed them, they fled into the night.

"What were those things?" I asked, pacing in his sparse living room. Tony shrugged and set the alarm on the back door. "Some kind of gremlin or goblin," I answered myself. "Your dad might know. Is he home yet?"

"He's been out all week," Tony replied.

"No, he's not," I said. "I saw him on Tuesday at Kermit's."

"You what?" he asked. I turned, and it suddenly dawned on me I hadn't told him. I relayed the whole story. "That dirty, rotten..." He launched into an expletive-laden rant. "I mean, I'm glad he was there to save your butt, but he could have at least called, right?" He finished his rant with a heavy breath and plopped down on the sofa. Dog, the biggest and oldest of the pack, licked his hand.

"He's probably in deep cover or something," I suggested while stroking Shep's head. "Why don't you call him?"

"Nah, his phone's off. Probably took out the battery, too. You know how paranoid he is." He let out another sigh as he stared at the ceiling. "I bet he forgot I even exist."

"He didn't forget. Dads can be cold and distant and unfair and make stupid rules and are demanding..."

"Are we still talking about my dad here?"

"Sorry. Point is, our dads aren't perfect, and they might not be the best at affection, but they do what they think is best for us, right or not, they try." I sat back and furrowed my brow like it was the first time my words had occurred to me. A long silence hung between us as we both considered what I'd said.

"So." Tony cleared his throat. "Chicks. Sports."

"Farts. Draft Beer," I responded. "Man stuff." We both laughed.

"Yeah, that's enough with the touchy feelies." He stood up. "You wanna tril' it up?"

"So very badly," I replied. We stayed up until halfway through Empire Strikes Back, talking and laughing the whole time. It was a good night, if you ignored the monster attack, which we were more than willing to do.

*   *   *

On the outskirts of town, Cisco pulled his axe out of the head of the creature. It was definitely not a racoon, but it didn't seem to have any particular defenses. A chill went down his back as he scanned the forest for more of the creatures, being careful not to move his head too fast. The night vision goggles he wore were almost as old as he was, and the elastic strap that held them to his eyes was worn, and scarcely strong enough to hold the heavy goggles up.

The flood light in Tony's back yard turned off and the bright green dimmed a bit. Seeing nothing further, he raised the NVGs and sighed. "Getting paid to babysit. Good call, Cisco," he said to no one in particular.

He walked back to his car. He cast one last glance back into the forest. He thought he saw a white shape moving, but when he flipped the goggles back down, it was gone. Nothing but a slightly distorted view of trees. It wasn't until he got to his car that he had a thought. He placed the goggles to his eyes again. The static was gone. He looked back at the trees and started the car. In the morning, he'd go to the library and do some research. "Maybe this gig won't be boring after all," he mused.

CHAPTER 10

The Reason

"I told you to tell me if the situation changed," my mom scolded.

I held my head down and pretended to be very interested in my chemistry homework. I regretted asking her if she knew what those gremlin creatures were. "I didn't get eaten," I said meekly. "So..." I winced as she slammed her hand down on the table.

She was not amused by my ability to detect loopholes. "No, but they tried," she retorted. "And you have a habit of getting into 'almost killed' situations. One of these days you'll forget the 'almost,' and if you make me go to your funeral, I'll kill you."

Shame and frustration wrestled inside me. There were people that cared about my safety, that was undeniable, but being scolded about taking risks for simply riding a bike? And what would telling her right away do but worry her? *I can't wait to be an adult, when all my decisions would be my own,* I foolishly thought.

"Sorry," I said flatly.

She crossed her arms.

"Sorry, Mom," I said more sincerely.

She still didn't look pleased, but left me alone with my homework. I was suddenly less interested in the effects of beta decay. Maybe she had a point. I had been sticking my nose in places it didn't belong. *Curiosity killed the cat,* I told myself. I wasn't even old enough to vote yet. I didn't belong investigating groups of homicidal bikers or international paranormal crime rings or evil wizards. So what if I'd heard that Kel was coming to town? Best to let the people in charge handle something like that. I tried to focus back on my homework.

Then again, I *was* sixteen, I'd be off fighting in a war 300 years ago. In a lot of cultures, I was basically a man. What was the point of all those martial arts lessons, hours learning to shoot, and a decade of private tutors if I couldn't be trusted to ride my bike home? I threw my pencil across the room.

I stood and walked to the end of the hallway where it landed. I heard voices, and they didn't sound like they were having a good time. I crept closer. "… just found out about it, what did you want me to do in the last forty seconds?"

"You're right, sweetie. We should just sit back and relax as our son rushes headlong into danger."

"He said they ran *from* it." My father paused. "They went to Two Dog's. Can you think of a safer place?"

"Home, for one."

"Dixie, you need to make your mind up. Is he a man or your baby?"

"Both." Something about her voice made me assume she had just crossed her arms.

Somehow, I'd managed to power through an entire weekend's worth of honors homework in only a few hours. On Monday, we sat at our usual table in Archie's. Bixby was pouring over something on his tablet. I was scooping the last bit of cheese up from our platter of Irish nachos. I noticed someone standing next to me. I looked up to see Topher Beck with his arms crossed. "Can I help you?" I asked. Travis stopped his explanation of why he'd decided not to go to college.

"You lost me my spot," Topher exclaimed.

"Did you try saving your seat?" I asked, still not sure where this outburst was coming from.

"On the *team,* dumbass."

"I'm not *on* the team, genius," I replied. I felt the hairs on my neck stand up as my adrenaline pumps kicked in. "How could I take your spot?"

"I said you *lost* me my spot," he snapped back.

"I don't even know what position you play."

"I'm Q.B.," he stated, as if that was obvious.

"Oh, I didn't mean for you to think I *care* what you used to play," I said.

"Coach told me how you wouldn't join up as a tackle so he had to keep Sunshine," he elaborated without prompting. "If you had, he wouldn't have thrown me out a window."

"He wouldn't have thrown you out a window if you hadn't been bragging about running train on my sister," Kyra cut in. Myra blushed and looked out of the window.

"You really are an idiot," I said. "Urchin was right."

"Watch it," he warned.

I started to stand, but Riley held my arm.

"So Coach had to call up a replacement and now Boy Scout has my spot."

"I'm sorry, I don't speak Keith."

"Bradly," he spat the name.

"Oh, man," I said with concern. "I feel so bad, I didn't know." Topher began to smile that intolerable grin of his, and I turned around. "I should call Gary and congratulate him."

My friends didn't have time to respond to my quip. I was pulled by the hood of my zip-up sweater. Automatically, I raised my arms and slipped out, but this deposited me unceremoniously on my back. My feet were still under the table. I punched up and connected with Topher's face as he leaned over to hit me. His friends jumped in, then my friends did, too.

The benches in the Quentin holding cell were hard and uncomfortable. I examined the new rip in my hoodie. "O'Connor," the officer yelled. I looked up to see Topher walking past with his parents, smiling. I stood up and looked for mine. They were not there. I guessed that was my dad not helping me with my mistakes. I was led into an interview room where I was cuffed to the table and made to wait a long time. I couldn't tell how long because my watch and phone had been confiscated when I was being processed, along with the rest of my personal effects. The clock in the room didn't help. The second hand was ticking, but after every tick, it snapped back to its original position. After approximately eleventy-billion ticks, the door opened to reveal Chief McKinsey. I gave a polite smile, which he didn't return. I tried not to think about what happened last time an O'Connor and a McKinsey were alone in a police station.

"You are a brave young man," McKinsey stated in what seemed to be a rehearsed way. "Like your father. But you also share his penchant for getting into trouble." I said nothing, waiting for him to continue. "This wouldn't be a problem, normally. Young men should be rough and ready. That's what I always say. But when you make trouble around my daughter," his voice turned dark, "I take exception."

"I didn't!"

"Is it true that you punched Topher Beck first?"

"No!" I said. "He pulled me out of my seat!"

"And this justifies battery?" he demanded

"Yes!" I said. "I know when a fight's happening and I make it a point not to get hit more than the other guy."

"I see. You recognized it as a fight from all of your experiences with them?" he asked as he leaned forward on the table.

"Right," I said half a second before realizing it was a trap.

He stood up, clearly pleased. "I did some digging on you." He pulled a file out of his jacket. "You've been in jail before." My blood ran cold. "'Possession of a weapon on school property,'" he read out. I said nothing. He pulled out a clear plastic bag and placed it on the table. Inside was a silver folding knife.

I winced and realized I'd forgotten to take it out of my bag. I felt like I was plunged 50 feet into the Arctic Ocean. My hands shook.

"Now, Scott," he whispered. "My daughter says she loves you." My eyes shot up, a smile inadvertently graced my lips. "A father has to listen when his daughter says things like that." He sat down carefully in his chair. "She told you about how sick she was in the past?"

I nodded, not trusting my voice.

His tone was suddenly soft. "We thought we would lose her forever. Her mother was devastated, I was lost. But then she was cured. Miraculously cured. We were given a second chance." He leaned forward in his chair. "I almost lost her once; I will do *anything* to protect my daughter," he said in a dangerous voice. "I will bury you under this station if you take one more tiny step out of line."

I gulped in response. Then the door exploded open, and my dad stood there with a face I'd never seen. He radiated pure wrath. Two officers had their guns drawn on him, and he looked ready to kill everyone in the room. The Chief stood quickly to face him.

"I'm taking my son," my dad said. "Now."

"He had a knife on him," McKinsey replied, only slightly shaken.

"And?" my father asked. "We've been in town a month and he's had three attempts on his life. You can't see why he might be worried about his safety?"

"It's against the law to bring weapons to school."

"It's a stupid law."

"Nonetheless, it's his second offense," McKinsey retorted. The two men stood eye to eye, and I could feel the pure aggression that poured out of both of them.

"I wasn't at school," I offered.

Leon turned slowly to me. "Did you stop by your house on the way to Archie's?" he asked me.

I looked away.

"Can you prove that the knife wasn't planted there by anyone else? Can you prove that he didn't pick it up from a stash? You didn't pick him up at school, did you?" my dad asked.

Leon said nothing.

"I'm taking my son home now," he stated firmly. The Chief began to object. "I'm taking him home now, or I will kill you, *then* take him home." I heard violence in his tone. It wasn't a shout of anger, but that made it feel all the more dangerous.

"Did you just threaten the chief of police?" Leon McKinsey asked him.

"I *warned* him," he replied in a deadly tone.

Leon spent several moments mulling over his options, but he held a hand up to the officers, who lowered their guns.

"You're free to go," the Chief told me. "But remember, one more toe out of line…"

My dad was silent most of the way home.

"I thought you would leave me there," I admitted, breaking the silence between us. We hadn't spoken to each other outside of third period in weeks. "I thought you were going to let me deal with my mistakes." I looked back down at my phone, willing Riley to send a message.

He grunted. "I'm not going to leave my son in a cell. Especially when it's because he got jumped."

"But you said I had to deal with my problems-"

"Even *I* need backup," he said. "You may be a 'man' now, but you ain't an island. And you're always going to be my son."

"Thanks either way, Dad."

He let out another grunt, and then he turned up the volume on the stereo as a Skillet song he liked came on. I understood this as the end of the conversation and took a deep breath.

I pulled out my phone and sent a message to Riley. Are you OK? Soon a little splash animation told me she'd seen it. I waited. Had her father already told her to leave me alone? I saw that she had started typing.

Just a little shaken up. Are you okay Trav said you were still being interrogated when he got out what happened

I had a talk with your old man, I replied.

oh? What did he say

Are you sure you want to know? Honesty is a gift and a curse.

just tell me

The short version is he didn't want me putting you in danger so he threatened me.

omg really!!!!! ill talk to him

We are pulling up to my house, TTYL. I like you

<u>Lol I like you too</u>

Like, I thought. *We both know that's not the right word.* A part of me was terrified at the thought of saying it out loud. I'd said it to my dad, but that may have been out of desperation. "Everybody gets one person that they fall madly deeply in love with that will fall madly, deeply back," he had said. "Throughout the ups and downs and ins and outs, all the fights and triumphs and kids and mistakes and victories, you get one person who would love you through it all. They might not always like you, but..." Part of me was sure I had found the right one, but part refused to let me say the word, in case it was wasted.

*   *   *

James didn't budge when he walked into the woman at the mall. She, however, was knocked to the ground, landing on her hands and knees, spilling her cup on the tile floor. The giant looked down at her. "Watch where you're going," he ordered.

"Nope," Tony responded. "Try again." James shot him a glare, which was ignored as Tony helped the woman to her feet. "Sorry about my friend. He has issues."

"Is one of them being a dick?"

Tony shrugged. "One of them, yeah. We're trying to work on it, isn't that right, bud?"

James looked like he stepped on glass. "Sorry?" he asked awkwardly.

The woman rolled her eyes and stomped away. Tony sighed and shook his head.

James took this action personally. "What's her problem, besides being a--"

"Bud, you can't just bowl people over, then get mad at them for existing. You want people to like you, don't you?"

"No."

"Well, I do, so..." His phone rang. He pulled it out of his pocket and read who was calling. He sighed and answered it. "Yeah, Pop? What is it?"

"Where are you?"

"I'm at the mall with James. Where are you?"

"I am at our house."

"Well, that's new." Tony sighed.

"Is that your dad?" James asked. "Tell him I'm out of elk."

Tony took the phone from his ear. "I already told him."

"Just now?"

"Tony, I want you to come home," Two Dogs interrupted.

Tony rolled his eyes. "Doesn't feel great, does it? Why?"

"Your attitude is reason enough."

"Are you serious?"

"I am always serious. Either come home now, or I will track you down. You will not like what happens after that."

It took Tony half an hour to get back home. When he got there, the garage door was open. He stepped off his bike and approached the classic car that sat parked inside. A shiny engine hung from a cherry tree. The door to the house opened. Two Dogs stood not in his usual hunting jacket and hat, but in a stained beige jumpsuit and a ball cap. The bill of the hat was lined with LED lights. "You made it in time."

Tony looked from his adoptive father to the car. "In time for what?"

"In time to help me install this engine."

Tony examined the chrome block. "Where did you get this?"

"I helped someone with a gremlin problem. This was how he repaid me. Duke helped me move it in, but I wanted to install it with you." Timothy moved between the car and his son. "But first, we need to discuss your attitude."

Tony let out a disappointed groan. "What attitude?"

"The attitude you have had all year. You do not have outbursts." It was an order, not an observation.

"What outbursts?" Tony's father stared into his eyes. "And how would you know what my year's been like? You haven't been here more than ten minutes."

"I am here now."

"How long are you staying this time? Long enough to change clothes? Or are you going to use your bed for a whole night?" Tony retorted sardonically. "Why are you even here at all? Just stay gone."

"Tony." For the first time in years, Two Dogs' voice held none of its stoic tone.

Tony took half a step back before doubling his resolve. He turned away. "I'm done here."

"You are not done until I am." Two Dogs grabbed Tony's shoulder.

Tony ducked the grab and spun, bringing his arm up to slap his father's arm away. Two Dogs was too wily for this. He grabbed the offending arm. Something inside Tony broke. Some long, dormant, animalistic instinct called him to attack, and in that moment, he listened. He threw a punch. Two Dogs released the other arm and leaned back.

Tony wasn't sure what happened next, only that he was suddenly laying on the floor, his father's hand on his neck. He wasn't choking him, only holding him down. Timothy Acothley stared into his son's mismatched eyes.

After a minute of struggling to break free, Tony finally relented.

"Are you done?" Two Dogs asked.

Tony nodded. "Yeah."

Two Dogs released him and stood. "You are a long way from being the alpha." He held his hand out.

Tony used it to pull himself up. "Sorry."

"Think nothing of it. You are young. These things are expected. I do not take them personally."

"Right," Tony replied. "So, can I still help with the Cobra?"

The door opened and Duke emerged in a dull orange shirt with a logo that read "Lee Motorsports" on one breast and "Duke" on the other. "I miss sumthin'?"

"Nothing that you should not have." Two Dogs replied.

* * *

The next day, I was running late. I'd slept through my alarms because I had been up all night, alone with my thoughts. I slid into World History with a second to spare. "Welcome, Mister Rabbit," Tony Two said and pointed at my seat. "Desdemona awaits."

"You should be teaching English, Mr. Garcia," A pale, black-haired girl named Kate said. "Mr. Lee says Shakespeare was a hack."

"Mr. Lee is not as cultured as I am, Ophelia," he replied.

"Sorry I'm late," I said to Riley. "Alarms all broke."

"Oh, don't worry, I just thought you were avoiding me," she said with a smile. "Next time, a text would go a long way."

I nodded in response and saw what I thought was a big cat through the window, but a moment later realized it was humanoid.

"Do you see that?" I asked. She turned her head, and her hair blocked my view for an instant.

"No," she said.

Whatever it was had gone. I opened my backpack, but my eyes kept glancing out the window. Something about it didn't sit right with me.

"So what are we all doing for Homecoming?" Myra asked at lunch. She held a flyer in her hand.

"What's that?" I asked. She and Riley turned their heads slowly and looked at me like I had uttered base heresy.

"Homecoming dance? You've never heard of a Homecoming Dance?" The redheaded socialite asked shrilly.

"Not everyone cares as much about social whatnots as you do, Sis," Kyra said in my defense.

"Homecoming," Riley said before the twins could get started. "Is one of the three dances TRALA has each year. It happens after the Homecoming Game," she explained.

"Oh, that," I said. Then a thought occurred to me and I sat up. "Am I supposed to do something for that?" I asked her. "Is this the one where people make giant signs and ask out celebrities?"

"That's prom," Myra said. "And you only get to go to that if you are a senior or if a senior invites you." She shot a glance at Travis. "So anyway, I'm thinking we rent a limo..."

"Mee, the dance is like fifty feet away from the game," Kyra said.

"...From our house," Myra continued, ignoring her sister's interruption. "My date is playing in the game, so he'll meet us there." She smiled. "Riley is going with Scott, obviously."

"Well, he hasn't asked me yet." Riley teased.

"Don't be stupid," Myra snapped uncharacteristically. "He's just dumb about these things." I chose not to take offense at the accurate charge. "Travis and Bixby, who are you taking?"

"Each other," Travis said plainly. I was the only one surprised by that.

"Oh, finally," Kyra said.

"Not like that," Travis replied. "Just because two friends are gay, that doesn't mean they're interested in each other. I don't assume you're going to go with Urchin."

Kyra made a grossed out face.

"I hope I'm not Urchin in that scenario," Bixby quipped.

"Wait," I said. "You're gay?" They turned to regard me. "Not that there's anything wrong with that..."

After school, Riley and I walked together. "Is it a big deal that I didn't ask you?" I asked. Everyone else had something come up so I decided to walk her home. She looked up from her phone.

"No," she said, shaking her head. "I know you aren't good at that kind of stuff."

"What stuff? Dances? I can dance."

"No, romantic kinds of stuff... did you just say you can dance?" she asked.

"I mean, not well," I shrugged. "But I could learn for you."

She smiled at me sweetly. "You are full of surprises," she said as she stopped and placed a cold hand on my face. The wind that had been blowing at us was suddenly blowing to our sides. I brushed the hair from her face and leaned in to kiss her.

BEEWOOP! The noise from the siren made me jump. Her dad drove up in a marked SUV. He looked at me sternly before waving Riley to join him. She stood at the window with her arms crossed. He sighed and lowered it.

"It's okay Dad," Riley said. "Scott's walking me home."

"That's not very reassuring," he replied.

Anger flared up in my chest, but Riley held her hand out towards me.

"I need to talk to you about something," he said.

She exhaled in frustration. "Sorry, I'll see you tomorrow."

I nodded. I then looked past her, at Leon. She got in and placed her backpack on the floor. I turned and began to walk away.

She said I'm not romantic, I suddenly thought to myself. I turned around and dialed her number before they drove off.

"Scott?"

"I forgot to tell you something," I said.

"What?" She turned around to see me through the rear window.

"I like you," I said.

She smiled. "I like you, too."

I ended the call and saw her pull the headphones I'd gotten her down onto her neck.

I was halfway home when my phone rang. Riley's ringtone sang a pop song at me from my pocket. She'd insisted on picking it out herself. "Hello?" I said as I answered it, but it was her father's voice I heard. It was distant.

"--go over this again?"

"I know, but..." Riley's voice also seemed far away. She'd pocket dialed me. Again. *Hang up,* a voice in my head warned, *this is not your conversation, hang up now.* Soon enough, I wished that I had.

"I know how you feel about it, but this has gone on long enough. It's starting to get dangerous."

"*Starting* to get dangerous?" Riley's far away voice mocked. "Can I remind you that if it weren't for him, I might be dead, or worse? Do you know what he sacrificed for me?" She sounded like she might have been crying.

"I know, but there are people, things, that are targeting him. Anyone next to him is going to be hurt, and I can't let that be you. You have to end it."

For a moment, I forgot how to breathe.

CHAPTER 11

Don't Speak

Unbidden, the sound cut out as my thumb ended the call. The wind blew at my back, but I didn't notice. *End it.* The words rang in my head like church bells echoing through the canyons on a Sunday morning. I hated those words. Once again, they stood between me and what I wanted. Would she defy her father as I had? Why had my thumb done that?! Because it had moved on its own, I couldn't know what her answer would be. I couldn't call now, could I? Through a great force of will, I managed not to throw my phone somewhere in the upper atmosphere. I wasn't sure how long I stood there. Long enough to draw attention to myself.

"Hey, Kid," said Cisco from his car. I couldn't believe I'd been so distracted that I didn't hear the loud rumbling of the black Chevy Nova. I looked at him. "You okay?" he asked.

Honestly, I shook my head.

"Get in," he demanded, and he reached across to pull the door handle.

"Thanks," I said blankly and sat down. I closed my eyes. Somewhere in my brain, I knew getting into a car with a stranger was an idiotic idea, but I couldn't will myself to care. *What was the point of being safe?* I thought.

"Either your dog died, or it's woman problems," he said as he put the car in gear.

"My dog died a couple of years ago," I said.

"That narrows it down," he observed. "The trick is to not get tied down. Love 'em and leave 'em. That's the way to do it. Every day a new town."

"You've been here a month," I observed. "Why didn't you leave when you killed that coven? The Van Hellsings lit out right away."

"Figured that out, did ya?" he asked.

"It didn't take Hercule Poirot. Hunters come, vampires die."

"Yeah," he laughed. "Well, I picked up another gig. A paying one."

"People hire Hunters?"

He smirked. "Occasionally. I heard about a big fish that might come to town, so I'm keeping an eye out."

"Is it Kel?" I asked.

"You know about him, huh?"

"He's an old family friend," I said sarcastically.

He shrugged and hit the eject button on his cassette player when the last song ended. He handed me the tape. "What do you want me to do with that?" I asked. He pointed to an open plastic case that held at least twenty thick jewel cases. I read the name of the cassette and looked for the matching box. "So why aren't you letting BOSS handle it?"

"I don't work for those corporate stooges. I don't trust 'em. Bunch of stuffed suits."

"Those stuffed suits have the resources to--"

"Then why haven't they caught him?" Cisco demanded. "It ain't cause they don't have enough money. They got enough to spend on a fancy school for their freak kids." He looked at me. "No offense."

"Yes offense," I retorted. "My dad helped found that school." He gave me a side-eyed glance.

"Your dad The Slayer?"

I nodded.

"For a hard-ass, he's pretty soft."

"It's called mercy," I said. "Not all sinners are evil. And all kids deserve an education."

"And putting them in a school with regular kids like you is a recipe for pain. What happens when a skinwalker gets hungry?" he asked defiantly.

"That's why all the teachers are BADASS," I said. The Banishment, Assault, and Defense Arm of the Silver Sword was the BOSS equivalent of the SWAT team. They were the most battle-ready Custodians. All of them had experience in combat.

He laughed.

"Something funny?"

"Just that there's someone in your org that loves acronyms." He turned around a corner down the road out of town.

Just then, I realized something. We were driving the opposite way of my house. "Where are you taking me?" I asked.

"Hunting," he said plainly. "Why, you got a hot date?"

I looked at my phone. Still no messages. "I guess not," I said and put it away. "Are you sure I'm not too young?" I stared out the window. I wasn't paying attention to the trees. They were just brown and green blurs.

"Nah. I was younger than you my first time. Nothing like killing a bloodthirsty, man-eating beast to break you out of your slump."

"I'm not in a slump it's just…"

"Yeah, I don't care," he said.

I ignored him. I wasn't talking for *his* benefit. "…parent drama," I continued. "My dad hates hers, vice versa. Real 'Hatfields and McCoys' stuff."

"That's great," he said. He picked a new cassette without looking, and with one hand, opened the box and shoved it in the player. While we listened to the guitar intro of a heavy metal song, a Metallica B side I'd not heard yet, my phone buzzed. It was a message from Riley.

We need to talk.

It was like all the air had been sucked from the car.

Cisco sighed. "I am giving you this one chance to talk about feelings, but then *you* gotta be the bait."

I exhaled through my nose and told him the whole story.

He was quiet for a bit. "I told you he was a dick," he finally said. "Maybe it's for the best." He pressed a button and the other side of the album started. "I used to have a girl. Lisa was her name." He smiled at the memory. "She used to do this thing…" He looked over with a grin, then seemed to remember I was a minor and sobered up. "Hunting is a lonely life. We don't get fat paychecks like your old man does. We don't get stability or family. We just see a monster needs killing, we know it's the right thing to do, and then we skip town."

"I'm not a Hunter." I reminded him as we slowed down. He rolled the car onto the side of the road at a mile marker.

"You are today, Kid," he said, pointing at the trees. "There's a haunted house up there needs cleansing." He took the keys out of the ignition and got out. I sat there, looking for any sign of a house. "You coming, Kid?" he called from the back of the car.

With a sigh and a look at my phone, I opened the door. I tossed the bringer of bad news to the floor and walked back to join him. He was looking through a large duffel bag that was sitting on top of two others.

"Let's see here. Gonna need these and these, a couple of those," he said, handing me an arm full of supplies including a can of kosher salt, some fireplace tools, and finally a double-barreled shotgun. "And this." He looked at me as he placed two metal cartridges in the breached chambers. "Sorry kid, you can't have one, you're too young."

The walk to the alleged cabin was grueling. I didn't mind, though; I reveled in the pain in my legs. Anything to distract me from my other pain. Finally, after half an hour, we reached it. It looked exactly like a haunted house should. It was an old, dilapidated wooden shack that was half crumbled, and none of the windows had any glass. He directed me to pour the salt in an unbroken circle around the house, which took five and a lot of sweeping leaves with my foot.

Cisco made himself busy inside and gave me instructions to run in if I heard screaming. "Don't let me get killed by some hippy ghost," he said.

I was almost done with the salting when I caught a whiff of gasoline. "Are you insane?" I asked. "You want to start a fire in the forest?"

"We're in a clearing. Besides, I brought a fire extinguisher." He watched me complete the circle and nodded. The sun was beginning to set. It always set earlier up in the mountains. "Just under the wire," he said.

I looked up and jumped. Suddenly, there was a man with an axe in one hand and a head in the other standing in front of the doorway. He was covered in silvery blood. My blood ran cold, and a shiver went up my spine. It was the first time I'd actually seen a ghost.

He stared at us with a snarl. Without a sound, the figure rushed at me, and I took a step back, dropping into a plow guard with the fire poker in my hand. It stopped at the line of salt.

Cisco chuckled as he lit a torch. "When I burn this mother down, the salt will stop him from escaping. "Only two things reliably cleanse a malicious spirit," he recited.

"Salt and fire," I finished.

Cisco looked impressed. He tossed the torch high in an arc. Right before it reached the roof, the spirit moved inhumanly fast and caught it in the hand that still somehow held the head.

"Hmm, did not see that one coming." Cisco narrowed his eyes at the specter.

Acting quickly, I threw the half-empty container of salt at the roof. As it landed at the spirit's feet salt sprayed out. The spirit vanished and the torch fell.

The fire burned for over an hour. We stood and watched the flames dance in the night. Cisco was right. This felt good. "You seem like you know what you are doing," I said as the Hunter sipped a beer. "And you aren't as whacked out as the Van Hellsings. Why don't you try to join BOSS?"

He laughed in answer.

"Well, you'd get paid, you could have a semblance of stability... you could still hunt and do good."

"What did we do here tonight?" he asked.

"We killed a spirit," I answered.

"And how much paperwork did we do?" I was silent. "BOSS is well and good inside the system, but the system is broken. If Hunters had access to the same resources, The Sindicate would be gone for good."

"It *was* gone. It came back."

"It came back because a BOSS agent brought it back." He took another sip. "And they ain't eager to take *him* on."

"My dad would," I said stubbornly.

"And if he didn't have to work with the system, how much faster could he do it? If he wasn't running around teaching, how much sooner would he be acting?"

I said nothing as I watched the fire turn to embers. There was no sign of the spirit. "I need to get home," I said at last. "Or I will have survived a murderous ghost only to be flayed by something more terrifying, my mother."

The drive home was quiet, save for the ringing of classic rock on the stereo. I had Cisco drop me off a block away. "Thanks again for the free therapy," I said as I closed the door. I leaned over to say one more thing I had been thinking about on the ride home. "Hey, Cisco? If you find out about Kel... let me know, huh?"

"Sure thing Kid," he said, and then sped off.

"You took your time coming home," my mother said offhandedly. "What is that smell?"

I sniffed my shirt. It smelled of gasoline and smoke. I shrugged in answer to her question and sank into the couch.

"What's wrong, Scott?" my mother asked with a touch of concern in her voice.

"How can you tell anything's wrong?" I asked.

She placed her hands on her hips.

I slowly pulled out my phone and showed her Riley's last message.

"Oh," was all she said.

I put it away and shrugged. "This was after I accidentally heard her dad telling her to break up with me," I admitted. Suddenly, the weight that had been taken off my chest and I sat back down.

It took her a long time to say anything. "Well, sweetie," she finally said. "If she *does* break up with you, and only if you want it, I can burn down her house."

*　*　*

After I went to bed, my mom flipped the page of her worn out bible. The cover was scuffed, many of the pages had small tears, and I was sure it was held together with highlighter ink and the power of prayer. It was one of her most cherished possessions. My father walked in and spotted her sitting at the table.

"You didn't have to stay up on my account."

"You didn't have to stay out so late," she replied. She looked up from Ephesians and smiled. "Did you get 'em?"

"Yeah. I sent the remains to Frank. Pretty sure I know what he'll say."

She closed the book. "Scott, ask me why I'm not happy."

He paused. "Okay."

"You remember why we had to move all those times eight years ago?"

"Yep," he replied, already knowing where this was going.

"And then you told me Kel was taken care of, and the Sindecate was gone?"

"That is a thing I said."

"And then, out of nowhere, we had to uproot ourselves and move to a BOSS stronghold because Kel wouldn't be able to reach us here?"

"Mmhmm."

"Are you now trying to tell me that Kel is, in fact, attacking us after you made your son leave *all* his friends?" He didn't answer her quickly enough. "Scott, am I going to have to hurt someone?"

He sighed. "Likely."

"Why is this so *hard*, O'Connor?" There was an edge to her voice few besides her husband would notice.

He raised his eyebrow. "So when are you going to tell me what's actually wrong?"

"I just did."

"That's what was wrong a week ago. What happened?"

She sighed. "My son is growing up, and I can't stop it."

"It sure beats the alternative."

She feigned anger. "You dare use my own spells against me?"

He reached for a hard cider from the refrigerator. "Okay, what happened now?"

She leaned back in her chair and crossed her arms. "He overheard Leo trying to break them up and then she told him they 'needed to talk.'"

He looked up at the ceiling.

"Act less disappointed. You were right."

"Why would I be happy about it? I'm not a monster." He shook his head and took a sip.

"Not a heartless one, at any rate."

"Not anymore. You saw to that." He approached her and leaned down.

She smiled and kissed him. "You're gosh darn right." She pulled herself onto his lap and rested her head on his shoulder. "What are we gonna do?"

He placed his hand on the small of her back. "Let him deal with it. Hope he comes out of it stronger."

"You're a good dad, but you'd make a God-awful mom."

*   *   *

The next morning, I didn't bother with my standard routine. Arriving early only made the inevitable come sooner. I had seen enough TV to know what "We need to talk" was code for. I poked at my mysteriously flavorless cereal for five minutes before I realized I would be late if I waited any longer. I dumped the mostly-full bowl into the sink and walked out the door, making it halfway to the street when I realized I had forgotten my backpack. Before I was a quarter of the way to school, the rain started. I briefly considered turning around, but I knew my mom would just drive me. She'd tell me it was best to rip the bandage off. I turned up the volume in my headphones and continued walking, ignoring all the shapes and figures around me, even the dark figure that observed me from the shadow of an alleyway.

By the time I got to school, the rain was coming down in buckets. My grey shirt was dark with water when I got to history. I sat down without another word, ignoring whatever Mr. Garcia's sardonic quip of the day was. Riley was likewise silent, pretending to be very interested in the Visigoths. As the bell rang, I picked up my stuff, none of which had been set up the whole class, and was somehow the first out the door.

Luckily for me, Mr. Keith had already separated our seats weeks ago, accusing us of being unbearable to look at, but by the time the bell to end the second period rang out, Riley was already walking toward the door where she stood waiting, and I knew my procrastination could no longer continue.

"What's wrong?" she asked as we walked down the hallway. "And not 'nothing,' you promised the truth."

I cleared my throat, but nothing would come out. I couldn't find the words. I pulled out my phone and brought up her message.

"Oh, that," she said. "I didn't mean it like 'We need to talk,' I just wanted to talk about matching outfits. What color suit you would wear."

"But," I began but paused. *Rip it off,* my mother's voice said in my head. "You pocket dialed me yesterday." I paused again and she gave me a confused look. "After your dad picked you up." A dawning look of comprehension came to her face. "And those headphones are really good at picking up voices." She looked horrified.

"Oh my God," she said. "So then when I texted… oh my God… Scott no, I'm so sorry, but no."

"No?"

"No, I'm not breaking up with you," she said.

"But your dad said…"

"So did yours. Did that stop *you*?" she asked firmly.

I shrugged. "At first."

She raised both her eyebrows. "And now?"

"No," I admitted. "But what if he was right? I *do* tend to attract danger."

"Scott, you are not an island," she said softly. "You are not Spiderman. You don't have to face the world alone." She placed her hand on the back of my neck. "What you *do* have to do…" she said softly. "…is get a dry shirt. Because right now you smell like a wet dog."

Five minutes later, I was changing into my gym shirt. It had the same design as Riley's signature blue hoodie, but the school logo was in black.

"Forgot your umbrella?" a man's voice said from behind me. It was Coleman, the school's safety officer, not that anything he wore differentiated him from a regular cop.

"I was a bit distracted this morning." I chuckled as I hung up my wet shirt in the locker. I saw out of the corner of my eye that he was fingering his baton. It was one of the old tonfa style black nightsticks my dad liked to wear when he went out on a job, and not one of the extendable ones most police wore.

"So what's the deal with you and little Riley?"

"Little?" I asked with a raised eyebrow.

"Yeah, she'll always be that cute ten-year-old in my eyes, I guess. I'd hate to see her get hurt.".

Something about his tone suddenly made me feel less than safe. I closed the locker and put on my backpack. "Yeah. Me, too." I moved to leave, but he blocked my path. "Where is this all coming from?" I demanded. "I've been with her for weeks and you said nothing."

"Before, you were the guy who saved her," he said, looking into my eyes. He was a little shorter than I was, and a lot pudgier. I thought I might be able to force him out of the way if I wanted to have another visit to a jail cell again. "But now you're the guy putting her in danger."

I stared at him. "I'm not putting her anywhere, except maybe on a pedestal."

"You need to stay away from her."

"You'll have to *kill* me before I do that," I said.

He looked me in the eye again before stepping to the side. I sighed in relief and walked past. When I looked back, he was staring at me. Lightning flashed, and in that instant, there was a shadow with dull red eyes standing behind him, but it vanished before I could see it clearly. It was there and gone so fast, I wasn't sure I'd seen anything that wasn't subconscious. I shook my head and got to class four minutes late.

CHAPTER 12

<u>Be True to Your School</u>

"So, you're going with red?" Myra asked Riley and me. She was writing notes on her phone. Homecoming had become the only subject she would allow at the lunch table.

I nodded as I inhaled a cheeseburger. I hadn't realized how hungry skipping breakfast would make me.

"You're going with gold?" she asked, pointing at Travis and Bixby. They looked up from their private conversation and nodded. "And Kyra is, and I quote, 'anything but pink.'" She gave a dirty look to her sister, who shrugged nonchalantly while biting into an apple. "Since I have an inventory of our nice dresses, I think I have an outfit picked out." She showed a picture of a pink gown. Everyone but Riley made half-hearted appreciative noises.

"That's a cute one," Riley said, pulling out her own phone and showing Myra a picture of her dress, making sure I couldn't see it. Myra made a whole-hearted, appreciative noise.

"So what you're saying is that you have more than one dress?" I asked, drawing another heretical look.

"If the dress fits, buy one in every color," Kyra chimed in. "It's what's written above her walk-in closet," she explained, indicating Myra.

"You buy weapons, I buy clothes. We play to our strengths."

"Found it!" Bixby yelled. He looked around at all the heads that were suddenly turned to him. "What?"

"What have you got?" I asked him. He handed me his tablet. On it was a hand-drawn sketch of the gremlin. There was text under that read:

> "Homunculi are false life creatures animated by their master's magical energy. They have a rough semblance of sentience. They do their master's bidding, though they can often misinterpret overly specific orders. They have also been known to act as spies, though the process of recalling the information destroys the creature..."

I looked up at him. He had a triumphant look on his face, as though he had bested me, or some other worthy opponent.

"You've been looking for those creatures all this time?" I asked.

"Well, I didn't know what it was," he said. "Not knowing is annoying."

I handed the tablet back to him. "Okay, but why did they attack?"

"I don't know that, either," he said with a frown. "Do you know any wizards who want to kill you?"

As a matter of fact, I did.

* * *

After lunch, Bixby looked around at the unfamiliar room before stepping out of the elevator. His normal IA room was packed with computers and usually one or two other students. This was the opposite. It looked like they had transplanted it from Hogwarts. Glass vials with colored liquids sat bubbling on their own on a stone table. A chalkboard on the far end read "Theory of Theurgy" in large white letters. Professor Mogrim, who normally taught chemistry, was reading from a tome that rested on a plinth.

"What is this?" Bixby asked.

Mogrim looked up. "It is a classroom," he said coolly. "What do you know about the arcane?"

"Like, magic?" The teen shrugged. "Not much. Just that it has to do with the manipulation of energy to create results not normally possible, like flight or spontaneous eruption."

"Doctor Burrows has suggested you have more than a passing interest."

Bixby shrugged one shoulder. "I mean, isn't it kind of... evil?"

"It can be. That isn't an inherent part of its nature." The bearded man swept his hand above his head and snow fell lightly around him. "As you said, it is elemental manipulation. On its own, it is no more 'evil' than a car."

"So why the stigma?"

Mogrim stroked his long white beard. "Most humans, a majority so large that you would be allowed to say 'all,' cannot even sense the energy themselves, let alone manipulate it. Even among those who can as see the energy fields around them, the ability to alter it is almost unheard of." He paused. "Though their desire was great, the ability was out of reach. This leads to desperation. To some, eldritch energy is like an addictive drug. Just like mundane narcotics, this can lead people to seek the energy any way they can get it..." He never looked away from Bixby's eyes. It was clear he was watching for something.

"So they make pacts," Bixby guessed.

"Correct. Many beings have access to this energy and are willing to trade. Their favors are rarely wholesome."

Bixby nodded in understanding. "Why are you telling me any of this?"

"Knowledge is better than ignorance, for those who understand it. That would be enough reason, however you have a leg up, as it were. You are not fully human."

"I--what?!" He looked at his hands. "Just 'cause I'm a sinner doesn't make me less than--"

"You misunderstand me. It was not an insult. Unlike a majority of your friends, your parentage is not solely that of Homo Sapiens."

"Still trying to figure out how that's possible. My dad's Dursley levels of human, so if I'm not, Mom's got some 'splainin' to do."

"What is your relationship with your mother?"

Bixby narrowed his eyes. "She died giving birth."

"Hmm," Mogrim turned.

Wanting to distance himself from the sensitive topic, Bixby changed tack. "Okay, let's put a pin in that wild claim. Doesn't it take years and years to learn this stuff?"

"Ordinarily, yes, but you are a polymath, and a genius. You should have a firm grasp on the basics soon enough."

"Uh, thanks?"

Mogrim shook his head. "It was an observation, not a compliment." He sat on a stool that remained hidden behind the heavy base. "I have refused all but three pupils since coming here. You are the first I've entertained in many years." The squat professor studied Bixby from his perch.

Bixby bit his lip. "I assume it's a lot of work."

The white bearded professor nodded.

"Is it worth it?"

"If you succeed, you will be able to bend the laws of nature. If that seems a worthy goal, then the road may yet be worthwhile."

"Is it dangerous?"

"It is perilous. And at no point will I guarantee your safety."

The teen raised an eyebrow. "So I risk my life, and maybe even my soul, for the power to lift rocks? It doesn't seem like a great trade."

"It is no trifle. I can summon a storm, or fly without wings. I could transform myself or others into whatever I wish. To wield magic is to wield pure power."

"My soul for power still doesn't seem like a great trade."

The mage nodded. "I thought you might say that."

Bixby shrugged. "Sorry to disappoint."

Mogrim smiled for the first time. "My boy, that is the reason I agreed to train you."

*　　*　　*

For me, Friday came on fast. Spirit week had ramped up and the whole school seemed to turn blue and red. Even I got swept away with school pride, participating in the destruction of a Blomgren Bull effigy. The pep rally was a rocking affair. The cheers as the members of the football team were announced shook the roof of the gymnasium, which was in the process of being converted to a dance hall.

"And your quarterback, *Garryowen Bradley*!" a cheerleader yelled into the microphone. The cheers were renewed.

"Well, *he* made a name for himself," I observed when the cheers died down.

Gary walked from behind a curtain to join the rest of the team, smiling humbly and waving at the crowd.

"Winning will do that," Urchin said from beside me. I did a double-take. "He's our own little Tom Brady."

"You go to the games?" I asked.

"'Course, I go to the games."

"Right, cheerleaders." I guessed.

"See, I knew we were frens'." He nudged me. "But also to support King Arthur down there."

"You've afflicted yourself on him too, huh?"

"Are you jealous?" he teased.

"Nope," I said. "I'm basically shoving you into the arms of another."

"Don't be bitter, Bella," he said with a grin. "But he's also got a 'Main Character' vibe and I want to hedge my bets."

As I regarded Urchin, who was scanning the crowd, Gary stepped up to speak. He had to wait for the cheers to die down. "Thank you," he said with his arms up to quiet the crowd. "Thank you TRALA!" More cheers. "When I arrived here just a month ago, I had no friends, and no idea what to expect. You took me in and made me feel like family." He paused for the commotion to subside. "So I figure the least I can do is *beat the bulls*," he finished with a yell, causing the entire Gymnasium to erupt with a "Beat the Bulls" chant, followed by the fan-favorite cheer: "Trala-la-la-la-la-let's go!"

Because the dance would take place so shortly after the homecoming game, Myra demanded everybody go home immediately and get ready, even though we were let out of class right after the pep rally and the game itself wouldn't start for several hours. I supposed the girls might need more time than I did. I walked slowly home, covered in blue and red confetti, drawing the ire of more than one Blomgren student on my way. That I had a "No BS" pin on my chest did little to endear me to them. I waved playfully at them, and they looked away.

I was ready after half an hour of arriving home, but I had more than an hour before I had to leave if I walked. I waited at the dining room table while scrolling through my Sploosh Pool, getting updates from old friends and new.

"What are you doing?" my mother asked when she walked into the kitchen.

"Just waiting to be picked up," I said without looking up from my friend Zeke's shared rugby meme.

"Looking like that?" she inquired.

I looked at my outfit. "What's wrong with it?" I was wearing my old suit. My former rugby coach had demanded we wear suits on the day of our games. Coach Berg called it "Comporting with honor." The only change was that I'd bought a red shirt to go with the black suit.

"The short list?" She took a deep breath. "It barely fits you, you aren't wearing a tie, and you didn't bother to take your 'Kia Kaha' pin off." She put her hands on her hips. "And where's your corsage?"

"My what?" I asked.

I spent the next hour getting ready again. As I sat, trying to figure out my tie (my mother had flatly refused to let me wear a clip-on), she sat at the table with flower clippings and wire, putting the finishing touches on a corsage, which I understood to be a type of miniature bouquet that I was supposed to strap to my date's arm. "How do you know all this stuff?" I asked her.

"I'm a mom," she said, looking up from the finished arrangement. She let out a deep breath and wiped some stray hairs behind her ear. "Let me handle that tie."

"But, where did you learn to make corse-ages?"

"Corsages," she corrected, looking me in the eye. "I wasn't *always* a mom." She looped the tie in an elaborate knot. "Now, you look ready." She brushed my shoulders and held my arms as she looked up. I thought I saw a tear in her eye.

When I stepped out of my mom's Dodge Charger in front of Morgenstern Manor, she rolled down the window "Call me when you want to come home." I gave her a thumbs up. She put the car in gear and leaned out the window. "And you want to come home before midnight," she ordered.

I turned and gave her another thumbs up. I didn't have to wait long for Travis and Bixby to arrive in a sleek, white Lexus. They stepped out of the back seat and thanked the driver, whom Bixby called Dutch. They wore complimenting outfits. It looked like they had gone all out. Travis wore a gold suit and bowtie with a white shirt. He wore a golden top hat with a white band. Bixby was the opposite, with a white suit and a gold shirt. I let out a wolf whistle.

"You clean up nice," I said.

"Shut up, baby, I know it," Bixby said as he mocked model poses.

"Holy crap."

"No need to overdo it," he replied, still moving from pose to pose.

"Not you," I said. I pointed to the doors of the manor, which had opened to reveal three girls.

"Not bad." Travis mused. *That's the understatement of the year,* I thought. All three looked stunning, even Kyra, who had picked a simple, blue gown. Myra was wearing the swoopy pink dress she had shown before that revealed her midriff. The most beautiful of them, though, was Riley in her red dress. It was modest compared to Myra's, but it still lit fires in my brain. As they approached, the gate opened.

"Wow," I said, unable to take my eyes off her.

She blushed. "Wow, yourself." The limousine pulled up, and I opened the door for the group. Riley was the last of them in and she held my proffered hand, looking me in the eyes for a moment. *Wow, indeed.*

The band played the TRALA fight song as the well-dressed crowd cheered wildly. Garryowen had just thrown the ball forty yards to the insanely-quick wide receiver to tie the game on the last play of the half. Despite my adamant hatred of the game, I found myself cheering as well. The cheer was cut short when we noticed one of the Blomgren players had crushed into Gary. The cheers turned to jeers.

"Is he okay?" Riley asked me.

I shook my head. "He's holding his arm. I think it got trapped in the tackle."

After a few minutes, when the EMTs took a look at him, he stood and walked off the field under his own power. The crowd clapped and then started to disperse. I stood to use the restroom when I saw it again. The crouched figure. It was on the far side of the bleachers, behind the lights, so I couldn't see it clearly.

"Are you okay?" Riley asked. I blinked, and the figure was gone.

"In general or right now?" I replied.

"If you're going to brave lines, could you get me an Ellenel?" she asked, referring to her favorite lemon-lime soda.

'Braving' was the right word. By the time I'd paid, halftime was almost over. I was leaving the snack bar with a pair of soft drinks when I almost ran into a teacher. "Sorry, Mister... Dad," I said. He took a break from surveying the crowd for rule breakers to look at me.

"Is one of those mine?" he asked as he continued scanning the lines.

"What are you doing here?" I was confused. Had he already gotten back?

"I work here, Junior," he said, watching a pair of juniors sneak to a shadowy place under the bleachers.

"What about Kel?" I asked. He slowly turned to look at me. "I thought he was being moved from Site B?" I continued.

"Where did you hear about that?" he asked calmly.

"I overheard it," I admitted. "McKinsey was talking to someone on the phone. I thought it was you."

"What *exactly* did he say?" he asked.

"Kel, at midnight from Site B, something about the eldrium mine."

"Kriff," he exclaimed, and checked his watch. "Kriffing rodders," he cursed again, and pulled out his phone. "Tony. Meet me at the van. Bring Tony. I'll explain on the way." He hung up and held me by my shoulders. "I have to go now. If anything...weird happens, you tell Keith. I need you to keep an eye out." He pulled something from his jacket and put it in the breast pocket of my shirt. It was heavy and metallic. He looked at me for a long moment and nodded. Then he turned and ran, leaving me with two drinks and a hundred questions.

I sat back down and distractedly handed Riley her drink. She was absorbed in the game. Topher had come on to replace Gary and it was not going well. That all seemed secondary. Something nagged at me. Who had Leon been talking to, if not my dad? Even if it had been someone in BOSS, surely, they would have told the Slayer, the only one who had come close to taking Kel down. "Beck fumbles the ball and Rojas takes it... touchdown, Blomgren." Cheers rang out from the opposite side of the field.

By the fourth quarter, The Bears were down by ten. The raucous energy was fading from the crowd. I could hear the egg timer tick in the back of my mind. If BOSS knew, then surely they would have sent as many teams as possible. A cheer went up as the horn sounded, signaling the start of the fourth quarter. The Quarterback was no longer Beck, but Bradley again. I couldn't believe that Keith would put him in after that nasty injury. The ball was snapped and he backed up a handful of steps and rocketed the ball to the wide receiver. "Bradley to Jordan again. Jordan with the stutter-step… Touchdown! The Bears are within three!"

The Bulls answered back with a touchdown and a conversion. I tried to distract myself by explaining the key differences between Gridiron and Rugby to Riley as the game went on. To her credit, she pretended to care about the nuances, but I still couldn't get the buzzing out of my brain. *What if the person at the end of the line wasn't BOSS at all?* I tried to push the thought from my mind.

Gary threw the ball up in an arc. There was a disquiet whisper, followed by a deafening roar as the band played the fight song again. "Bradley to Jordan, *again,*" the broadcaster announced. "They're back within four." Gary walked calmly back to the bench and received various pats. The special team lined up again. This time, the punt looked like a grubber. It was kicked along the ground instead of through the air. One of the green and white Blomgren players reached down to grab onto the ball. He had barely touched it when James slammed into him with enormous force, and the ball bounced away. A TRALA player jumped on it. I saw Keith and Gary talking to each other as the ball was set up and the different lines went out to play. Gary finally made it to the huddle, and a hush fell over both sides of the field. There were seconds left, no time for a second play. Gary called the hike. He sidestepped a defenseman and started running down the line. He juked and broke through, running the ball with thirty yards and only a trio of defenders in front of him.

"He'll never make it," someone behind me said. Then I noticed Day Jordan running alongside, but he wasn't blocking. I recognized the maneuver. I held onto Riley's arm in anticipation. Just as two of the defenders both converged on Gary, he tossed the ball laterally in an underhand pass. Jordan picked up speed, caught the ball, dodged the only defenseman near him, and cruised into the end zone. The noise was deafening. I caught sight of Coach Keith, who looked right at me and made an "I see you" gesture.

CHAPTER 13

<u>Step to Me</u>

"Ladies and gentlemen, your Roosevelt Bears and their consorts," the DJ said in between songs. A spotlight shone on a curtain on the stage. Out walked Gary and Myra, arm in arm.

"It's weird, right?" I asked after telling Travis what was going on. Travis was silent. "If you tell me I'm crazy, I'll believe you. I want to believe you."

"I wish you were," Travis said. "If BOSS knew, They'd almost have to send him. Which means if they didn't, then either someone at BOSS is on the take…"

"…Or McKinsey is," I finished somberly.

"I'm what?" Riley asked.

I winced. I hadn't noticed her approach. Travis cleared his throat and walked away. I silently cursed him for his cowardice.

"Do you want to dance?" I offered. She didn't take the bait.

"Scott, I'm what?" Her face was suddenly stern. She clasped her handbag with both hands.

"It's not about you," I admitted. I looked intently at the standing table.

"So it's about my dad?" I nodded. "Just tell me what you were saying."

I looked at her finally. I wished I could make anything up. But a promise had to be kept.

"I think he might be dirty," I sighed. The look of outrage on her face was too much, and I had to look away.

"How can you think that?" she demanded. "How can you *possibly* think that?"

I swallowed and steeled myself; the cold truth was my only way forward. "I told you about the conversation he had with my dad? Well, he wasn't talking to him. He never said one word to him." She looked incredulous. "So he either told someone else at BOSS, and they decided Kel wasn't a priority..."

"Or?" she demanded.

"Or..." I took a deep breath. "He wasn't talking to BOSS and he sold us out. Best case, he told Hunters. Worst case... is that he's working with Kel."

Her hands were trembling. "Take it back. Now," she demanded.

"It's not unthinkable," I said unwittingly. "He has a history of selling people out."

She leaned back and blinked. Her eyes widened. "What?"

"He used to work with my dad and he sold him out."

"Your dad? The idiot?" My eyes shot up. "I asked my dad about that, and he told me the whole thing," she said. "He tried warning him, but like the idiot he was, he plowed right along, almost getting his friends killed."

Her fury rolled over me like a wave. "Hold on, how did this become about *my* dad?" Hot anger flooded through me in a flash.

"Isn't everything? If he snaps, you go running!" Her voice increased in volume. "I put myself out there to be with you and it wasn't enough, because Daddy said no."

"We got past that!" I said furiously. How could she be bringing this up now? "Remember the part where I'm your boyfriend *against* his orders?"

"And now because Daddy said something, it must be true!"

"Yes!" I yelled. "Because he didn't turn traitor *ever*. He stays by his friends and his family and he does what's right." She seemed at a loss for words so I pressed. "How did your dad get such a nice house on a cop's salary?" I was livid. The calm, logical voice I tried to trust the most had been obliterated. There was only rage.

"You two are a great pair," she said. "Perfect in every way." She laughed mirthlessly. "Just a couple of martyrs. You judge goodness on willingness to throw your lives away for other people. Do me a favor and don't do me any more favors, you self-righteous ass."

"Fine, I won't," I agreed, outraged that she was bringing up the first promise I wouldn't make.

"Promise?" she spat back.

"Yeah!" I said. I noticed all of our friends standing around us mouths, agape. I needed to break something. The rage was going to drown me. I kicked the table and it skittered across the floor. She winced. Did she really think I would hurt her? Was she actually acting afraid? Someone placed a hand on my shoulder. I reacted instinctively and barely caught myself from punching my cousin in the face. He didn't flinch.

"Let's go," he said.

I gave Riley a hateful look that I never would have given if I had been in my right mind.

"Fine," I spat. "I'm done here. *We're* done here." The sight of her crying at my words didn't fill me with satisfaction, but only because the hungry rage beast wouldn't let me be fulfilled. *What is wrong with you?* Some far-off voice said in the back of my mind. I ignored it. I turned and stormed away, aware that I was being followed. When I could stand it no longer, somewhere near the staff offices, I let out a rageful yell. It came from every part of me. I yelled until I was empty and bent over.

Then I cried. I didn't care that I was being watched. I sat with my head in my hands. I sobbed and cried out and prayed. In the end, when I was out of tears to cry and sat up, I saw Tony and James standing off to the side. My cousin stood with his black shirt half undone, with his hands in his pockets. James wore a pure white suit that was entirely too small in the chest and shoulders. Neither were looking at me.

Someone sat down next to me. "So on the on again off again card, I think this makes five times," Urchin said. "Two more and you get a free ice cream scoop."

"I don't think there's going to be another on again," I said in a dead voice. I had nothing left, even for sarcasm.

"Oh, well, no ice cream then. It was a good, long run."

"It was a month."

"That's like, ten years in high school time." He patted my shoulder. "At least we can put this whole melodrama behind us and get some action."

"Urchin, get out of here," Travis said as he approached. Tony and James stood in his way.

"I'm not here to start anything."

Tony looked at him for a moment before letting him pass.

"Is she okay?" I asked in the same dead voice.

"No, Scott, she's pretty far from okay." He stood above me. "What the hell is wrong with you?"

"I don't know," I said before Tony could interrupt. "I just lost it." I hid my face in my hands again. "I can't believe that happened." The sudden weight of my actions bore down on me. The entire school saw that. Saw me blow up. Saw me rip out the heart of one of the sweetest girls in school.

"Why didn't you just make something up?" he asked.

"I promised her I wouldn't lie."

"Even if you had lied and she caught you, you wouldn't be as bad off as you are now."

"That's not the point," I explained. "Even if I could lie, I said I wouldn't. I made a promise. Even if she never found out, I would know."

"Well, I hope your honor is a good kisser," Urchin mused.

"Maybe it's for the best. Both our dads wanted us to end it," I observed.

"Yeah, but now you won't be invited to any more pool parties," he replied. The buzz started again. "All of those bikinis lost, like tears in rain." Somewhere in the back of my mind, the egg timer dinged.

"No!" I shouted. How could I be so dense?

"I know, tragic," Urchin sighed dramatically.

"Not that, shut up!" I leaned forward and looked at Travis. "The Chief warned Riley I was being targeted. For the last few days, I think I've been followed." He didn't reply. "What if he *knew* I was listening? What if he's on the take, but he wasn't talking to one of Kel's goons? What if he was *performing*?" I stood up. "What if the plan was for me to feed the info to my dad in a way that wouldn't raise suspicion?"

"That's a lot of what-ifs, and even so, he still has a plethora of people who trust him at BOSS, it's really just your dad--"

"Exactly! My dad would absolutely believe it if he thought I wasn't supposed to hear it. But what if I was? If he told someone at BOSS, and my dad heard it came from Leon, he'd be suspicious."

Travis stood. "Even so, if you'd told him earlier, Scott would have told Doctor Burrows, at the least. That'd be a huge risk for Leon to take."

I thought about it. My dad and the director of BOSS were on familiar terms. He'd even been over for dinner last week. "It is, but from what I know about Kel, if he tells you to do something, it's more dangerous to refuse."

"Okay, but why tell you weeks in advance? That just gives more time for your dad to prepare."

"It was the only time he knew we would be in the same place. Plus, if Leon's feeding him info, he's got to have others. The second my dad requested a mission, Kel could change his plan. Then when nothing came of it, my dad would be crying wolf again, and he would lose a little credibility. But if he rushes in unprepared..." I gulped. "It's a trap." Suddenly, far off screams rang out down the hallway.

*   *   *

Riley rushed past the crowd and into a small alcove, just away from prying eyes. Her two best friends flanked her. "That self-righteous, uppity... ooh!" She slammed her hand into the wall. Myra placed a hand on her back, and she spun around. "I hate him!" she insisted.

Myra gave a doubting grin. "Sure, you do."

"I never want to see his stupid face ever again."

"I know."

The weight of it all finally crashed down on her. The embers of her rage died down, and she saw clearly again. She sank to her knees. Gary and Bixby joined them. Myra handed her friend a tissue and rubbed her shoulders. "What happened, Mac?" Bixby asked.

"Do you not see her crying?" Kyra demanded. "Give her some room."

Riley sniffed. "What have I done?" she asked the floor.

"Hey, now, it's okay," Myra whispered.

Riley dabbed her eyes and sniffed again. "Sorry."

Gary squatted down and placed a hand on her shoulder. "Crying's an acceptable reaction." My roar rang out from the hallway. "Shouting can be therapeutical, too."

She faked a smile at him. "Thanks."

"If you ever need anything, I'm here for you."

"I know," she whispered.

"Hey, Gary, can you give us a minute?" Myra asked.

He smiled. "Sure, let me get out of your hair. Let me know if you need a punch or something." He stood and walked back a bit towards the dance floor with Bixby.

"Mac, what happened?" Myra asked softly.

"He started talking about my dad. Saying he's dirty." She dabbed her eyes again.

Myra grimaced. "That's... a pretty serious accusation."

Kyra rolled her eyes. "And super topical for a dance."

"Sarcasm not helping, Kee."

"Whatever. Who does that?"

Riley shook her head. "It's my fault."

"Like hell."

"Again, Kyra, not helping." The pretty twin lifted her friend's chin. "Mac, I don't want to ask this, but I need to know… did you..?"

Riley's eyes filled with tears again. "Oh, God, what have I done?"

Kyra shook her head. "Now who's not helping?"

"He's going to hate me forever." Riley whispered.

"No he's not," Myra replied

"You didn't see his eyes. He hates me. I've created another James."

"He loves you. I've seen it. He's just… heated."

"Does he really? Think about it." She looked Myra in the eyes.

Her friend frowned. "That's a question for another day. Right now, we need to do damage control."

There was a bang and a shriek. The doors to the gym were flung open and a group of ninjas ran into the dance. "Hello, kids." The voice chilled Riley's blood. "How's the dance?"

"Who are you?" One of the football players asked.

"Oh, yes, introductions." One of the ninja stepped forward. His pale green eyes darted erratically around the room from behind his green oni mask. In a motion so quick, Riley barely saw it, he pulled his sword from its sheath and opened the Day Jordan's belly. Someone screamed. Many people screamed. "I'm not a patient man. Someone fetch me Scott O'Connor." He held his sword above the student, who was trying to keep his insides in. "No one?" He slowly slid the blade into the athlete. "I know he's here." He spun around to face the two football players that were charging at him. He sliced upward, disappeared, and reappeared behind them, bringing the sword down in a flash. They both fell to the ground next to their teammate. "Round them up," he commanded his cronies.

*   *   *

My dad scanned the facility with his binoculars. "I don't like it."

"This was *your* idea, mon frere." Tony One hid ineffectively behind a large tree. The three men overlooked the clearing. The lights in the gravel field were all off, and several earth movers were parked around the quarry.

"No one made you come." He stuffed the binocs in his jacket pocket. "I told you it was a trap."

"Yeah, we're gonna just stop following you into danger now that I have a cushy teaching job. Stop acting brand new." Tony Two pulled his twin Baretta 92fs out one at a time and checked their magazines. "So what's the play? Obi-Wan it or...?"

My father remained silent, deep in thought. "I don't see that we have a choice. We stay together, no point in letting him pick us off one by one."

"I agree, picking off bad."

"Oui."

"Still…" He let out a sigh. "Let's make our way around through the tree line. No sense getting a crossbow bolt in the eyes." He pointed with his hand and mimed weaving between trees. "See if we can get to that building and have a look around before getting spotted."

"What's step two?" Tony Two asked.

"Violence, likely."

"Ooh, goody."

The trio made their way as silently as they could, at last standing at the edge of the tree line again. There was nothing between them and the target building but open ground. My dad didn't like open ground. He took time to scan the area. His sunglasses didn't hinder his night vision in the slightest. With a sigh, he counted off on his hand and the three of them dashed off. They didn't stop until they made it to the building. Then the lights turned on. Three spotlights highlighted the trio.

"Scott!" The unhinged voice rang out through the gravel field. "I knew it! I knew you couldn't resist. Welcome to my trap."

"Told ya," Tony Two muttered.

My dad shot him a look. "I told *you*."

"It's no use hiding," Kel called out. "Besides, 'in front of a building' is a terrible hiding spot."

Tony narrowed his eyes. Kel still had an annoying habit of speeding up his speech the longer he went on. Still, if it meant he wouldn't be talking as long…

"But it's so comfy," my dad retorted. "Come on down so I can show you."

Evil laughter filled the space. "I do so love your jokes. Very well." A green light appeared on top of one of the gigantic earth movers, followed by a man in a white puffy jacket and earmuffs squishing down the wild hair on his balding head. His eyes glowed with purple malice. More lights filled the place, and three enormous shapes landed among the dozens of armored figures that wore black wraps.

"That's cheating," Tony Two complained.

"If you aren't cheating, you don't want to win," Kel retorted.

Tony One adjusted the armored sleeves he wore, opening his hand and making a fist to make sure they were securely fastened. "Bon, time for the other half of the battle?"

"I'll take the big guy," my dad muttered without moving his lips.

"You can take all the big guys you want," Tony Two replied.

"You see, Scott, I am at least two steps ahead of you," Kel began. "Now, if you want to surrender peacefully, I'll let you die quickly, if not--"

My father pulled his gun from its holster and fired a shot. It bounced off a purple light that had been invisible until that second.

"You mule-molesting goat stealer! I was monologuing!"

"You talk too much," Tony Two replied without a hint of irony. He began firing, dropping a ninja with each shot.

The mob came in all at once. Scott emptied his magazine quickly and dropped the gun before swinging out with the sword that appeared in his hand. He kicked out and swiped left and right. The ground shook as one of the scaled trolls landed almost on top of them. The three men had to dive away from each other. Exactly what they didn't want.

The creature was enormous. "Don't kill them! I want them to suffer." Kel's voice was still somehow audible, despite the din of battle. The creature looked at its master with a look that could only have been confusion. Tony Two and his best friend knew better than take the lull for granted. Tony fired a shot from each gun before rolling away to stand. The bullets flattened against the scales and fell to the ground. My father's sword found more purchase, but was rewarded for the strike by a blow from the massive club. He flew ten feet into a crowd of the ninja. Their numbers had dwindled, but there were still too many of them.

Tony One gave the behemoth a standing uppercut directly to the testes. It roared and stumbled. The big man, who was dwarfed by the creature, jumped onto its back and applied a neck hold. This worked surprisingly well until a second one showed up. It brought a massive club down. Tony One tried to avoid the strike, but was still dealt a glancing blow that shattered his arm. The creature that was freed from the grapple was unable to display gratitude as it lay in the gravel with a crushed skull.

The second creature raised his club again. He received four rounds to his armpit. None of the 9mm bullets could pierce his skin, but it drew his attention long enough to notice Tony Two throwing a grenade at Kel. It caught the projectile in its left hand, then noticed the second grenade. It dropped the club and caught this one, too. Then Tony Two tossed the V-Bang, a modified flash-bang grenade that fired off seven blasts of captured sunlight. Tony hoped this creature was enough troll that he maintained the weakness to sunlight. As the creature began to petrify, the grenades it still held exploded, shattering his hands. Tony didn't have time to celebrate. Kel drew up energy, muttering sounds that amplified the harmonics of magic, and fired a green ray. Tony only avoided the blast because Scott tackled him. The two men scrambled to get back on their feet.

The remaining half dozen cybernetic ninja samurai advanced, now joined by the third giant. My dad turned and parried a strike from a hidden ninja, but it cost him. The enormous mutant swung the morning star like a baseball bat. My dad sailed back, blood flying everywhere. He came down on a fallen tree and laid there, unable to breathe. Tony brought his guns up, but caught a katana to the thigh and went down. A green ray hit him square in the chest, and he couldn't move. All of his strength was sapped from him.

My dad was broken against a tree, his back folded unnaturally. He gasped for air.

"Do you like my new pets?" Kel asked as he floated toward him. "Years and years of genetic modification, but! I finally have my dragon." Kel touched the ground and pushed his foot into my dad's chest. "And now I have revenge." He looked at his watch. "By now, my other pet will have dealt with your whelp."

Tony One writhed in pain mere feet away. He was bleeding out and only had one functional arm. Tony Two would have sighed if he had enough strength to breathe.

"Oh, but you're going to have to wait to join him. I intend to extract my pound of flesh." He raised his hands to the air. "Where's your god now, Scott?" He laughed maniacally, then looked back down maliciously. "I'll make you pray to *me* before the end."

*　*　*

At the dance, five of us looked around the corner. Two black-clad figures with swords in their hands stood facing the interior of the gym. Several people were crouched, looking on in terror at the stage, which was blocked from my view. There were hushed and panicked whispers.

"Where are you, Baby Slayer?" a sing-song voice called out. "I'll kill another one. Grab the principal." I made a move to walk toward the fight, but Travis and Tony pulled me back.

"Are you insane?" whispered Urchin in a tone I'd never heard from him before.

"Obviously. Now let me go." I heard the melodic voice counting down.

"If these guys were sent by Kel, do you really think they'll stop when you're dead?" Travis asked. I thought for a moment, the four other boys watching me intently.

"Okay, so we compromise," I said, wincing as I heard a scream cut short and a sickening thunk.

Less than a minute later, my plan was in motion. "Ah, there she is, the girlfriend." the voice said as I snuck up behind one of the black-clad figures. I held my tie wrapped around my left hand and the knife my father left me in my right. The steel was blue, and light danced on the surface.

"No!" came Riley's terrified scream.

"Let her go!" another voice shouted. Then a commotion.

I didn't see what was going on, I was too focused on my target. I used the scuffle to close. At the same time, the male voice that had jumped to Riley's rescue cried out in pain. I pounced on the figure to the right. I covered his mouth with my tie hand and shoved the knife into his back. It slid between the plates of his armor and he shuddered. As he fell, he took the knife with him. I turned to his friend, who had just noticed me. He thrust at me with his katana and I dodged to the side and blocked his arm with my tie held taut between my hands. I stepped in with an elbow strike to the throat. While he was distracted, I grabbed his sword hilt, pulled it away from him, and twisted the blade down and around. I stepped again and he was impaled through the heart with his own sword. His blood poured out greenish white. It looked like tree sap.

I spun back to my first victim and stole his sword. More of the black-clad figures approached. They looked like someone had tried to put Ninja robes over black samurai armor. I held the sword in front of me. It felt enough like a longsword that I thought I should be able to use it effectively, even if it only had one edge and a slight curve. But even the best swordsman couldn't expect to fight three skilled opponents while wearing a black cotton suit for armor.

"Well done, Baby Slayer," the sing-song voice said. The speaker stood elevated. He was dressed like the others except his mask was bright green. I risked a glance to the stage that until recently had a DJ, though, judging by the number of bodies, the DJ might have still been up there. He held Riley by the nape of the neck. "Now surrender, or I kill your lady-love."

"Your news feed is a little slow." I sounded braver than I felt. I began circling. "She's not my lady-love anymore."

"Oh, so you won't mind if I do this." He moved quickly and brought his wicked-looking knife to her throat.

"No!" I shouted and took a step forward. The ninja samurai brought their swords up.

"Scott, you promised!" Riley shouted with panic in her voice. I looked into her eyes, then I glanced behind her.

"Sorry, but she's right," I said as I retreated a few steps. "I did promise her I wouldn't try to save her." I knelt and yanked my blue knife from the disposed-of ninja's back. "Though I can promise you this. If you hurt her," I held my sword out, "I'm going to kill you," I said grimly.

"You *are* funny." The ninja/samurai on the stage laughed. "Too much like your father. Always rushing headlong into danger."

"I'm not my father," I said.

"No, you are just a boy, thrown into the deep end too soon. You have no rope." He lowered the knife and pointed it at me. *Now was as good a time as any*, I thought.

"Maybe not. But that's Riley McKinsey you've got there, and I have something you don't have," I said with a smile as the other five ninja samurai moved to surround me.

"If you say 'Honor' I'm going to scream," he said.

"No, I have a James." I smiled menacingly.

"Wha--" Was all he got out.

Urchin ran from the back of the stage and jumped. He broke Sing-song's grip and dove off the stage holding Riley. At almost the same time, James burst through the curtain and tackled the ninja from behind. Chaos broke out. I faked a lunge forward and one of the mooks took the bait. He thrust, and I cut down, severing his hands and pouring more green-white sap-blood on the floor. I saw the leader disappear from under James and reappear above him. He slashed with his wicked knife and his sword. He received a kick to the face from Tony for his efforts, causing his mask to go flying. I suddenly had to focus on my own fight. My odds had increased now that the fight was on. All but two broke off. Still not great odds. I moved towards the one on the right and slashed, immediately moving my blade for a parry. As I lifted his sword I punched out with my knife, making sure to avoid the black lacquered armor. With a violent shudder, he collapsed. No time to celebrate, I cut behind me to give myself room. By sheer luck or blessing, my sword caught his. I turned and jammed my knife into his knee. The enchantment on this knife proved fatal for these creatures. It shuddered as well.

I heard a scream of pain and saw Tony grab his leg. Sing-song had stabbed him with that wicked knife. I bolted to help. He teleported again, this time right behind me. I dove forward, which saved me from the brunt of his attack, but the knife nicked my leg. Even a cut that small sent spasms of pain all along my body. I tumbled to my side and thrust out to catch him if he had followed.

He stood laughing and wiggled the small blade. I slowly stood. "Come on then," I grunted. "I have a threat to keep."

He teleported behind me, and again, I narrowly avoided impalement, but got another cut from the pain knife. I turned and feinted throwing my knife. At the same time, I reversed the grip on my sword and shoved it behind me. I felt it shudder. I turned around. He had impaled himself on my blade. He looked at me, his green eyes a sea of shock, respect, and anger, and fell over.

I looked around. There were bodies on the floor. I didn't know how many were students and how many were the ninja. Riley stood up. She was crying. She ran to me and jumped to hug me. I spun around, holding her. I pulled us apart and looked in her eyes. Then, as if in slow motion, I saw Sing-song vanish, only to reappear vertically behind Riley. It took him a beat to ready the thrust, which gave me enough time to spin us half a turn. I pushed her away just in time. The sword that was shoved into my back missed her by less than an inch as it exited my chest. I looked at the bloody blade. It shrank back and nothing was holding me up anymore.

Someone shouted "No!" and I fell to my knees. Riley ran to catch me. It was strange, I thought being impaled would hurt more, but I just felt cold. There was a flurry of sound in the distance, but it was too muffled to make sense.

I felt somehow detached from reality. I hardly felt the burning pain in my lungs. "Good thing I brought my red shirt." I joked, but then I coughed up something wet and warm.

"Scott!" Riley's voice was now the only sound in the universe. Her face was the only thing to see. If I could look into those eyes forever… "Scott, I'm so sorry."

"No," I coughed. Air was getting scarce. Better use the last of it well. "I'm sorry." I reached up with my cold hand. "I broke my promise."

And then I died.

CHAPTER 14

<u>One More Light</u>

The world was light. The sky was pure white. The ground was… nonexistent. I floated in the æther, formless. I didn't have a body, nor did I have a head. I just *was*. I was comfortably warm. If this was being dead, it wasn't so bad. I don't know how long I hung there, time had no meaning. Without warning, the blue giant was in front of me in his full splendor. Four wings beat slowly as he wrapped himself in a cloak of another pair of his own wings. One of his four faces, this one human-looking, peered down at me. *I guess now is yet my time,* I thought.

If you wish it to be. But far greater things are planned for you, he thought into my head. No, not my head. I didn't have one of those anymore.

Planned? I just died. What else is there to do but sit on clouds?

The giant had no visible reaction. *You think death is a barrier to the will of the King of Kings?* it demanded.

I… no?

The world needs you, Scott, son of Scott, son of Scott, son of Richard, son of Jesse, son of Robert, son of James, son of Michael, son of Sean, son of Seamus, son of Connor, it thought into me.

How can the world need me? I'm just a kid. **Was** *a kid.*

David was younger when he saved Israel. All things are possible through Him that made the universe.

Fair enough. You said I had a choice?

A vision of what must have been heaven appeared. It seemed to be a massive city. Streets paved with gold and motes of light floated around everywhere. I saw other giants like mine. I finally recognized them as angels. We hung above it. The colossal temple in the center radiated holiness and fulfillment. Ten million voices sang out in the most beautiful song I'd ever heard.

The almighty decrees this be your choice. If you so choose, you may rest in eternal life.

Definitely that one, I thought to him. *There's nothing back there for me.* It was an easy decision. We began to descend. The angel's eagle head peered at me discerningly. *What 'greater plans,' out of curiosity?* I thought.

Your world is in peril, was his simple reply.

Is it ever not? He didn't respond. *What happens if I just die now, or stay dead, or whatever?*

Another will be chosen. Likely not as capable. But the Almighty shall make them worthy.

And will I be punished if I don't do it? We were getting near now.

You will not. This is a choice given to you. You must make it. No reward will be given, nor punishment received. You must decide. His fiery gaze shifted to me. *If you wish to continue serving the Lord.*

If I had lungs, I would have sighed. *Fine. Fine. Fine!* I took one last look at Heaven. *What do I need to do?* We stopped descending, and the vision vanished.

He raised his arm, and the world turned to light as a million images flashed in my mind in a single second. If I hadn't already been dead, I would have passed out from all the information pouring into my mind. I felt warmth in my chest. What was more, I had a chest again. The light became a single point, and suddenly, I was being jostled around. The bright white lights were many, and I heard a voice yelling.

"I've got a pulse," said a female voice. My chest was cold and wet. My shirt was gone and needles were sticking in me. I heard a beeping noise. I looked around. Two people were leaning over me. The woman looked at me. "Scott? I need you to stay with me, Kid."

"Uhh," was what I could manage to say. There was a clear plastic mask on my face and breathing was agonizing. I tried giving a thumbs up, but there was an I.V. needle in my arm.

"Just hang on," the male said. "You're gonna make it."

"Cool," I said drowsily.

"E.T.A. one minute," a man in the front said. I blinked up at the ceiling of the ambulance. I guessed by the pain shooting through my lungs that the fight hadn't been part of my dream. The ambulance stopped suddenly and the doors burst open. I was pulled out on the gurney, the bright white inside replaced with momentary darkness, then the lights at the entrance of the hospital shone down on me.

"Status?" a second female voice asked as I was being quickly wheeled into the emergency room.

"I've got a sixteen-year-old male found unconscious, multiple lacerations. Blood pressure and O2 sat. was low with absent lung sounds on his right side. We did a needle tee and started bagging him en route when he coded. We got R.O.S.C. about one minute ago but is still altered and slow to answer our questions. Two eighteen gauge I.V.s in each A.C. with about a thousand C.C.s of fluid on board."

I blinked slowly up at them. I was fairly certain some of those words were in English. I was tired.

"Is he from Roosevelt?" the doctor asked.

"Yeah," the paramedic replied.

"Thanks, Marc," she said. More people rushed to my gurney. "Do you know your name, sweetie?" she asked me.

"Scott," I managed to say. Sleep tried to overtake me. I closed my eyes and she lightly slapped my cheeks.

"Scott, you need to stay with us," she warned.

"Nah," I mumbled under my oxygen mask. "I'll be fine." I closed my eyes again.

When I woke up a few hours later, I was in a room with many beeps. My nose was so dry it felt ready to crack. I couldn't be sure that they gave me the same terrible bed as my last hospital visit, but I suspected it. There were still needles in my arm with a series of tubes leading to different colored bags with writing on them I'm sure someone understood. The fog in my brain was clearing.

"Hey, there he is," a familiar voice said. I looked across the room to see Tony sitting in the bay opposite. Curtains blocked the other two beds.

"Hey, Tony," I said in a voice that was cracked. "Long time no see."

Within seconds, my mom was at the side of my bed. Tears filled her eyes.

"Hi, Mom," I said with a dopey smile. Whatever was in those bags was still affecting me.

"Hi, Sweetie," she said, stroking my hair.

"Did we win?" I asked. She blinked and wet drops fell on my arm.

"Of course you did," she replied. Her smile seemed sad somehow. My brain was breaking free of the drugs. My dopey smile disappeared as I suddenly remembered the previous night.

"Is everyone safe?" I inquired. She didn't answer, which was all the explanation I needed. My memory was becoming clearer. "Is Riley safe?" At the mention of the name, her eyes turned momentarily murderous.

"She's alive," she said. Her tone told me she wasn't happy about that.

"What about--"

"Sweetie," she interrupted. "You need rest."

"But Mom, it was a trap," I insisted.

"I know," she whispered. "Tony told me."

"They were after me. If anybody died--"

"Scott no," she tried to interrupt, but I kept going.

"--then it's my fault," I said.

"The only one to blame is the psychopath that sent those deadheads," she said harshly.

"The what?" I asked. The name sounded familiar, but I couldn't place it.

"I'll explain in the morning. For now, rest." She kissed my forehead.

The next morning, I was feeling as good as new. Aside from the new scars on my chest and back, there were no other ill effects from being run through the night before. While I welcomed this news in the hope that this time I could escape a second night in the hell bed, I understood why it had drawn so much attention. Mr. Fuller, the school counselor, sat interviewing me in a private room. "And you just now unlocked this ability?" he asked.

"Well, I've always been a fast healer," I offered. "Are you sure you all aren't just making a big deal over nothing?" I tried one more time.

"Mister O'Connor," Mr. Fuller said kindly. "I was there last night. I saw it happen. If three hundred people suffered that wound, maybe one would survive. It's a miracle you didn't die."

"I did die." I reminded him. "For ten minutes."

"Can you see how that doesn't make it less odd?" he queried.

I sighed and leaned back. "Does this mean I'm a Sinner now?" I asked hopelessly. The last thing I needed for what little social life remained was to be marked as a Supernatural Entity. I was already the guy who lost his temper and broke up with one of the most popular and well-liked girls in the school, and I was the reason the dance had been attacked.

"I'm sure you are aware that a student's S.E. status is strictly confidential," he offered.

"Right. The rule no one follows," I quipped.

"Quite," he said with a grimace. "I'm afraid it will be hard to keep this quiet from your friends."

"It's alright, Mister Fuller," I said. "Some of my best friends are..." I trailed off. They probably weren't that anymore. Travis might still be civil to me, but I doubted I would get the twins or Bixby in the divorce. Still, Sinner or not, I could count on Tony's loyalty. And now that I wasn't with Riley anymore, maybe James would be more friendly to me. Or at least less hostile. I felt like I owed him a steak for his role in the rescue.

"Now," Mr. Fuller picked up his notepad again. "Are there any other strange things that happened? New senses? Extra strength?" I shook my head silently.

Back in the shared hospital room, I was finishing up some green jello while Tony was telling me his side of events. "Then I got stabbed in the leg by that knife," he said. "It hurt like crazy, and I blacked out. When I woke up, I was here. I was hoping they would put James in with us, but he *did* get cut up pretty bad. Instead, we got Urchin."

I looked over to the bed next to mine, where the small acrobatic boy was pretending to be asleep. Despite warning us he was a coward, he jumped into battle with us, something I wouldn't soon forget.

"I'm much prettier," he said, his face still turned away from us. "Not that I'll be here long."

"Oh? You going home so soon?" I asked.

"Certain videos on the internet lead me to believe this would be a much different experience," he said.

Tony and I laughed at this. His reaction to finding out his nurse wasn't a buxom lass but a large Samoan man named Greg had been worth the price of admission.

"Well, thanks again for overcoming your craven nature and stepping up," I said genuinely.

"Had to. The fans were counting on me." He winked at the empty fourth bed in the room. Our revelry was cut short when the door opened and a tall woman with a tight, red bun stepped in, followed by the twins. I took her to be their mother. Kyra shot me a spiteful look as they walked to Tony's bed. Ms. Morgenstern whispered something into his ear. The smile melted from his face in an instant.

"No!" he said. "No. I don't believe it."

Myra's brave face broke, and she sobbed into her pink handkerchief.

"I'm sorry, Tony," she said in a sorrowful voice.

I felt a violent tingle rise into my throat. I prayed that she wasn't telling him what it seemed like she was telling him. He flung off the covers and ran from the room.

"Is James..?" I dared ask. "Ms. Morgenstern? Is he?" She turned to face me.

Kyra spoke before her mother could. "Why do you care?" she snapped.

I felt like a knife in my chest was being twisted. The weight of my actions crashed down on me. "I care," I said shakily. "Because it's my fault."

"You're damn right it is."

"Keraya Anne!" her mother scolded, then looked at me more softly than I thought she should. "James passed this morning," she confirmed. "They couldn't stop the bleeding." I couldn't fathom how strong she had to be, that her voice only carried a hint of a waver.

"I'm so sorry," I whispered.

"It was not your doing," she replied stoically.

"It was, though," I insisted. "Those things were there for me. James was in danger because of *my* plan."

"James' actions were his own. He knew the risk inherent in any action against armed opponents," she stated.

I stared off to the empty hospital bed. "He and I weren't friends, to put it mildly," I said softly. "But last night, he saved my life and the lives of a bunch of other people. He may have had a bad reputation, but he was a hero, and I'll never forget him." I blinked away the moisture forming in my eye. A single tear rolled down her long face.

"Yes, I know," she said, and she turned and walked out. Myra followed but Kyra stood there, glaring at me.

I didn't have the heart to look at her. "Kyra, I'm-"

"Why weren't you there?"

"I was."

"You know what I mean. If you'd been there from the beginning, they would have killed you and left, saving us all a lot pain."

The hatred in her voice, which would normally bring out the confrontationist in me, instead made me shrink into my bed. She was accusing me of the things I already blamed myself for. I couldn't mount a defense. What was the point?

"Get out," said a dangerous voice. I looked up to see my mother standing in the doorway with a bag of fast food in her hand. Her eyes were murderous. "Shut your mouth and get out," she repeated. It was the only time I had ever seen Kyra this close to scared. "If you ever talk to my son again, I'm going to grab you by your ginger, daddy-issues-having, mangy hair and I'm going to throw you at the ground until it stops being satisfying."

I believed her. Kyra did, too. She left without a glance. It took my mom a few seconds to calm down. She handed me a double cheeseburger and fries.

"That was amazing Missus O'Connor," Urchin said in genuine awe.

"Thank you, Urchin. I still didn't get you a milkshake," she said without looking up from her tablet.

"The boys in the yard will be so disappointed," he said, shaking his head.

By the time Tony got back, I had changed into actual clothes. Urchin and I were cleared to go home, but I wasn't going to leave my best friend when he might need me.

Greg pushed him in a wheelchair. He looked dazed. "He'll be alright, Scott," Greg said. "Eventually." He left us alone. I sat down in the chair next to Tony's bed as he climbed in. I didn't say anything, and we sat in silence as the minutes ticked away.

"I can't believe it," he finally said. "He was always getting into trouble and fights and stuff. 'Damn the torpedoes! Full speed ahead!' That was him. But he always seemed so... indestructible."

He sighed and leaned back, staring at the ceiling. "He's protected me for four years. That's how we became friends, you know? I was new to town, and some bully was picking on me for some reason or another. James just came out of nowhere and clobbered 'em. We've been together ever since. Until now." Tears were running down his face.

I didn't look, I didn't speak, I was just there. I put my hand on his arm and sat silently while my cousin cried. The same way he had stood to the side and protected me in my moment of weakness.

Eventually, he stopped, and I dared to speak again. "I'm sorry. I'm so, so sorry. I can't take back anything that's been done. I can't do anything to make his sacrifice more worthwhile. But what I *can* do is take down the madman that ordered the attack, but I'll need help." I finally looked at him.

His mismatched eyes shone with resolve. He nodded. "I'm with you."

*   *   *

Cisco sat in his car, staring at the entrance to the hospital. He gripped the steering wheel and squeezed. He almost jumped out of his skin when my mother knocked on his window. "Jesus, lady!" He cranked on the lever and lowered the glass about an inch. Then he saw her face. "You must be mom."

"Two Dogs said I should talk to you." She placed her hand on the door above the window and leaned down to look him in the eye.

Cisco sighed and looked back at the hospital. "Yeah."

My mom blinked quickly and looked up. "It's not your fault. Even *I* know that."

"Yeah."

"Look, there's things we can change, and things we can't. That whole night was a mess. Keith told me you tipped him off. If you hadn't, he would have still been on his way out of town. That's all you could do. You can't change that."

He looked up at her. He had expected a reaming for failing to do his only job.

"Figure out what you need to change so it doesn't happen again. That's all you can do."

Cisco looked down. "Yeah." He clearly didn't believe her.

She looked back toward the hospital. "Listen, if you really want to make it right, I've got an idea…"

CHAPTER 15

<u>Welcome to the Black Parade</u>

"Is Dad home yet?" I asked my mother when I woke up late Sunday morning. Her lack of reply told me he hadn't returned. It was a case of "No news is bad news." I tried to put it out of my mind. I had enough to think about without stressing over things I couldn't control. I had a lot of work to do. Though, my brain was having trouble unpacking the information. A live stream of our old church was playing on the TV. A knock on the door tore me from my contemplation. My mom didn't get up from the couch, so I answered it.

A tall man in a blue Italian suit stood in the doorway. "Doctor Burrows?" I asked. "What are you doing here?" Dr. Franklin Burrows was the head of BOSS. He rarely left the headquarters in Las Vegas. Upon hearing his name, my mom stood up slowly. A sense of dread started gnawing at me.

"Good morning, Scott, Joanna. May I come in?" he asked in a kind voice. He looked to be in his seventies, though my father had suggested he was older, and his long nose had been broken in several places.

My mother looked at him for a moment before taking in a deep breath. "Come on in Frank." He took a step in and gestured to the table.

"I assume you know why I'm here?" he asked as we sat down. Neither of us said anything. "No word has been heard from the members of Tactical Team Seven since Friday night. I'm afraid we must assume the worst," Franklin Burrows said somberly.

"They've been out of contact longer than that before," I suggested.

He smiled kindly. "There is a possibility that they survived, and their status will not be changed until we have confirmation either way. But I think it prudent to plan for the worst. I would like to invite you to join our internship scheme, Scott."

I raised an eyebrow. From what I knew of the internship, it involved training to work as an agent right out of school. I had assumed I was already in it based on the I.A. classes I had been taking. Either way, this was an odd time to bring it up.

"Absolutely not," my mother said firmly. "He's going to college."

"There is nothing about my suggestion that prohibits that. I just thought that he would benefit… that we all would benefit…" He took a deep breath. "In the event that the Slayer, the Priest, and the Gator are all lost…"

"I'm not my dad," I said. I didn't know why I had to keep reminding people of that.

"I apologize. I didn't mean to suggest… anyway." He cleared his throat.

"I don't know what I'm going to do after I graduate, but if I join BOSS, I want it to be on my own terms," I said.

He nodded and checked his watch. "I must be off. Many families to visit. Too many," he said as he stood and put his bowler hat on.

"I'm sorry. I wish I had been able to…" I said.

He smiled kindly at me.

"You did everything that could be asked and more. My offer stands any time you wish to change your mind." He shook my hand and walked to the door, pausing as he opened it. "Please know that your scholarship will not be affected by any of this."

"Why would it be affected?" I asked.

"Strictly speaking, Team Seven's operation was non-sanctioned." He left before I could think to say anything. I turned to my mother, who was staring a hole into the wall.

"What does that mean?" I asked.

"It was a threat," she said bitterly. "If he dies in an off-book mission, we don't get compensated."

"My dad might be dead, and he's bringing up money?" I demanded, suddenly angry.

"I don't want you to worry about that." She pretended to smile. "Visiting hours started a bit ago. Why don't I take you to see Tony?" It seemed like a good idea. We had some things to talk about.

My mother insisted on staying in the waiting room, so I was alone when I walked into Tony's room and found Myra at his bedside, her hand on his. She moved it quickly when she saw me. I scanned the room for Kyra, having no desire to be yelled at.

"I'll come back later," I said, and I closed the door. I began walking back to the waiting room.

"Scott, wait," Myra called after me. I paused and turned around. She had gone without makeup today, and she wore her hair plainly. Her face was soft.

"Yes?" I asked after she failed to say anything.

"Why haven't you been to see Riley?" Her tone told me she was curious, not accusatory. I couldn't think of an answer that wasn't sardonic. "She's in room two-oh-seven."

"I didn't know she was in the hospital. Is she okay?" I asked politely.

She shrugged. "She dislocated her shoulder when Urchin pushed her off the stage."

"When he saved her from a homicidal maniac, you mean?"

"Yeah, that," she said.

"Why would I go see her?" I inquired. "We broke up."

"You think that still matters?" she laughed. "You saved her life. I'm sure she's willing to forgive you."

A huge part of me wanted to take her up on her offer then and there, but my stubborn nature refused. I laughed humorlessly. "Well, I'm sure her dad would arrest me."

"Yeah, maybe," she admitted. "See you at school?"

"Yeah, maybe," I said.

"That's messed up," Tony said after I told him about Frank's visit. "What are you going to do?"

I didn't have an answer. If it came down to pride or financial ruin, I still didn't know what I would choose. The door opened and Two Dogs stood at the threshold.

"Hey Pop," Tony said merrily.

"I have your things," his dad replied. "How is your leg?"

"Better now. Still a little sore."

"Too sore to drive?" Two Dogs asked, holding up a set of keys.

"Are you kidding me right now?" Tony asked in disbelief. His dad tossed the keys onto his lap. The largest of them had a coiled snake embossed on it. "No way!" he said "The Cobra?"

"If you crash it, do not come home."

"Deal," Tony said, not looking up from the key.

Two Dogs looked at his watch. "I have a business trip. I will be gone a while. If you need anything, Dixie will help," he said, using my mom's nickname. He walked over to Tony and placed his hand on his son's shoulder. "Stay safe."

"Thanks, Pop, you too," Tony replied.

"So" I said to Tony when his dad left. "Sleepover?"

"Definitely."

I hadn't been looking forward to school. TRALA had been closed for a week to repair "damages to the boiler," which was the official explanation of the injuries. A boiler explosion seemed a weak explanation to me, but "attack by cybernetic ninja samurai under the orders of a psychopathic wizard" would probably have the Department of Education worried. Monday arrived eventually, though, whether or not I wanted it to.

My new magic healing factor didn't come with time control. Still, getting a ride to school in a classic 1968 Shelby Cobra GT500KR helped soothe my woes. The sleek beauty was a project car that Tony and Two Dogs had been working on together for five years. Two Dogs found it in the shed of a man who had a banshee problem. The result was a spectacular car.

One downside was that they hadn't installed a quieter muffler, so everybody knew we were coming. Tony parked it with a grunt that was drowned out by the roar of the engine as he turned the key. I helped him out of the car and grabbed his crutches from the back seat. We both took a step back and admired the car for another minute. I wasn't what I'd call a car guy, but I already loved this automobile. My mother, who *was* a car guy, apparently, had nerded over many of the details with Tony when he brought it over.

The two main advantages to riding to school were that it took less time, and the parking lot was on the opposite side of school from where I normally arrived, so there was less chance of running into Riley. What I hadn't counted on was the fact that Riley also arrived in the parking lot and had been walking around the campus to meet me every morning. I strolled alongside Tony with my dad's old "Not of This World" hoodie on, hood up so fewer people would notice me. I saw Chief McKinsey's police SUV pull into the bus lane, which was technically illegal, but I doubted anyone would call him on it. I put my head down, hoping she hadn't seen me.

"Scott?" Riley asked. Apparently, she had.

"What do I do?" I asked Tony, who could only shrug. I pulled my hood off and turned around when she reached me. "Heylo," I said awkwardly. She slipped her arm out of her sling and hugged me. I did not return it. I was too busy looking at her dad, who was scowling. If I was surprised by the hug, the kiss she gave me left me in shock. I leaned into it at first as a purely physical reaction. Then the little voice in my brain spoke up. *Band-aid,* it said. I pulled away quickly.

"What's wrong?" she asked. The confused and innocent look on her face was so ironic to the situation in my head, I almost laughed. "What?" she asked in response to my half-chuckle.

"Did you hit your head? Or did you just forget everything you said?" The wounded expression she gave would normally have been all it took for me to soften, but my heart remained hard. Tony nudged me from behind. I ignored him. Angry Scott was taking control, and I was letting it happen.

"I thought since you rescued me…" she began.

"I didn't do that to get back with you," I said.

Tears began forming in her eyes. "I just thought… when I had lost you forever... You died in my arms and--"

"Technically I died in the ambulance," I interjected.

"Much savage, very destroy, wow," Urchin said from beside me.

"Scott…" Tony whispered.

I looked around and noticed we were being watched. I sighed. This needed to end quickly. "Riley, I love you." The words formed on their own. She moved to embrace me, but I put my hand up. I hadn't meant to say it, but there was no helping that now. "I will always love you. But… you broke my heart. The things you said… well, you can't un-ring a bell."

She shook her head and opened her mouth to speak.

Taking a deep breath, I steadied my voice. "I don't think we're going to have much of a future. Your dad tried to have me killed and he lead my dad into a trap. That's not something I'm just going to get over."

The tears had left her eyes. She said nothing, but nodded. She put her arm back in the sling and walked away. I watched her leave and tried not to feel regret. In truth, all I wanted was to have her back. But I had a mission now.

"Wow, that was harsh," Urchin said from the other side of Tony. "You know she's going to turn into an evil ex, right?"

"How do you know I'm not the evil ex?" I asked.

"Fair point," he admitted. "Still, onwards and upwards. You never know what major hotties you'll run into on our way to take down the head of the cops."

"'Our?'" Tony asked. "Are you planning on helping? You know we're going against the Chief of Police, right?"

"I have a problem with authority," he responded.

"Let's get to work," I said.

I don't know what I expected when I walked onto campus. Leering looks, hushed conversation, not so silent insults. I received all of these, but also, something I didn't expect. Cheers. A handful of upperclassmen patted me on the back, and more than one girl slipped a piece of paper in my hand with phone numbers. I was confused.

"I told you girls loved heroes," Urchin told me as we walked. "Yes, that was me, I helped," he told an older girl when she smiled at the three of us.

"Yeah, but, it was my fault." I reasoned.

"Bro, you could have hid like half of them did," Tony said. "But you manned up. A lot more people could have been dead."

"Yeah, but everyone also saw me be a dick to Riley." I rebutted.

"Yeah, that's what they paid attention to on a night with teleporting assassins," Urchin replied, his voice heavy with sarcasm. "Your relationship drama. Pull your head out."

"Attention, students." An unfamiliar voice said. "Please report to the auditorium for a memorial for those we've lost."

"Smells like a setup," Urchin said.

"A setup to what?" I asked as the flow of students suddenly all shifted to head toward the gym. Our ID badges were scanned before we were let in. It only took half an hour for the seats to be packed. The windows were shuttered and the doors closed, leaving us temporarily in the dark. A spotlight clanked on, and the stage was highlighted. Nine photographs in golden frames stood near the rear of the stage. Each one had a black sash draped across it. The assistant principal, Mr. Mendenhall, walked to the podium that sat front and center.

"Thank you all for being here," he said in a somber voice. "We gather to remember those who perished in defense of our school. Principal Gloria Hepburn, Kimberly Gurandan, Daniel Gregory Burns, Gerold Jessup, Day Tiberius Jordan, Ricardo Angel Jose Guermo Lopez, James Matthew Morgenstern, Muhamed Rostami, and Alexander Sedarous." He continued. "The founder of our school would like to say a few words." He stoically walked off the stage and was replaced by Franklin Burrows. He was wearing an all-black suit. There were murmurs in the crowd.

"Greetings," he began. He straightened his papers. "The namesake of our school was chosen carefully. When we founded this temple of education, it was with the hope that our students would be upright and loyal. That they be young men and women of action and unquestionable moral fortitude. That all students be given a 'fair shake,' regardless of their backgrounds." He paused and scanned the crowd. "When World War One broke out in Europe, the President of the United States at the time did nothing, being unwilling to risk our youth to a foreign war."

He looked up from his prepared speech again to survey the silent audience. "Theodore Roosevelt's sons all went to fight, following their father's philosophy. One of them, Quentin, did not return. In a letter to a friend, Theodore wrote 'It is very dreadful that the young should die and the old be left, especially when the young are those who, above all others, should be the leaders of the next generation. But they have died with high honor, and not in vain; for it is they, and those like them, who have saved the soul of the world.'"

He once again looked up, allowing the words to sink in. "And I believe that these nine individuals ought to be honored, even if only by us. Therefore, the board of directors has voted to replace the founder's wall with these portraits. A memorial to their sacrifice." He turned his page. "Furthermore, I believe honors should be given to those who faced adversity head-on and risked death to fight against evil. Will the following students please join me on the stage: Garryowen Stuart Bradley, Travis Celendel, Scott Richard O'Connor the Third, Urchin Smith, and Tony Scott Acothley."

The five of us stood slowly and began making our way down to polite applause. "And will Myranda Lynn Morgenstern also join us?"

She looked confused, but began walking as well. On my slow way down, I tried to understand what the goal of this was. There was every chance that Franklin was trying to boost morale or even legitimately honor us. But it seemed like the type of man who would threaten a grieving widow would have less altruistic motives. Was this an attempt to win me over to the internship? Why would he want me there so badly he would put on this show?

We all stood in a line. I was made to stand stage left of the rest, next to Myra. The rest of the auditorium was a shifting group of dark shapes with the spotlight on my eyes. He looked at us all. "You all risked life and limb when nothing was asked of you." He regarded the other four boys. "I award you with the Roosevelt medal of bravery for services to the school beyond the line of duty." An attractive woman with curly black hair held a case open, and one by one, they received them around their necks. He then moved in front of Myra and me. "This is an award I wish never to give again. It is for those who have died in the active defense of our home."

"But, I'm not dead." I couldn't help but say.

"You did die, though," he said. "Your heart stopped."

"Well, technically. I got better, though." There was quiet laughter in the crowd. I felt a hand on my back. It was Myra's.

"Let me be the judge of what qualifies," he said, and I nodded finally.

I bowed to receive the medal. I saw it had the picture of a handsome young man on one side, and a biplane circled by four others on the opposite side.

"Myranda, please accept this medal on behalf of your brother."

She nodded and received it soberly. He stepped back and began clapping. A few students in the seats joined him, then more. Soon, there was the sound of shifting metal and the lights in the auditorium went up and I saw what the sound was. The school was giving us a standing ovation. Myra began to cry and I placed my hand on her shoulder.

"I should almost die more often," Urchin said.

"Really?" I responded. "I've been thinking about giving it up."

When the applause died down, Franklin had one more announcement. They had already found a replacement for Miss Hepburn. There was faint clapping as he announced Doctor Mark Julien, who gave a standard speech about coming together. I had lost the ability to pay attention. There was something more to this ceremony. I just didn't know what yet.

"Mister Burrows," I called out after him as he walked away from the auditorium.

He turned to regard me and held his hand up to the bodyguard that was moving to intercept me. "Mister O'Connor? Have you rethought my proposal?"

"I'm mulling it over, but there's something I need to tell you." I glanced at his two guards.

He nodded to them and they stepped back. "You may continue," the elder man said.

I shifted uncomfortably, suddenly less sure of my decision. "Well, when I was dead, I had this vision." He looked down at me with a kind smile. I took a deep breath. "I think Kel is trying to raise the Veil. Will you help me stop him?"

He raised his eyebrows in amusement. "Young man, Kel is at all times trying one plot or the next to bring about his world of magic. I assure you we have the situation well in hand."

"Okay but in my vision--"

"Scott, you do not have anything near the clearance level necessary for me to talk to you about such things," he interrupted.

"But I--"

"You are not a Custodian. Your only affiliation with the Brotherhood is purely familial. As such, outside of school hours, I cannot order you to investigate or not investigate any more than I can force you to work in a mine. There are rules that must be followed."

I looked him in the eyes, but his gaze wasn't patronizing or superior. "Is that your way of trying to convince me to join the internship?" I asked accusingly.

He chortled. "Young man, I offered that as an opportunity for your future. Even if you joined today, I would not help you dig into this. I'm sorry, but I have a lunch appointment. Good day." He placed his black bowler hat on his head, and I had the strangest feeling that he'd told me more than he said.

*　*　*

The door to Frank's temporary office opened and my mother stepped in. "Joanna, please come in."

She sat down in front of his desk. "What's the game, Frank?"

"Whatever do you mean?"

"Bringing up our finances in front of my son like that? You'd play that dirty to get him to follow in his father's footsteps?"

"I didn't mean to... well." He cleared his throat and adjusted the papers on his desk. "Yes. We need men like him."

"He's a boy, Frank."

Franklin regarded her. "You know what threats are out there as well as I do, Dixie. Someone's son is going to have to be a sword shining in the darkness. Yours has a better chance of surviving the dark than the others. I'm trying to mitigate tragedy."

She shook her head. "Don't try to get altruistic with me. I'm his mom. I'd let a thousand kids die before I'd let him go."

He was taken aback momentarily by her admission. "I wasn't aware you felt so strongly about this."

"Yeah, you did. My son isn't going to be your next project, so let's move on to what I'm going to ask next." She stood up and approached the decanter set.

"I can assure you I am doing everything I can to investigate--"

"You know where he was, and I'm betting you know where he is. Why aren't there tanks outside?" She took a sip of the brandy. She preferred a solid bourbon, but if needs must...

"The situation is... problematic." He leaned back and pulled out a pipe. "There are no less than fifteen eldrium mines in those mountains. All of them are owned by different corporations, all of them guarded."

"Scotty said he was somewhere called Site B."

Frank methodically packed his pipe bowl. "Our system seems to have been tampered with. We have no record of anything with that name." He reached for his match book. "But I'm afraid we might have problems more nebulous than a server crash." He brought the fire to the bowl, and the room filled with the smell of burning tobacco. He exhaled a plume of smoke. "The board is not convinced Kel is a threat."

My mother almost spit out her brandy. "Are you clinical? You know what he's done."

"I agree, but some doubt has been cast on Kel's involvement in certain events."

"Is that a fact?" She shook her head and set down the snifter. "Frank, you can't fight a war by committee. You need to sort your house out or it's going to tear itself apart."

He nodded and took another puff. "You may be right, but how do I disband the board without losing funding?"

"What's the point of the funding if you can't get done what needs doing?" She drained the rest of her drink in one go and set the crystal cup back down. "You better figure it out soon. If Kel takes another swing at my kid, you'd better pray he misses, or you'll have someone much worse coming after you."

CHAPTER 16

<u>One Way or Another</u>

"Hear me out on this," Urchin said as he stole another fry from my plate. "He shows up out of the blue? Where was he before? What's he doing now?"

I eyed him as he took yet another.

"For the last time, the principal is not a Sindicate plant," Tony said. "I know Mark. He and my dad go way back."

"But have you seen him and Kel at the same time?" Urchin asked.

"Have you seen *me* and Kel at the same time?" Tony responded.

Urchin didn't reply, but scooted farther away in the booth. "When's Norbert getting here, anyway?"

"*Travis* will probably be here soon. It takes about fifteen minutes to walk here," I impatiently responded. I had called Travis on Tony's strict insistence. Three underclassmen alone were not going to be enough to take down a multinational paranormal mafia. "And we don't even know if he's going to help."

"The missus got all the kids in the divorce, huh?" Urchin said. "That's rough, buddy."

"Something like that," I responded.

"Bro, you said he was with us in your dream," Tony insisted.

I didn't respond, but continued to watch the door until I saw him walk in. He was not alone. Bixby had joined him. Travis wordlessly grabbed a chair and Bixby slid in next to me.

"Alright, let's hear it," the older boy with a golden tan said plainly.

"Okay," I began. "So, this is going to sound a little insane."

"Scott, we go to a school with magicians and monsters," Bixby interjected. "Give us some credit."

I took a deep breath. "When I died, I was sent back on a mission from God."

"Wow. You were right," Bixby said.

"At first, I chalked it up to hypoxia or something, but then this happened." Without warning, I picked up the steak knife from the table and sliced into my forearm. Blood dripped down onto my plate.

"If you didn't want to share, you could have said…" Urchin trailed off, because I was no longer bleeding. I wiped the blood off with a napkin. The skin had already healed. Travis was silent for a while.

"So you have new powers," he said. "Congratulations on becoming a Sinner."

"Trav, let's hear him out," Bixby said.

Travis seemed unconvinced. He stood up.

"I need your help," I said.

"To do what?" he asked impatiently.

"Close the Veil," I replied.

He sat back down. "What do you know about that?" he demanded quietly.

"I know it's why this area has seen a spike in Sinner activity."

"Time out," Bixby said. "What even is that?"

I looked at Travis, who nodded once.

"Back in the beginning of this world,"

"*This* world?" Bixby interrupted.

"You wanna let me tell the story?" I retorted.

He gestured for me to continue.

I closed my eyes and brought forth the visions granted to me by the angel before my heart started beating again. "In the beginning of this world, there was no separation between humans and creatures of shadow. Giants, angels, demons, vampires, false gods, and all manner of beasts walked the earth freely." The words came without thought. "Humans were weak, though, seen as food by most. But God favored humanity, and he began to lower the Veil between humans and monsters. As time went on, it became harder for creatures of shadow to pierce through the Veil. Eventually, magic and false gods and monsters faded into myth. There are some points in our history when the winds of magic blow fiercely and the veil ripples. The Dark Ages, and the days of ancient Greece, for example. The Veil is rising near Quentin. It is what caused eldrium deposits. There is one who desires the destruction of the Veil. This would bring about another Age of Darkness. This must not happen." I finished and opened my eyes

"Why does he want to do that?" Bixby asked.

I shrugged. "Kel only cares about power. He thinks if he raises the Veil, he'll have his world of unlimited magic."

"What's so bad about that?" Bixby asked, placing a hand on his face-down tablet. "A world with more magic would be pretty lit."

"Well, you'll recall the 'humans as food' thing," I said. "And if it does lift, we will be ground zero for the emergence of an entire reality's worth of hungry creatures."

"And the ones who have successfully made it through thus far are the small ones," Travis said. "If the Veil is raised, it means the return of dragons."

"Among other things," I added.

"That sounds ungood," Bixby admitted.

"Say we believe you," Travis said after a while.

"We believe you," Tony and Urchin said in unison.

He turned his head to their side of the table. "How do you go about finding it? Once you do, how will you get to it? Once you do, how will you close it?"

"Right. That. I don't actually know," I admitted. He stared at me. "Plan making has never been my strong suit, okay?"

"That has been made apparent," he said.

"Yo, what is your *problem*?" Tony said in frustration.

"It's fine," I replied.

"But it's not. He's trying to save the world and you're supposed to be his friend. Where's the loyalty?"

"With Mac," Travis said. "She's been my friend for years, and I'm not going to suddenly team up with her evil ex just because he has a messiah complex."

I rubbed my eyes. I had a feeling this would be his reaction. I wished it could have been as simple as taking her back. Heaven knew that's what I wanted.

"Hey, you were right," Urchin said.

"Travis," I said. "Leon is somewhere at the center of this. I can't put Riley in the middle, I can't ask her to choose between a boyfriend and her father. I care about her too much."

"You broke her heart twice because you care?" he asked incredulously.

"It sounds a little stupid when you say it like that," I admitted.

"It sounds stupid because it *is* stupid," he snapped back.

"What do you want me to do, turn back the hands of time?" I replied. "I can't un-ring a bell, Travis. You want me to say I'm sorry? Hell yes, I'm sorry. I'm sorry that I have to do this thing and I don't really see a way forward without kicking my own heart in the nuts, or hers. I have to do what needs to be done."

Travis looked at me for a few seconds and stood up. "Bix, are you coming?" Bixby looked at me for a moment before nodding.

"Well, that was a good use of time," Urchin said after our two guests left. It was hard to argue with his sarcastic comment. "This whole thing would have been easier if you had just let Hottie McHotterton make out with you."

"What?" I asked.

"Get back in the door. It would have made it easier to get info from Poppa Cop."

"How?" I wondered.

Urchin sighed as if he was giving instructions to a three-year-old. "You need info on crazy wizard man, Poppa Cop *works* for crazy wizard man, who needs a better name, bee tee dubs, and Hottie *lives* with Poppa Cop. That's only two degrees of sep right there. Say one night daddy's working late, you round the bases and put her to sleep, then you're free to search the home office for evidence."

"Well, what if her mom catches him?" Tony pondered.

"Even better," Urchin grinned. "So here's what you do-"

"Okay, discounting the fact that I wouldn't be 'rounding bases' with anybody since I already closed that door, and even if I could change my decision, I wouldn't. I get the feeling that I have to do this the right way or there's no point in doing it at all."

"Fine, Pali-for-life, what's the next step?" Urchin asked with a disappointed look.

"Keep our ears to the ground?" I suggested.

It turned out that keeping my ear to the ground was harder to do than I had counted on. Between the increased October workload and the nearly omnipresent patrol car following me around, it was hard to get any investigating done. My life had turned upside down. My companions had changed as well. Instead of lunches with the clique, I ate outside with Tony. Occasionally, Urchin joined us. It was a few days before Halloween when a break came.

I stood next to Tony as he shopped for a new stereo at the local auto parts store. "Man, just get one with Bluetooth and let's go. Jung gave me an eleventy-hundred-word essay on hyperbole."

"Look, it's got to fit *and* it's got to look good. I don't want to put anything in Carol that's going to clash," he replied distractedly, referring to the car by the name he'd given her.

"Myra doesn't spend this much time buying shoes," I accused.

"Kid?" Cisco's voice came from the next aisle. I peered over, and the Hunter was standing with his father.

"Oh. Hey, Cisco," I said politely.

"I told you he didn't bite it, Pops," Cisco said to the older man next to him.

"Guess I owe you a cola," the man with a salt and pepper beard replied.

"Actually…" I began.

"Got it," Tony said and stood up. Pops' eyes narrowed. "Hey, I'm Tony. Scott's cousin." He reached over the shelf to shake hands. Only Cisco returned the gesture.

"Cisco, and this is my Pops, Alex."

"Good to meet you," Tony said with a smile, and held up a box. "I'm going to go pay for this." I nodded, and he left me alone with the Hunters. Cisco stuck his hands in the pockets of his leather jacket.

"So, did your lady problems clear up?" Cisco asked.

"Uhh, sort of," I said. "Did you find out more about Kel?"

"Uhh, sort of," Cisco said.

"You sharing info with BOSS now?" Alex murmured to his son. "You *know* who his dad is."

"I'm not my dad," I said. The answer was automatic at this point. "And just because my school is BOSS, doesn't mean I am."

"Told you, Pops, Kid here is Hunter material."

"Let's not get carried away," I said. "I'm not that, either."

"What are you then?" Alex raised an eyebrow.

"Just a kid trying to take Kel down."

They looked at each other. "What?" They seemed to be having a telepathic conversation. Finally, Alex looked at me.

"Meet us at Kermit's tonight at sunset. Leave your friend," he said.

"No," I replied firmly at once.

"What?" He seemed surprised at my defiance.

"I'm not going to a secondary location without backup," I stated.

A slight smile graced his lips. "You got the makings of a Hunter for sure. Fine, bring him, but make him wear a hood or something."

*　　*　　*

Kyra sat down next to her sister, who was consoling an inconsolable Riley. "Mac, it's been weeks. He's not worth the effort."

"There, there, Mac, pay no attention to the heartless old lady," Bixby replied, looking up again from his tablet.

Riley dabbed the tears away. "Sorry, Kyra."

Kyra sighed. "No, I'm sorry. I'm just…"

"Is there anything I can do to help?" Gary asked. He sat down at the table across from my crying ex-girlfriend.

"Do you have a time machine?" Riley asked.

"Depends," Urchin replied sitting down. "What would you do with it?"

"Kick Scott in the nuts, for one," Kyra replied before taking a sip of protein shake.

Urchin shook his head. "You don't need a time machine for that, just a reasonably quiet run up."

Kyra almost spilled shake from her nose. It took her a moment to recover as she coughed in laughter.

Gary smiled at the exchange. "Riles, I know there's not much I can offer in support, and you're sick of hearing how you're too good for him and you're better off…"

She nodded and rolled her eyes.

"All I can say is that it sucks."

"Super helpful, boss," Urchin said, redoubling Kyra's laughter. "I'm sure that's new info."

"I know it's not the same feeling, but when I lost my dad, I thought the world was ending," Gary said. "But it kept right on spinning, so I got back up. So, if I can give some advice, it would be to let it suck. Eventually, it'll hurt a little less, and you'll move on, but don't let any of us try to hurry you through your grief."

Riley smiled. "Thanks, Gare, that actually does help."

He smiled and bit his lip before returning his attention to his salad.

*   *   *

Kermit's looked the same as it did last time I'd visited, except there wasn't a line of motorcycles in front. Tony and I sat in his car with hoods up. "Are you sure this is a good idea?" Tony asked.

"Not even a little at first," I said. "Let's go." We stepped out of Carol and walked into the bar. It was much emptier this time. I immediately spotted Cisco in a nearby booth. We made our way over, trying not to draw any attention to ourselves.

"Wow, you came," Cisco said, impressed.

"Yeah, that's great," Alex said. "Sit down.You want to take down Kel? Well, you ain't alone." He pulled out a paper map and spread it on the table. It was marked up in red and black ink. He pointed to a valley floor in the forested area miles out of town. "We've been tracking a known operative. Last night, we followed him to a mining operation here. We're going to check it out tonight."

"And we're coming with you," I said.

"Did you come strapped?" Alex asked us as he opened the trunk of his car. The light shone dimly on three, large duffle bags. We'd followed the Nova through a mountain pass for almost an hour before turning down a dirt road. Now we were parked a mile or so away from the highway. It was a quarter moon, which offered enough light to see a little way into the forest.

"Strapped?" I retorted. "I'm sixteen. Where am I going to get guns?"

"You don't always need guns. Depends on what you hunt." He moved the duffles so the red one was on top, then unzipped it and started rummaging through. "Always have a diverse array of weaponry. You never know when you'll need a silver knife." He pulled a bolt action rifle out and attached a scope to it. "Store what you can't carry in your trunk, better if it's a false bottom." He slid in a magazine and chambered a round. "Rule one of hunting, Kid, stay strapped or get clapped. Always be carrying."

I felt in my back pocket for my blue steel knife. It was the only thing I had thought to bring.

"Did you bring your parasites?"

"No, I got dewormed last week," I said sarcastically. Cisco handed his dad a pair of binoculars.

"Parasites," Cisco said, handing me a smaller set. "Pair-a-sights?"

"Oh," I said. "I didn't know we were going hunting tonight."

"Rule one, Kid," he replied and closed his trunk.

We followed an old hunting trail to a small outlook. The two Hunters navigated it adeptly. I wasn't as used to traveling through rough terrain as it were, so it took me longer, and Tony insisted on bringing up the rear. His night vision had always been good. If I didn't keep looking back to spot him, I wouldn't have known he was behind me. He had grown up bow hunting with his dad and he had a natural talent for this terrain. Couple that with years of practice, and he seemed like a shadow slipping from tree to tree. I crawled up next to Alex and Cisco and pulled out the binoculars.

The mine site was a well-lit slate field. There were several cars parked seemingly at random points. A hundred feet away from a steel entrance to what I assumed was the actual mine was a ten-by-twenty bungalow. Bringing up the binoculars, I read the name on the side of the building,"Perkins Minerals." I watched the door.

It took at least an hour before anything happened. "Car coming. Truck or SUV," Tony told us in a whisper. Thirty seconds later, we heard the crunching of gravel and saw light moving through trees below us. Tony was right. It was a police issue Explorer. Leon McKinsey's car. I watched as he calmly got out with two other officers. Unlike the officers who were still in uniform, Leon wore a black coat and blue jeans. They stayed next to the Explorer as he walked inside the building. "Looks like you were right, Bro."

"Yeah, great," I said bitterly. My father used to tell me that the worst part of being a pessimist was always being right. Now I believed him. There was still a small part of my brain that said this might be innocent. He could be just checking in on the miners. Outside his jurisdiction. At night. In a manner that was right out of a mafia movie.

"He's coming out," Cisco said. The door flung open. He was shouting about something. I couldn't make out what he was saying. Luckily, Cisco could read lips. "...My daughter in danger, not part of... *damn*." He translated for us in a whisper. McKinsey had turned to look at someone still inside. A new figure emerged in a black and white tracksuit. He had pale features, green eyes, and a disturbingly familiar smile.

"Shit!" Tony and I said at the same time. We ducked down. "Was that him?" I asked Tony.

"Looks like it," Tony whispered. "But I thought Keith put a bullet in his head."

"Will you two shut up? They're talking again," Cisco said hoarsely. "...Relax more, Chief. I was just trying to draw out the Baby Slayer." I looked over the ridge again. Leon was walking down the steps. "I won't warn you again. I owe Kel, not you... Sue G. Gary? I think he said." The pale teleporter spoke again. "Is that why you set us up?" Leon turned and said something. "Then who are the four up on the... hill." We looked at each other for a second, then we got up and ran.

CHAPTER 17

<u>Breaking the Law</u>

Tony was the first up; he sprinted back down the path, disappearing quickly into the forest. Alex and Cisco were ahead of me. I took one look back and saw that Leon was standing by himself. Then I ran into a sword. "Hunnn," I said as the air was forced out of my lungs. I stumbled backward onto the ground. A strange thought occurred to me: my dad would be upset that I just ruined his old hoodie.

"Baby Slayer!" Sue said in a pleased voice. "They said you'd survived. I was hoping they were right. You were fun to kill."

"Bet," I grunted. "Didn't I kill you first?" I clutched my chest over my fresh sword wound. I could feel the muscles in my chest fusing back together. While it hurt a lot less than being run through, it still wasn't entirely comfortable.

"Let's compromise," he responded. Then he raised his sword and his face exploded. A fraction of a second later, I heard the loud boom of the rifle.

"Time to go, Kid," Alex called out. I looked back again and saw a group of black-clothed people with swords running at me, and several more getting into the cars parked in the lot.

"Oh, boy. Running!" I yelled to no one. I pulled myself up and grabbed the discarded sword before running as fast as I could back up the path. I almost got lost a few times as I sprinted in the dark. The trees tried to slow me down, but I plowed on, heedless of the scratching and pounding on my face. I heard Carol's familiar roar as Tony brought her to life. I also heard a branch snap behind me. I didn't dare look back. If they caught me, I was dead either way. I couldn't fight all of them, and I knew Tony wouldn't leave me. I heard another car turn over. I rounded a big tree and bounded to the car, Tony already had the door open for me. I chucked the sword blindly into the forest and sat down. As soon as I did, Tony peeled out in a cloud of dust and dirt. We went faster than was safe down the dirt road. The flying dust from the Nova's tires made it hard to see the dirt road, but luckily there were not any sharp turns until we hit the highway.

As soon as we hit the blacktop, the Hunters' car slid sideways as they made the sharp turn to go north. Tony shifted and we blew past them in a slide of our own. It was not as drastic because Tony continued going south, which was a much wider turn. We narrowly missed an oncoming truck. Tony shifted again and stepped on the gas. The trees were blurs as we came around the hill. A black truck had just turned left, and another sedan was about to turn the same way up ahead. I grabbed tightly to the strap by my head as we narrowly avoided the car by momentarily moving into the left lane. I turned back to look, and the sedan was turning around. "Company," I told Tony. He cursed and glanced at the rear-view mirror.

Suddenly, the road ended. We flew past the warning sign and Tony tapped rapidly on his brake pedal. He shifted down and pulled the handbrake lever. The back swung around and he slammed the gas again. We slowed down and stopped for a second as headlights flashed up and down in our direction. They were getting closer. The tires gained traction and we sped down a single lane, tree-lined path at forty miles an hour. The road looked little used. We sped around a right-hand turn, narrowly avoiding a tree. I let out a gasp. We hit a left turn too fast, but there was a turnout on that side. Tony managed to wrestle the car under control just in time. I saw white lights still flashing behind us. After another quick left and a right, we were briefly airborne as we hit the hard road again. Tony picked up speed but had to slow down for a hard left turn. The truck still behind us had to slow down a lot more for that turn, but it didn't. It lost the road and rammed a tree. Tony sped off, not daring to slow down more than he had to in order to make turns. We didn't breathe easy until we hit the main highway.

We pulled up to his house. "Who taught you how to drive, my mom?" I demanded.

"Actually, I took some lessons from Mister Lee."

"Lee, the English teacher?" I asked.

"English and driver's ed. Did you know he used to be a getaway driver?"

"I do now." We parked and hosed down Carol, at Tony's insistence. He had been lamenting the probable damage to his car ever since we passed the airfield that marked the northwest border of Quentin.

"Dude, is that blood?" Tony asked once we got inside and turned on the lights. "And is that a hole in your sweater?"

"Yeah," I said miserably. "Can I throw these in the wash?"

Tony looked at me blankly.

"Bro, even if the blood washes out, they've got massive tears! How did that even happen?"

I told him about being impaled and how Alex had saved me by shooting the assassin in the head.

"Well, hopefully, it sticks this time," he said. I ripped off my shirt and tossed it to the side. "What did your mom call those things again?"

"Deadheads," I replied as I rummaged through my overnight bag for a new shirt. I'd told my mom I was helping Tony with homework and wouldn't be home for the night. She only agreed because Tony had given her puppy dog eyes. "Some sort of cybernetic clone thing Kel invented to use for menial tasks. If Sue was one of those, they need a different name." I put on a soft shirt and plopped onto the couch.

"Why?" Tony asked, sitting in the recliner.

"From what I've heard, they were called that because they were mindless. Kel created them in spite after my dad wouldn't let him scour the morgues so he could use real bodies for zombies." I pulled a folder out of my backpack. "That's how the story goes, anyway. I skipped the colorful language and calls for beer."

*　　*　　*

At Riley's house, Travis shifted on the couch, earning a scowl from Kyra. "Sorry," he silently mouthed. She turned back to the screen. Ashley Judd was giving an impassioned monologue to Hugh Jackman. Travis looked at his watch as Van Morrison began singing again. The actors kissed and the music swelled.

The trio of girls cried as the camera panned away and the credits rolled. Bixby sniffed next to him. Travis never really got swept away by emotion, as much as he tried. "So, what's next? Something happy, I hope?"

"Wow," Bixby replied.

"Sorry, but it's been weeks, Mac."

Riley leaned back. "I know Trav, but I…" Her throat caught and her tears began anew.

"There, there," Myra hugged her friend close and stroked her hair while glaring at Travis. "You pay that mean old man no mind. Should we watch Chicago next?"

Travis sighed and stood up. "I'll get the ice cream." He stepped carefully past the pillows that were strewn about the floor and walked to the kitchen.

"Oh, hello dear."

Travis looked away from the refrigerator and saw Alice McKinsey had entered the room.

"Hi, Alice, am I in your way?"

She smiled. "No, I just needed to hydrate." She opened a smaller refrigerator door that held rows of drinks and pulled out a water bottle. Leon entered the room wearing a concerned frown. He patted his wife's bottom and nabbed the water from her when she took it from her lips.

"Thanks, love." He took a drink and seemed to notice the tall senior for the first time. "Sorry, Travis, didn't see you there."

"Leon, I'm glad you're here, I had something I wanted to ask about."

"Can it wait a minute? I've been in meetings all day."

Travis smiled politely. "Whenever you have time."

Alice noticed Travis' smile was plastic. "Is it still bad in there?"

He nodded. "Like a funeral."

Leon sighed in annoyance. "She can't still be that upset. The boy was a loser. She's better off."

"I'm inclined to agree," Travis said. "He's hot-tempered and childish, and not nearly as clever as he thinks."

Leon slapped his hand on the counter. "Exactly what I've been saying."

"We can't help who we fall in love with." Alice snatched her water back and looked pointedly at her husband.

"I have no doubt she'll get over it eventually." Travis opened the freezer door and pulled out two pints of chocolate ripple fudge frozen custard. "Until then, I get to sit through an endless stream of rom-coms." His phone dinged, and he pulled it out.

"Nice swords." Leon pointed at the crossed silver blades on Travis' lock screen. "You collect?"

"What? Oh, I guess I have quite a few." He swiped his phone screen and looked through his gallery, clicking on one picture, making it fill the screen. "I keep them at Bix's house. He has more room to display them than my hovel." The image showed a wall of at least a dozen ornate swords.

Leon took the phone and let out a whistle. "I've got a collection going, too, you know. It's not like this, but they've all got some historical significance." He handed the phone back and smiled. "Hey, how about you drop off that ice cream and then I'll show you what I got?"

Travis smiled. This was going to be easier than he thought.

*　*　*

I sat in history the next day, listless. The replacement teacher for Tony Two made Ben Stein seem exuberant. Mr. Barnes droned on about the fragmentation of Rome, and I couldn't even distract myself with Riley. The day after the memorial assembly, I'd switched places with a boy named Kevin. He'd seemed eager to trade. My new neighbor was named Jessica. She was a fairly pretty Asian girl, with sleek, black hair and she blushed every time she looked at me. I sighed again, my mind drifting to the previous night.

"I know, right?" she whispered.

"Huh?" I asked, snapping back to reality.

"Barnes is so boring. I hope Garcia gets back soon," she said.

"Yeah," I said sadly. "Me, too."

"Did you have him last year?" she asked.

"No. He's an old family friend."

"That makes sense," she said with a smile. "When you were in the hospital, he was in a really bad mood."

"Oh yeah, sorry," I said.

"No, I thought it was really brave, standing up to those awful Hunters. I think you're a hero," she whispered.

I smiled and blushed. Unbidden, I glanced at the window that Riley sat next to. She was scowling. She looked away when she saw I was looking. I turned forward, trying to pay attention to the lecture.

"So you went on an adventure without me?" Urchin said at lunch. "How do you expect me to gain levels?"

"Answer your phone next time," I replied sourly. We were within sight of the clique's table, and Gary was sitting in my old seat, next to Riley. He had just said something to make the rest of the table laugh. A coiled snake sat at the bottom of my belly, exuding hateful thoughts. Did she invite him for my benefit? Was she trying to get even with me for my conversation with Jessica?

"Hey," Tony said, snapping in front of my face. "Green isn't your color."

"How long has *that* been going on?" I asked, failing at apathy.

"You think a guy like Cap would try and steal your girl?" Urchin asked.

"She's not my girl anymore," I replied bitterly. *And whose fault was that?*

"Then why do you care?" Tony asked.

"Because humans are stupid and emotional." I sighed and forced myself to look at my lunch. "Anyway, I'm going to try to find out if they made it out okay, so I want to swing by Kermit's after school."

"Sure," Tony said. "But you help me wash Carol."

I awoke the next day and immediately looked at my phone. No texts or missed calls. I was getting worried, but there wasn't a lot I could do. No one at Kermit's had seen Alex or Cisco since they left with us. I rolled over and almost stepped on Tony's face. I hopped over him and headed to the bathroom. I looked at the closed door to my parent's room along the way. Mom was due home late tonight.

When I had finished my morning routine, I walked back to my room.

Tony was awake and sitting on my bed, looking at his phone. "Still nothing?" he asked.

I shook my head. "We can drive back, see if they're laying low in Greenville."

He shrugged. "It's worth a shot." He stood and grabbed his jacket. "Kind of a boring way to spend Halloween."

"Yeah, all things considered, I'd prefer boring."

"What are we gonna do if we can't find them?"

"Find who?" Urchin asked before eating a spoonful of cereal.

I didn't even bother asking how he got in my house. "Alex and Cisco. We were only talking about it all day on Friday."

"I was distracted. Gabriela was wearing this top that--"

"Anyway," I interrupted. "Are you helping or just eating all my food?"

"What do Sam and Dean look like again?" Urchin asked.

"Alex and Cisco?"

"Yeah," he said. "Old guy and a young guy? Brown leather jackets? Ruggedly handsome?"

"Yeah…" I said slowly.

"Well, the good news is that I know where they are..."

"That's really bad news," Tony said. We sat in his car on the opposite side of Main Street from the Police Station.

"Well, we have to do something," I said.

"Do you have a bulldozer in your back pocket?" Urchin asked.

"I left it in my other pants," I replied. "You guys stay here. I'm going to ask some questions."

"Listen, Thor, that is such a bad idea that even I wouldn't do it," Urchin said from the back seat.

"Well, in the absence of good ideas, a bad one will have to do." I opened the door and stepped out as my friends expressed their displeasure.

"Can I help you?" the woman at the front desk asked. She was heavyset, and her curly hair was an unnatural shade of red. I hadn't planned this far in advance.

"I heard a friend of mine was arrested last night."

"And your name?" she asked, pulling a clipboard out from a pile.

"Scott O'Connor," Leon McKinsey said from behind me.

I turned. "Leon McKinsey," I replied.

"That's *Chief* McKinsey to you," he said sternly.

"For now."

"Talk with me in my office," he said.

"No thanks."

"It wasn't a request." He placed his hand on his hip where he carried his gun. I briefly considered my options. I doubted he would start shooting in the lobby, but I needed answers. I might be able to get something from this guy. My trepidation of going to a second location with a man I knew wanted me dead lost out to my curiosity.

I shrugged in response. "What the hell, why not?"

Inside his office, the 'Chief' didn't mince words. "What are you doing here, Scott?" Leon sat behind his desk.

I stood near the doorway. I knew running wouldn't do me any good, but I wanted to be as far from him as possible. "Following a lead," I responded.

"You aren't a detective," he observed.

"And yet..." I crossed my arms and leaned against the wall. "Why were those two men arrested?"

"What are you going on about?" he sighed.

"You brought in two men. Father and son. Leather jackets."

"They were trespassing," he said warily.

"On public land?"

He was silent.

"Because I know for a fact that you didn't pick them up in Quentin. You picked them up in county land. That's the sheriff's job, Leo," I said leadingly.

He slammed his hands on his desk. "You are an annoying little prick. I will never know why my daughter had feelings for you," he said in a growl.

"It was my winning smile," I said flatly. "What do you care about her?"

"I would do anything for her," he shouted.

"You'd do anything for *you*," I snapped back. "You don't care about her, you just don't want to feel sad." I pushed away from the wall.

"Don't dare assume my motivations, boy. You know nothing about me."

"I know enough. The only thing I can't figure out is why you'd sell out to Kel of all people."

He glanced at the picture on his desk for a fraction of a moment.

The egg timer went off. "Kel gave you the cure," I said.

He remained silent. The door opened behind me and two uniformed officers rushed into the room.

"We heard banging, Chief. Is everything okay?" one of them asked. The other looked at me suspiciously.

Leon smiled. "It's about to be."

I sat in my cell, banging my head against the wall. I should have listened to my friends. I was stuck in a cell and not even the one that contained the two people I was there to see. I was stuck once again in Leon's realm, and this time, my dad wasn't around to save me. I opened my eyes when I heard footsteps. It was Leon, there to gloat.

"What do you want?" I asked in a bored voice. Being alone in an iron cage for two hours had put me in a bad mood.

"I want you to stay out of my way, and away from my daughter. Promise me that, and you can go free. I know how important promises are to you," he said slyly.

I stood up and ran at the bars. He took a step back.

"No," I shouted. My temper was at its limit. "You set me up, you set my dad up, and you sold out everything you used to believe in." I grabbed the bars and fixed him with a hateful stare. "And I'll tell you this: the only reason I'm not with Riley *right now* is the fact that I'm going to take you down if it kills me," I growled.

He smiled in response. "I was hoping you would say that."

Two large men with tattoos walked down the hallway. I backed up from the bars. They stood a head taller than me and looked like they tossed around large pieces of farming equipment for fun. The door opened, and they stepped in. "Play nice, Junior." The casual reference to my father sparked something in me. A righteous fury. I tried to get at him but was shoved roughly back. The cell door clanged shut.

Leon walked away as the two thugs approached. Gone was any idea of an attempted parlay. There was only violence left. I dodged a clumsy swing as I charged the first one and lifted a leg as I drove into him. He toppled, and I went down with him. He grabbed onto me and I tried to wriggle free. I felt a sharp pain in my back. I punched out and caught the one on the ground in the wobbly bits. He let out a grunt and released me. I stood up in time to get a faceful of hand. I punched again and again at the arm, but was lifted and became airborne for a moment before crashing into the cage. I heard a loud crack in my ribs, but whatever was in my back fell out with a clatter. I stood up again and leaned to the side to avoid a massive punch to the head. Instead, his fist clanged on the bar. He shouted in pain and grabbed his arm. I took a steadying step and kicked as hard as I could against his knee while he was distracted. He went down, and I booted him in the face. He crumpled. I was lifted again from behind. I threw my head back and lights flashed in my eyes as I hit his face. I kicked down and caught his leg. He didn't go down, but he let me go again. I spun around with an elbow to his face.

He went down, but I followed. I punched him again in the face and felt a bone crunch. I didn't know if it was mine or his, so I switched hands. All the anger and frustration I'd felt for the last two weeks came loose, and these two would be the ones to suffer for it.

When the rage was sated, I stood huffing and puffing in the middle of the cell, my shirt stained with blood, very little of it mine. The two men groaned. My wounds had already healed.

"Wow," Urchin said. "You are going to need to invest in more shirts." I tilted my head to the side. "Are you going to be a good boy?" he asked.

"I thought I told you to wait in the car," I said.

"I thought I told you I have a problem with authority," he replied. He turned his wrist, and the cell sprang open. "Now it's time for running. I love this part."

I followed him out. There was ringing down the hall. It sounded like a fire alarm. "What is going on?"

"I've always wanted to be a part of a jailbreak. You're just collateral damage." He smirked.

"Aren't they going to be upset that I'm gone?"

"Maybe," he said as he peered around a corner.

"They know where I live," I said.

He looked at me and sighed. "You can't escape from jail if you were never in," he explained. "You really think they're gonna hold a minor for hours and then put him in a cell with violent felons and actually write any of that down?"

"I hadn't thought of it like that," I admitted.

"That's why I'm here, to inexplicably do what needs to be done. This way, now." He sprinted down the hall, leaping over a trash bin sideways. I ran around it.

"Did you also get the Hunters out?" I asked.

"They got moved while you were locked up," he said. "Can you fit through that window?"

As it turned out, I could. We met up with Tony, who sat with the car running a block away, and we drove to my house.

"Was there a point to this episode?" Urchin asked.

"Well, I tried visiting people in jail, didn't see them, threatened the chief, got beat up, and now I'm a fugitive. So, no, classic filler," I joked.

Urchin patted me on the shoulder.

"You must have gotten your bell rung harder than you thought, bro," Tony said. "You're talking like *him*. And we need to address the amount of blood you're leaving on my seats. Should I get them reupholstered in red?"

"Well, one thing I know is that I need to pack more shirts in your trunk," I said, looking at what had been a shirt with one of my favorite anime characters on it. Now it looked like a horror prop. "Hopefully, my mom is still at work. I do not want to have to explain this."

"Uh-oh," Tony said.

"What, is she home?" I asked. My house had come into view. While the driveway was empty, two people were standing on my lawn. We pulled into the drive and I hopped out.

"Travis, Bixby. What are you doing here? I thought you were done with me."

"I was," Travis said. "But Bixby insisted we keep digging."

"Yeah, I wasn't a fan of being eaten," Bixby said. "I found out McKinsey Manor was bought by a shell for a shell for a shell…well anyway, the short version is this: that house was built by one of Kel's companies and sold for pennies."

"So you found out he's crooked, thanks for the news," I said acerbically.

"That's not the news," Travis said as he pulled out his phone. "That's what led us to look around. That's when I found this." He showed me a picture of a sword. It was intimately familiar. I grabbed the phone and zoomed in. There were intricate runes along the blade, and I recognized them. I looked up.

"This is my father's sword."

CHAPTER 18

<u>Boomerang</u>

"Where did you find this?" My voice trembled somewhere between shock and outrage. I had to remind myself to breathe. We were all sitting in my living room, except for Travis, who was standing.

"In his bedroom," Travis said. "I recognized it right away. I snapped this when he wasn't looking."

"He showed it to you?" I demanded. Anger was flooding my thoughts. Tony put a hand on my shoulder to calm me down.

"He was bragging about how he'd wanted this piece for his collection for years and he finally got it," Travis said.

"How did *you* recognize it?" I asked.

"I'm a Sinner," he said. "I was once on the wrong end of that sword. The Slayer showed me mercy. You don't forget even a single detail of something like that."

I looked at him, trying to measure him. He took off his sunglasses for the first time. His eyes were silver, bright, and gleaming. They resembled chrome orbs, but there was a swirling aspect to them. He looked back at me with his mercurial eyes. The others in the room shifted uncomfortably. He replaced his glasses. "Your dad gave me these to help me fit in." He turned to look out of the window. "It took me a while to remember what I owe him."

"I'm not my father," I reminded him.

"No, you sure as shooting aren't," he replied.

"Will you help me?" I asked him again.

He turned to face me. "I'm with you."

"Me too," Bixby agreed.

"You know I'm coming," Tony said.

I looked at Urchin, who was staring at a family portrait. He finally seemed to notice the room was looking at him.

"Look, I'm only here for the fan service," he said.

"So what's the next step?" Tony asked me.

"It might sound selfish, but I need to get that sword back. We can kill two birds if we also get into Leon's study. And we need to do it without alerting security."

"Why don't we just go to Mac's Halloween party?" Bixby asked.

"Okay, we can do that. Tony and I will need masks to go incognito."

"Why?" Bixby asked. "You have an invite." I stared at him blankly. "Did–did you ignore *all* of her messages?"

I continued to stare, but this time with a guilty face.

He rolled his eyes. "Is it too late to change my answer?"

I sighed and pulled out my phone and unmuted my conversation with Riley. There were forty-three new messages.

<u>Hi. I know what we said, but I still want you to be a part of my life. I hope that's okay,</u> The first one read. A smile crept onto my face as I read through all the little updates. And there it was, an invitation right above <u>Scott, please come. I need to talk to you.</u> It was dated the twenty-ninth.

"Well, I guess that's that," I said. "Crap, now I need a costume."

"Bix and I will meet you there at six," Travis said.

"Urchin, do we need to swing by your place to pick something up?" Tony asked.

"For what?" he asked, coming out of the bathroom.

Tony did a double-take. We hadn't seen him leave the room.

"For... the Halloween party at Riley's." Tony said haltingly. "Do you need a costume?"

"I'll just go as a teenage heartthrob." He messed up his hair. "Okay, I'm ready."

*　*　*

At the edge of town, Howard Keith took a final drag of his cigarette and flicked the butt away. He held the smoke in his lungs for a moment before exhaling it away. He'd forgotten how good the nicotine felt. He'd managed to quit years ago, but he still relapsed in times of stress. Having half of his team killed at a school dance definitely qualified as a stressful situation.

"Good evening, Bandit."

Keith jumped at the sound of Two Dog's voice. "Jeezus, TD. Snap a branch or something. Yer as bad as that Urchin kid."

"That is an impressive rifle," Two Dogs said, gesturing to the long gun that leaned against the wall.

"That's Charlene. My very favoritest rifle." He picked it up and slid the bolt back. "She started out an M1A, but that was years ago." He slid out the box magazine and handed it to the Navajo man. Two Dogs checked to make sure there was not a round still in the chamber and pointed it at the base of a faraway tree. "I kitted it out with all my favorite goodies. She can fire SLAP rounds with no issues."

Two Dogs looked up at the blonde man. "To what end?"

"A few years ago, me and Icebeard was workin' a job in Germany at some castle in the forest. They had these magical talking dogs. Anyway, these wolves had hides so thick that the Seven-Six-Two APs I was firing weren't doin' anything but tickling 'em." He sniffed and spit. "Ended up havin' to shoot 'em in the eyes."

"That sounds reasonable." Two Dogs handed the rifle back, and Keith reset the bolt before slamming his mag back in.

"So, what brings you out here?"

Two Dogs adjusted his Stetson and gazed at the forest. "A hunch."

"Be more vague."

"I have been tracking something large. It is strange, like nothing I've seen before."

Howard placed his hand on one of the box magazines strapped to his vest. "What's it look like?"

Timothy shook his head. "I have not seen it, but the tracks look like some species of troll I have not yet encountered."

The Bandit froze. "A troll? In California?"

"A troll with claws. It drags a club behind it. It is at least ten feet tall, and I suspect it has wings."

"You can tell all that with tracks?"

"If you know what to look for, yes."

Keith let out a low whistle. "Well, I guess I'm goin' trick or treating with you tonight." He ejected the magazine and replaced it with the smaller one that he had been fiddling.

"I welcome your company. Please try to keep up."

*　*　*

Tony, Urchin, and I were parked in front of the wall around Riley's house.

"And we're sure this is a good idea?" Tony asked.

"Not even a little at first," I replied. The small clock on the dashboard told us it was five minutes to six.

"So your dad had *all* this stuff in the garage?" Urchin asked, picking at the patch on my combat shirt. Tony and I had looked around through bins, searching for costume ideas when we came across a box with tactical clothing that hadn't been put in his closet yet. We decided to go as "Tacti-cool kids."

"He likes to take work home with him," I said, then I turned to Tony. "Leon's not likely to be home. Halloween is always a busy night for cops." *Not to mention custodians,* I didn't say. "Couple that with it being a Saturday *and* a full moon…"

"Long night for Leon," Tony concluded.

"Hey, I get you wanna put the small guy in the back, but is there a way you can make this thing a four-door?" Urchin asked.

Tony looked at him like he had just asked to kick a dog. I noticed Bixby's white Lexus pull up to the gate.

"Showtime," I said, interrupting their argument.

The house was lit up in purple and orange lights. Inflatable ghosts were popping up randomly from fake tombstones. Music drifted from the backyard, and I could tell before entering that the house itself was going to be full. "Okay," I said before opening the door. "We do this in groups. Trav, Bix, and Urchin, you try to get info. Tony, you stay with me and keep me from doing something stupid." Tony scowled at this. "Fine, *try* to stop me."

"It might already be too late for that," he said.

I opened the door and at least twenty people were dancing to some EDM remix of an old, spooky song. Travis' group immediately broke off from us. Tony and I entered and attempted to navigate the crowd.

"Scott?" Jessica asked. She was wearing a skintight cat costume. "I didn't know you were coming."

"I, uh, got an invite," I said, not paying much attention.

"Yeah, but, you know… with Riley and all?" she noted.

I looked at her. She bit her bottom lip.

"Do you know where she is?" I asked. She shrugged. "It was nice running into you. I'll see you later." I walked away, not noticing the disappointed look on her face. I had to focus on getting upstairs somehow. I tried to make my way through the crowd, a majority of whom were wearing low effort costumes. I walked past one of the football players, who was wearing a shirt that said, "Costume."

I ran into Gary, who was wearing a child's plastic knight set. We reached out and stopped each other from falling. "Scott? Are you okay? What's wrong?"

"How much time have you got?" I asked. He raised an eyebrow. I looked out at the crowd. "Have you seen Riley?"

He hesitated. "She went upstairs for something," he said. I started to move away, but he held onto my arm. I looked dangerously at him. He didn't flinch. "What do you want with her?"

"Does it matter?" I asked. He fixed me with a serious stare. I sighed. "Are you and she..?"

"Dating? No."

"No, or not yet?" I tried not to sound accusatory. He glanced up the stairwell. "Gary. Get your hand off my arm."

"Don't hurt her again," he warned.

"Darn, you foiled my clever plot," I replied sarcastically. I pulled my arm away from him. Once free, my expression softened. "Look, I know this comes from a good place," I admitted. "She wanted to talk to me. I'm not trying to start anything."

"Okay," he said calmly. "But be careful."

I turned and tried to make my way upstairs as quickly as possible.

"Watch it," someone said as I pushed between two people. I tried to keep moving, but a hand grabbed my shoulder. I turned to find Topher in a skeleton costume that was little more than paper bones stapled to a black skinsuit.

He started to say something, but I jerked my shoulder free. "Shut it," I said. "I've got no time or patience for your crap, so shove it back up your butt." There was an "ooh" sound coming from the people around us.

"You wanna go for round two?" he asked, cracking his knuckles.

"Didn't I tell you to shut it?" Before he responded, I turned and walked away. There was a gasp from multiple people and I turned to defend myself, but he was already on the ground. Tony was on top of him, pummeling him in the back of the head. He paused and looked at me with a small shrug. I nodded and rushed up the stairs while no one was looking.

I tried to remember which of the doors were which. I knew which door was Riley's so I started there. I paused as I heard her voice. I leaned in close. "I don't care, I have to tell him," Riley said.

"The only thing he needs is a kick in the--" Kyra began.

"Mac, have you thought about this?" Myra interrupted. "Once you take that step… you can't un-ring a bell, as he likes to say."

"I know," Riley replied. "He needs to know. I can't keep this secret forever. He's going to find out eventually, and if he hears it from me, maybe he won't hate me forever." Deciding that this conversation should be private, I continued down the hall. The next door should be the study, but that was Urchin's job. I assumed Leon's bedroom would be near his study, so I decided to check the door opposite.

"Excuse me, the party's downstairs," Riley said.

I had just passed her bedroom door and was about to reach the study. I froze. A thousand conversations played through my head at once and I couldn't understand any of them. I turned around.

"Scott?" She was dressed as a fairy princess. She dabbed her eyes so her makeup wouldn't smudge. "You came. Thank you."

"I wasn't going to. But…" I trailed off. I let a long silence hang between us.

"There's something you need to know," she said and reached out her hand halfway to me. "Come with me." I looked at her hand for a long time. Finally, I reached across and grabbed it. She led me to her room. Myra and Kyra were inside. Myra was wearing a nurse costume that was cut too low and too high. Kyra wore a black gi with a green belt and a black snake coiled in a yellow circle. She took a threatening step toward me, but Myra held her back.

"Are you sure you want to do this?" Myra warned.

Riley hesitated, then stood up straight and nodded.

Myra stood and locked her arm around her sister's. "Let's go, Kee."

Kyra didn't move at first. She glared warningly at me. I stared stoically back. Finally, she let herself be dragged away. Riley closed the door behind them, then I heard it lock. My entire spine tingled. I was alone in a room with a girl. My mother had warned me against such things. I took a step back to maintain distance.

"Scott, I don't even know where to begin," she sniffed. "I've missed you."

I didn't know what to do with my hands. I opted to stick them in my pockets. I tried my best to avoid eye contact. "I've missed you too," I managed.

She smiled ruefully. "You were right. I found out…" She took a steadying breath. "My dad has been helping Kel." I wasn't surprised by this. "And I know why." She looked at me and I gestured for her to continue. "Remember when I told you I was sick? Well, I was almost dead when Kel gave us the cure. That's why… that's why he…" I didn't help her finish, this was something I needed to hear from her lips. "He set the trap for you and your dad."

I expected to be more satisfied with that, but looking at her, I could tell it was tearing her apart. I wanted to hold her and say everything was fine. But I didn't, because it wasn't. My face was shockingly stoic. "Why are you telling me this?" I finally asked.

"You need to know," she said, looking at the ground.

"I already knew all that. That's why we broke up in the first place," I reminded her.

"Then I guess…it's because…I'm sorry." She looked up and tears were falling down her face. "You were right, and I'm sorry."

I sighed again. "This… doesn't change anything. I'm still going to take them down. And anyone who gets in the way."

She nodded. "He betrayed everything he taught me to believe in," she said. "If I thought it was just because he owed my life to Kel, I could forgive it. But when I confronted him about it, I knew it was just his own personal vendetta. I know you hate me now, but Scott, you need to know. Your dad is still alive."

"What?!" This was the first actual piece of news. My mind exploded with questions. I settled on the most obvious one. "Where?"

She shook her head. "I don't know, it was something he said, thinking it would make it okay. I think he's a prisoner somewhere. That's all I have. I hope it's enough to--" I didn't let her finish. I reached out and pulled her into a tight embrace.

"I don't hate you," I said. "I never did." We pulled apart enough to look at each other. "Truth is, I like you."

She smiled up at me. "I like you, too," she whispered.

We kissed a deep and passionate kiss. A kiss that tried to make up for all the hurt and separation. It went a long way to doing just that.

"And we're back up," Urchin said from the doorway. I quickly looked to find the whole gang there.

"Urchin," Riley exclaimed, stunned. "That door was locked."

"Weird. Anyway, Boss Man, we have the stuff, and check this out--"

"My dad is alive?" I guessed.

"Okay fine, ruin the big reveal. But *I* know where he is," he replied.

I looked back at Riley. "Where's your dad's room?"

CHAPTER 19

<u>The Animal</u>

"Did you see the size of that thing?" Keith whispered loudly. He watched as the enormous creature barreled through the forest. He tried to line up a shot, but the trees blocked him. "What the hell is that thing?"

"I have a theory," Two Dogs replied. "Scott and the Tonys told me they found a laboratory a little while ago. In it were several hybrid creatures."

Keith raised his eyebrow. "O'Connor said they found something big. I didn't expect it to be Kel splicing pig and elephant DNA."

"I believe this is more likely a troll spliced with a dragon." He lowered his binoculars. "You may get a chance to utilize your sabot rounds."

Howard stood and shook his head. "Lucky me."

Two Dogs watched the trees part. "We need to move quickly."

"I hope you understand my lack of eagerness. Did I mention the size of that thing?"

"Did you see what was leading it?"

"I swear, Dogs, if you make me bring up its size again…"

"It was one of the creatures my son told me about. They followed him to my house, and the dragon troll just turned north."

"I think we need to move quickly," Keith agreed.

*　　*　　*

Back at Tony's house, we sorted through a box of items that might be useful to our mission. "Kicking down the door was a bit much," Tony said as we sorted through the things we might need to bring.

"It was exactly enough," I replied with a smirk as I picked up a silver knife. I tossed it into the bag. I looked at the sword. The inside of the fuller was etched on one side with small, swooping Hebrew letters that I couldn't read. I liked holding it. It was perfectly balanced, and the edge was razor sharp. We had split up from the group and returned to Tony's house for supplies. The plan was for Bixby and Travis to join us as soon as they were ready. The dogs in the back started barking. Tony looked up from the can of salt in his hands.

"I'm just saying…" his voice drifted off.

"What? You think Leon's really going to report--"

"Shh. Can you feel that?" he whispered.

I couldn't hear much over the dogs' incessant barking. I knew enough to listen when I was being warned. Tony's pack were well trained, and wouldn't be this loud if it were a simple raccoon. I felt a thud and held the sword in my right hand, turning to look in the backyard. The floodlights flashed on a giant creature with ruddy green and copper skin landing in the middle of the yard. It was so tall that we could only see its bottom half out of the window. I recognized the way it moved its legs with a rush of dread.

"Down!" I shouted. No sooner had we dropped than the roof vanished in one swing of a giant mace. Suddenly, through the flying debris, I saw the creature in full. It was over ten feet tall, stocky, and covered in dull scales. Wings that were too small for it furled out behind. Its long snout had many sharp teeth. It lifted the club again. "Time to move," I shouted, and we rolled in opposite directions. The weapon, which was just a large metal ball at the end of a long metal stick, hit the floor so hard, the boards split and bent. I was lifted from the ground, landed on my feet and ran.

"What the hell is that thing?" Tony shouted. "It's not a dragon, is it?"

"How should I know?" I asked. I jumped back and narrowly avoided being clutched by a clawed hand. I swung out with my sword. It sunk in a few inches, and the only thing stopping it from being ripped from my hands was that I'd learned to hold on tighter. I rolled in the same direction, which put me in line with the club again. Rolling again, I jumped over what used to be Tony's back wall. "I can cut it, at least," I said.

"Good for you," Tony said as he ran to the far side of the yard. "I might as well be sticking it with a needle." He chucked the knife that was in his hand. It was bent out of shape. I pulled the blue steel knife out of my pocket and threw it with all the accuracy I could manage while jumping out of the way of another swing. He caught it, but I'd lost focus and was snatched up. The thing lifted me to its face.

"No snack for you!" I shouted and aimed a thrust at its eye. It made a squelch as the point of the blade pierced the eyelid. I pulled back the sword and readied for another strike, but instead, I was thrown. I don't know how I held on to the hilt as I flew through the wooden fence and rolled to a stop twenty feet away. My leg felt broken. The only thing that eased the pain was that every part of my body screamed with pain, and a brain can only process so much. I struggled to get to my feet as my bones popped back into place.

I hobbled faster and faster, ignoring the shooting pain from my leg. Tony was quick, but I didn't know how long he could hold out. If he took a hit like that, it would put him out for a lot longer. His four dogs barked and growled as they tried to take nips at the giant's heels. The giant made them seem tiny. They jumped away every time it reached down. I got to the hole in the fence and my last rib clicked back into place. Tony had just jammed the knife into the giant's knee, which buckled, but he couldn't dart out in time. He was picked up in a big hand.

I rushed in, and the giant swiped one-handed with the club. I didn't have time to dodge. I brought up my sword in a futile attempt to block. When the mace made contact, a bright light blazed from my blade and the club shattered. The ball went flying through the fence behind me and the shaft swung quickly back. This caught the creature by surprise and it stumbled off balance.

There was nothing for it, I had to keep pressing. I darted in and cut at his arm as it came back around. The blade dug in but didn't stop the momentum. I was clubbed over by its forearm. One of the dogs jumped up and latched onto the arm that held Tony. I tried to get to my feet again, ignoring the ringing in my ears. The monster grabbed the dog with its free hand and clenched it. There was a terrible crunch and a whine. It dropped the dog to the ground.

"No!" Tony and I shouted. I thrust into the wrist near Tony and buried the sword to the hilt. The creature roared, but that only drove me. Tony dropped to the ground and leaped impossibly fast. He roared back at the beast and latched on. I twisted the sword and pulled it out, moving to be ready to accept the next blow that would come my way. It swung at Tony instead, who moved behind its head and latched onto its ears. The other giant hand moved to swat at him but got stuck on the grass, or rather, the grass reached out and grabbed it. I didn't stop to question it. I drove the sword into the monster's gut. It roared in pain. Another sword joined mine a foot above. Travis had joined the fray. He drove the sword in his off-hand even higher. We both pulled out and stepped back. The other arm clubbed at us. The creature was bleeding green blood from several spots now. It ripped free of the grass vines and slammed both hands at its head. Tony jumped ten feet, did a twist in the air, and landed on all fours. It was at that moment that I realized he was different.

Instead of his normal brown skin, he was covered in hair. He looked more like one of his dogs now. "Tony?" I wondered. He looked at me intensely with those eyes. The egg timer went off in my head. "Puppy?" I heard Bixby's voice behind me, but whatever he was saying wasn't in English. A loud WOMP rang out, and I saw a clawed hand trying to break a clear barrier. I swung my sword in a loop to get a better grip. *Killing now, questions later.*

I thought, and we charged. I leaped to the side and cut at the claw that was headed toward Tony, he bounded at the beast, swiping at the knee, digging deep with his claws. Travis took the other hand and it dropped with a thud. Bixby threw some sort of frozen ball of energy and got it in the face. I leaped and sliced clean through the throat. It gurgled.

I swung my sword one more time for good measure. With a loud crash, the thing fell the rest of the way to the ground. I looked around as I caught my breath. Tony was with the other dogs, sniffing their fallen comrade. Out of the heat of battle, I saw it was Girl Dog, the second oldest of the pack. She looked to be in rough shape. The dogs and Tony whined at her.

"Someone want to explain this?" Travis pointed to Tony.

"I can," a calm, low voice said from inside the wrecked house. Two Dogs was standing there in his long, brown coat, wearing a cowboy hat. Next to him was Mr. Keith, who had forgone his traditional suit in favor of a tactical vest and cargo pants. He had a long rifle in his hands. Timothy stepped through what used to be the doorway. "But it will take some time to do it right. Suffice it for now to say, Tony does not suffer from a heart condition. The medicine he takes is designed to suppress the monthly transformation."

"Does he know?" I asked. The older man shook his head. "Why not?"

"Hey, I know it's medicine man story-time, but if we don't torch this thing, It's going to get back up soon," Mr. Keith said.

Travis and Bixby volunteered to help while Two Dogs approached his son and pulled out a syringe. "He has not needed to know until recently," Tim continued.

"The first day of school," I said. "He saved me in the alley."

"Yes, it seems his connection to you suppressed his instinct to hunt. Loyalty has always been his greatest virtue." He plunged the syringe into Tony's neck, and the werewolf passed out. I looked on as the hair started to shed and his features began to look more human. "Some Hunters found out, and I have been leading them down false trails. And looking for a way to tell him."

"Is he going to be okay?" I asked.

"He will awaken soon. It may be impossible to say if he will be 'okay.'" Two Dogs picked up his adopted son and carried him into the wreckage.

I found a toppled chair and turned it upright to have a seat before addressing Travis. "You guys came just in time."

"Had to stop for these," Travis said, holding up two swords that were a little longer than his forearm.

"And I see you decided to add 'mage' to your resume, Bix," I said.

"Mage may be too strong a term. I've been working on it with Professor Mogrim all year. I only really know three spells," he replied.

"Is one of them 'build a firepit?'" Keith interrupted.

"No, Professor Mogrim seemed reticent to show me fire magic."

"Yeah, that sounds like him. Bad news for you lot." The football coach handed the short boy a plank that was once part of a fence. Bixby grimaced and held the wood with two fingers.

We worked together and quickly placed the kindling around the body. True to Keith's words, the giant dragon creature's wounds were beginning to close. He fired a shot into the creature's skull to buy us more time. Soon enough, the monster was engulfed in flames.

"I can't go to the bathroom around you people without some tragedy occurring, can I?" Urchin said as we watched the bonfire that was once a giant.

"I *did* notice your absence," I said casually.

"What was I going to do against that thing? Joke it to death? It was dumber than Becky, wait… no, yeah, dumber," he said.

"So now that Big Ugly is taken care of," Keith began. "What are you kids doing out here?" He pointed at the blade in my hand, which was no longer glowing. "And where did you get that sword?"

I looked down. I'd half-forgotten I was holding it. I hadn't cleaned it yet, but there was no blood or dirt on it. "I took it back from Leon. And now we're going to save the world and rescue my dad," I said bluntly. Lying took more energy than I had. I briefly told him about Kel trying to lift the Veil.

"Oh, is that all?" he said. "Are you insane? Five kids against Kel?" He flicked his spent cigarette into the fire and fumbled in his pockets for another smoke.

"It has to be done," I said simply.

"By you?"

"We're the only ones willing to do it. Are you going to try and stop us?"

He looked taken aback. "Stop you? Nah. But what kind of teacher would I be if I let a bunch of kids storm a castle by themselves?" he asked with a grin.

"So what's the plan?" Tony asked as he stepped from the wreckage of his house. I looked at him. He had a brown motorcycle jacket over his tactical vest. There was a large, red line across his forehead, but otherwise looked none the worse for wear.

"You good?" I asked simply, turning my attention away from the fire.

He nodded unsurely. "I'm going to have to be." He looked at his father, who was as stoic as ever. "I guess I have even more reason to remember my meds." He chuckled. "Are we… still cool?" he asked.

"Can't think of a reason why we wouldn't be," I said. Before the conversation continued, My phone rang. It was my mother. I briefly considered not answering, but that wouldn't work in my favor.

"Where are you?" she asked. I could tell by her tone she knew the answer somehow.

"I'm at Tony's," I said.

"Scott *Richard* O'Connor, you'd better not be planning something stupid."

I glared at Coach Keith.

He put his hands up in defense. "Sorry kid, but I'm more scared of Dixie than I am of you."

"Mom, I--"

"Don't you 'Mom' me young man. I'm going to be home in five minutes. You'd better beat me there."

"I wouldn't be doing this if--"

"Four minutes and forty-five seconds." The line lost sound. I looked panic-stricken to Tony.

"How fast can we get to my place?"

The answer was exactly three minutes. We blew past every stop sign and almost ran over a score of trick-or-treaters. We beat her there, barely. I could hear the rumble of a diesel Semi-truck when I stepped out of the car. By the time I'd unlocked the door, I saw her trusty long haul big rig. It was a twenty-year-old Mack truck with a purple night sky paint job. There were forked lightning bolts painted from front to back. I stepped into the house. She ran the giant truck up the lawn. I heard the familiar sounds of the engine being shut down. She stepped down from the cockpit angrily. She was the only person I knew who could seem angry from behind.

"I'm home," I offered.

She walked into the house, pushing me to the side. "Tony, out," she said as she threw her pack to the table. Tony knew better than to argue. He gave me a reassuring pat on the back and closed the door behind him. "Are you *insane*?!" she shouted. "Have I not lost enough in one month? Now you want to take away my *son*?" She started pacing.

"Mom--"

"And you were just going to traipse off with your little friends to fight Kel?"

"Mom!" I shouted. "I have to do this."

"You think your father would want you to die trying to get revenge?"

"Not revenge, rescue."

She blinked, but pressed on. "Oh, so he's a noble dip--"

"Mom, I need to--"

"Says who?" she demanded.

"God!" I shouted back. I took a second to calm myself. "When I died, an angel said I had to stop the Veil from rising. That's why I came back."

She was silent.

"We know where to go, we found a map, and we have to do this tonight, I just know we do. I don't know how I know, but I know."

She looked at me like she was losing something. When she finally spoke, it was in a whisper. "Okay. Okay, I won't stop you." She turned and walked into her room.

I sighed in relief. There were countless ways that conversation could have been worse, and precious few that could have been better. I opened the door to find six people on my doorstep.

CHAPTER 20

Move

"As far as I can tell, there are two distinct sections, the mine and the lab," Bixby said as we watched the 3D rendering of a facility he'd put up rotate on my TV screen. It had many passageways and levels. There was a large, dome-shaped room at what looked to be the center. Bixby highlighted it. "This looks like the center chamber, and if I read the ley lines right, it should be where Kel is trying to do the thing."

"Raise the Veil," I corrected.

Tony raised his hand. "Is that what those moving lines are?"

"Yep. I've read some of his notes already, and it looks like he's using the natural magical currents to tear a hole. I'm not going to bore you with the minutia. Anyway, the problem is that while there are likely to be guards, there's no shift list or even a logistics report to look at to guess the strength," Bixby continued.

"He's prol'ly using Deadheads," Keith chimed in.

"Howard is correct," Two Dogs confirmed. "In past assaults on Kel's labs, the vast majority of his security has been provided by them. It stands to reason that they would be in use here."

"Great. Is there a way to guess their numbers?" Bixby asked. They both shook their heads. "Magical. Continuing, the map I found may be out of date. It also rather unhelpfully does not list any room names. Do the professors have anything to add?" he asked.

"None of the laboratories have been structured around a pattern," Two Dogs said.

"He likes to keep us guessing," Howard Keith agreed. "Maybe half are flat-out traps. About the only thing you can count on is that there will be cameras everywhere. He likes to watch."

"Who doesn't?" Urchin asked.

"If there *are* cameras, I might be able to access them when we get in," Bixby suggested. "That should give us some sort of leg up."

"Okay, so what's the plan?" I asked Timothy Acothley.

"Scott, you are the mission lead here," Two Dogs said.

"That's right," Howard agreed. "It's your farm, how do you want to hump this pig?"

I looked around the room to see all eyes on me. After scanning the rotating schematics and the photos of the large open gravel field, I tried to come up with an idea. "Bix, assuming we can get in. How do we stop the spell?"

He stroked his chin. "For his ritual to succeed, he needs to channel a ridiculous amount of energy into a runic circle. He'll then use the circle to force a breach in the Veil."

"So if we broke the circle?"

Bixby shrugged. "The stored power would dissipate.

"Okay. Here's the plan..." I trailed off as my mom walked into the room with an armored vest on and two bandoleers strung around her shoulders. She indelicately put a duffle bag on the table. "Mom? What are you doing?"

"I told you, you could go," she explained without looking up. "But if you think you are going to run around saving the world without parental supervision, yer knocked."

"But--"

The sound of her closing the break on a sawed-off shotgun one-handed cut me off.

"Told you she was scary," Howard muttered.

It was past ten by the time we arrived at what I had called "Checkpoint one." That didn't give us a lot of time, according to Bixby. He'd told us that the ley line would be most power-ful at midnight, so that was most likely going to be when Kel's spell would complete.. I rode in the front of my mom's semi. The rest of the assault team sat in the back area. Howard and Tony were in the red pickup in front of us. They turned left down the road Tony and I had taken with the Hunters. We stayed on the road and waited with the lights off.

"There's something I need to give you," my mom said, piercing the quiet.

"Yeah?" I asked.

She reached down and pulled a package out from under her seat. "This was going to be your present from your father and me," she said. "I don't mind giving it to you a few hours early. Happy Birthday, Scotty."

I carefully took the package. Inside was a cross pendant made with three handmade iron nails. It was the same as the one my father wore.

"Wow, all my mom ever got me for my birthday is... well, I'll let you know if it happens," Urchin said.

Ignoring him, I hugged my mom.

"I love you, sweetie," she said. "Whatever happens, know that I love you."

The radio clicked. It was the signal.

"Love you too, Mom."

The engine roared and Dixie Thunder rolled down the wide, dirt road. I could hear shots ringing out and echoing through the valley. Tony and Howard had already started. When we rounded the bend, I saw that so far, the plan was working. A large group of black-clothed figures was coming out of the building. My mom shifted gears and sped up. There was a dull thudding as she ran through the mob. She shifted again and maneuvered the truck into a slide. As soon as she slowed down, I opened the door and rolled, Two Dogs coming a second later. I sliced through an approaching ninja. Two Dogs pulled out two giant pistols, made longer by the silencers attached to them.

The door closed and the truck sped around for another pass. Two Dogs and I ran to the bungalow building. I was about to block a strike coming from one of the deadheads when it flew backward as Two Dogs shot it. The sound was almost deafening, even with the silencers attached. I kicked down the door as Dixie Thunder came in for a third pass. Two Dogs entered and fired off two shots. I peeked inside. The only person standing was Two Dogs, holding up his twin Desert Eagles. How he fired them without his wrists breaking was beyond me, but I could take a sword to the chest and walk it off, so I didn't judge. I pressed a button on my earpiece. "Room clear," I said into the radio.

The big rig had kicked up so much dust that Howard had stopped firing. The truck swung by one more time and Bixby jumped out. He ran with his satchel hugged in front of him. He hadn't closed the door. A Deadhead tried to jump up but was kicked in the face by Travis as he moved to the front and jumped out. Urchin tossed him his swords and closed the door. Together, we kept the doorway clear while Bixby set up his laptop. Our sniper team trotted up to us as we watched my mother driving in circles trying to run down fleeing figures.

"Well, the good news is that I have the cameras. The bad news is that they know we're here," Bixby said. I moved into the room to join him. "Even worse news." He pointed at one of the camera feeds. There was a man with hair that stuck out at all sides standing in a circular chamber. Purple light was swirling around him and the floor was glowing.

"Alright, That's where we're headed. Guide me--"

"Scott!" Bixby said, and another feed popped up. This showed five men tied down on tables. I recognized them all. I instantly felt like going to them, but it would have to wait.

Then I noticed what he was pointing at. There was a clock counting down. It was at 31:42 and it was going down by the second. It was plugged into a block of white, claylike substance as well as a bright yellow cord that wound around the room and was wrapped several times around each man's neck. "That's C4 and det cord," Bixby said.

"Any more bad news?" I asked ruefully.

"Yeah, it's the room farthest from the central chamber. Unless you grow wheels and an internal combustion engine, you can't do both. Looks like he knew we were coming," he said.

I cursed loudly. I pressed the button on my radio again. "Alright, stage three," I said. I depressed the button. "Two Dogs, you stay here with Genius," I said using Bixby's code name for the mission. "You keep us updated and on the right path," I told Bixby.

It only took a few minutes of running through the labyrinthine halls to completely turn me around. My group reached another intersection. I looked down each corridor with no clue.

"Alpha, hang a right. Three deadheads waiting for you," Bixby's voice in our ears said.

"You have to say 'over' when you finish, over," Keith replied over the radio.

"Sorry… over."

I checked my watch. Only fifteen minutes left until midnight. Tony ran and dove into a roll past the corner. I swung up at the arms of the creature as soon as the blade came swinging down, the arms came off easily. Travis rounded and blocked another sword, stabing forward with his off-hand blade. Tony had recovered and stuck the blue steel knife into the side of the third one. We looked at each other. These tiny fights weren't challenging, but they were taking up time we didn't have. We made our way past a room that was empty, save for some faintly glowing hunks that Travis said was eldrium ore.

There were wires and glass containers scattered throughout the room. I couldn't tell what type of experiments were being done, just that a lot of effort had been put into it. "Bravo, you have a straight shot to the door, but it's at least a thousand feet away, over," Bixby's voice said.

"Genius, this is Bandit. What's our welcome party look like? Over," Bandit asked.

"Just a door."

"Check Roger, *over*." We continued down the hallway at a jog. If Bixby hadn't been leading us along, we would have been lost in this labyrinth forever. As it was, we barely made it with five minutes to spare. We came to a locked door.

"Genius, this is the Kid, how do I get this door open? Over." I said into the radio.

"One second," he replied, then the door whirred. "Over." I looked at the others. They looked at me. I shrugged and kicked open the door.

The large, white domed room was buzzing with power. Kel floated in the center of the circular chamber, kept aloft by sheer force of magical energy. The radio buzzed and clicked.

I walked intentionally toward the mad mage.

"Scott!" Kel said, "Well, Baby Scott. Good. Behold! My ultimate triumph."

"Shut up so I can kill you," I said.

Tony began walking around the circle.

"By the gods, you *are* just like him. Those were the first words *he* said to me!" A thrum of power surged, and the other Alpha team members were knocked back.

I held firm. It was like trying to walk into an incoming tide.

"You need to stop," I said. "For all our sakes."

"Ah, I see, the redemption angle, eh?"

"If you lift the Veil, we will all die."

"*You* will all die. I will be like a god! Besides, the veil is already rising, I'm just helping it out a little." He turned his hand to me. "Look, just let me have this one little thing and then you and I can duke it out in a battle for the ages."

I reached into my pocket. "I'm not trying to save you, I'm not even trying to fight you," I said as I pulled out a ball-shaped object. "I'm just giving my friend time to sneak up on you." He turned in mid-air and caught Tony with an invisible hand. At the same time, I rolled the grenade to the center of the circle and Travis launched himself up. He was caught by an invisible force as well, but he opened his mouth and a stream of white-hot flame shot out.

"Woah!" Kel yelled. He dropped both boys, who jumped away. Kel spent a few seconds containing the fire into a ball. "Now *I* have the fire. Prepare to…" He looked down at the grenade rolling in a circle a foot below him. "Clever," he said, and it exploded. The fire disappeared as he focused on protecting himself from the blast.

I caught a piece of shrapnel in my leg, but I could still move.

Kel tumbled fifteen feet in the air before stopping. "Damn," he said as his magical energy began to dissipate. "Do you know how long that took to set up?"

"Ask me again when I start giving a crap," I said as I twirled my sword.

"What are you going to do from down there?" he asked. But suddenly, giant gold wings exploded from Travis' back. "You have a dragon? I want one!"

Travis jumped with a mighty flap of his wings. He lifted off the ground and chased Kel around the ceiling. Kel maneuvered more easily.

"Wait! I remember you. You're that dragon we found in Norway! I was wondering where he put you." He stopped running for a second when he realized Tony had pulled out a brick of C4 with a timer on it. He began to cast a spell, but narrowly missed being impaled by one of Travis' swords.

"You're fighting *me*!" Travis roared.

"Quite right. Tsujigiri! Here now." The pale deadhead with a personality appeared behind Tony. He readied to strike.

"How many times am I going to have to kill this guy?" I asked, and bodied Tony out of the way. I caught a sword slice to the back that was mostly stopped by the plate in my armored vest.

"That's my line, Baby Slayer," he said.

I turned to face him, sword at the ready. "What *are* you?" I asked as a plume of fire burst overhead.

Travis flipped around and tried to keep with the mage, who wasn't constrained by physics. He didn't need to catch Kel, just keep him busy long enough for Tony.

Tsujigiri smiled evilly. "Come find out."

I thrust from my ox guard and spun around with a wrath cut as he vanished. He caught my blade and smiled. "I see my tricks aren't going to work with you anymore. Fine, sword against sword."

I shifted, and the swords both moved to one side. Mine was on the inside. I plunged my point and he spun away, swinging. I blocked his swipe and swung around for an overhead strike. He parried and spun his sword around to counter with a lunge. Bringing my sword around, I deflected his blade up, so I could let go of my hilt with my left hand, and held his thrusting sword arm. My sword dropped and I pivoted, bringing it up and around behind my back and cutting into his head with the false edge. His eyes went wide as I reversed momentum, and without letting go of his arm, brought the sword back around, cutting through his neck. I had no time to celebrate.

"Oh, no, you don't!" Kel shouted from the ceiling. He summoned a violent, green ball into his hand and dove at Tony, who was setting the explosive up.

Travis was behind him. I ran as fast as I could. With a great leap, I spun to save my best friend. Kel slammed into me, but the spell he hit me with fizzled. His eyes went wide as my sword entered his gut.

We tumbled, and he stood slowly. "Not another one," he said in frustration. He stumbled back away from me, clutching his wound. "You will pay for your insolence. You have insulted my pride, my magic, and my goat! I will--hold on." His watch was beeping. "I don't want to miss this part." He listened for something that never came. He frowned.

Travis landed and twirled his blades.

"Well, congratulations, Little Scott. It seems like you have learned a lesson Big Scott never could, how to have more than two friends." He stood up as Tony, Travis, and I approached him. "Que sera." He turned on the spot and a circle appeared below him. He waved and then fell into it. The circle closed immediately behind him. The chamber was quiet. We'd saved the world, if only temporarily. We smiled at each other, surprised we were still alive.

CHAPTER 21

<u>All Saints' Day</u>

"You boys need to answer your damn radio," Howard Keith said between deep breaths. He was bent over, his rifle slung behind him. Tony and Travis stopped talking to each other. Less than a minute had passed, and we were still trying to figure out the best places to place the C4. Though most of the glow had left the symbols, there was still some residual light. Travis had reabsorbed his draconic wings into his back.

"I think the radios died when we got hit by waves of pure magical energy," I said. "And you need to do more cardio. Did you get to them in time?"

"Yeah, but there's something you need to know," he panted. My smirk faded. No good news ever followed those words. "You need to get there like now." He unplugged his headset from his radio and handed the black box to me. "I'll take care of things here." He surveyed the damage. "What the hell happened to your back?" he said, turning to Travis, whose shirt now only consisted of a front, arms, and various scraps.

I paid no attention to their conversation. A lead ball was forming in my stomach. I sprinted down the hallways as quickly as I could, Bixby leading me through the labyrinth, and Tony running right behind me. When I got to the open room, Urchin was helping Tony Two to his feet. My mother was standing next to the table my dad was on. I slowed down to a stop just on the other side of the threshold. Maybe I thought that if I didn't walk through the door, my worst fear of what waited for me in the room wouldn't come true. Tony nudged me from behind. I stepped in and approached the table. My dad looked to be in bad shape. He was severely emaciated. He was lying half-naked on the table, eyes bright white. A short, red beard had grown on his face. He raised his hand to me, and I took it.

"Dad…" I started to say.

"Shh, no time for that," he croaked. "Dixie already told me everything. And I'm proud of you." He tried to smile, but winced in pain.

"We're going to get you out of here, Dad. We stopped Kel," I said, trying to keep the dam in my eyes from bursting.

"Good man," he said. "I knew you would."

"Someone help me carry him," I said, but no one moved. "What's wrong with you all? Tony, help me." He took a halting step toward us.

"No," my mother said. "We can't." Her eyes were already wet.

"What?"

"The only thing keeping him alive is the gris-gris," Tony One said sadly. "Kel wanted to torture him the most."

"He about died so many times, Kel… tied his life to this place," Tony Two said. "If we move him, he'll die."

"Who told you that? Kel?"

"It's all written down here," Bixby said over the radio. "These notes are meticulous. I'm looking for a flaw, but… Over."

I looked around. "Then we'll keep this place intact. Tell Keith not to blow the chamber."

"I can't." Bixby said quietly "I can't," he repeated more loudly. "Keith gave you his radio. They've already placed the charges."

"We can go back and undo them." I slammed my fist into the table. "If he knew you were like this, why did he still set the bombs?"

"I told him to," my dad said.

"What? Why?"

"Had to be done. We have to stop the rising of the Veil."

"Dad, there has to be a way to--"

"No, it's time," he grunted.

"We can save you. Dad, I *need* you." I felt like a small child again.

"Glad to hear it," he replied. "Too bad it's bull. You're ready to take up the mantle. I've run my race." He smiled and looked to the ceiling. A shudder went through his body, and my mother let out a sob. He turned to her. "Dix, I never told you I loved you enough."

"You told me once. You would have let me know if it changed," she said with a bitter smile. Her voice cracked.

"Still. You were so much to me. I'm going to tell you again. I've loved you since Vegas, and that *won't* change." He held her hand. "Tonys," he said. "You two…" He searched for the words.

"Yeah," Tony Two said after clearing his throat. "You, too."

Tony One walked to him and kissed him on the forehead. "When you get there, you say 'hey' to Nana, hear?" the giant man said through his tears.

My dad tilted his head in acknowledgment. "Tony Three," my dad beckoned.

Tony made his way up. He was crying, too. "I'm here, Uncle Scott," he said.

"There's a lot of things… I wish I had the time to tell you. But… know that I'm proud of you. When you see Frank, tell him I was right." He looked at me finally. "Scott. There's even more I need to say to you." He winced again.

"Not to spoil the moment, but Bandit and Drake just armed the bomb. You have thirty minutes," Bixby said over the radio.

"It's gonna take us at least twenty to get out of here," Urchin said seriously.

I looked at him. He didn't have a quip for maybe the first time since I met him. "Yeah," I coughed, trying to get rid of whatever was growing on my adam's apple. "Go on. I'll catch up in a second."

As they left, Alex and Cisco paid their respects as well. Then we were alone.

"Son," he said softly. "It's up to you now."

I shook my head. "There has to be a way, I could carry you out, or--"

"Stop it, Scott. Let me be. I know you don't think you're ready, but you gotta be."

I bowed my head. It was all too hard. It was all wrong. We'd won. It was time for the happy ending. "You have my sword?" he asked.

"It's right here," I said, handing it to him. He seemed to take a modicum of comfort at the feel of it in his hand.

"This is Spirit. This is the sword of a saint. There's not enough time to explain now. You'll find out soon enough." His body seized again. "Scott. I've done a lot of things in my life. It might seem like I cast too big a shadow. But you will more than make up for it. You are the one thing I take pride in. I love you, son." My eyes met his. There was no holding back the tears. He opened my hand and placed the hilt in it. "It's yours now."

"I love you, Dad," I said.

He brushed my cheek and smiled. "I know. I love you too, son. Now go. No point in both of us biting it." He held my hand as I backed away until we could no longer reach each other. I wondered if I had the strength to turn away. There he was. The strongest and toughest man I ever knew, lying shirtless on a table. There was no way I could stay until the end. He would die alone.

Suddenly, the sadness was washed away with anger. I set my jaw and looked dead ahead. He smiled again. I turned and left. They were the heaviest steps I'd ever had to take. I felt like I was the one who needed to be carried out. I walked out to find the small crowd gathered by the semi. I went to my mother. Words seemed pointless. We could only hold each other. There was a loud boom, and a dust cloud flew from the mine entrance. A second explosion, this one made of purple and green light knocked us all from our feet. The sky was lit by an aurora. Gradually, over the course of a few minutes, the light dimmed. I closed my eyes. It was over.

*　　*　　*

I sat, staring at the blank television as my mother spoke to someone on the phone. I tried to feel anything but emptiness, but the only thing strong enough was the bubbling rage seething just below the surface. There was a knock on the door. I stood to answer, if only to give my body something to do. I opened the door to find Riley in a black dress. I couldn't think of anything to say. She pulled me into an embrace. I felt something akin to comfort. I returned the hug. Suddenly, the ice around my heart began to melt. I thought I could maintain a somber exterior, but when I tried to release the hug, she kept holding me. "I am so sorry."

That was all she had to say before the dam burst. I cried and held her until her shoulder was soaked. With a great effort, I pulled myself away and wiped my eyes. "Sorry," I said.

"Sorry? For crying? Scott, let me tell you something. You can be tough and rough to the rest of the world, they might judge you, but I will never for a moment think of you as weak because you have emotions. If you need to sail through a storm, at least let me be your safe harbor," she said fiercely.

I gave a weak smile. "Did you practice that?" I asked.

"A little." She looked past me.

I turned to see my mother standing with her arms crossed. She was staring down Riley.

"You got balls, girl," she said. "The shit your family pulled. You willing to risk my wrath just to comfort my son for a minute?"

Riley looked back at her. "Yes," she said simply.

My mother gave her an appraising look, then she nodded and returned to the table to look at coffins.

"Hey, Kid." I looked back to see the Hunters. "We came by to pay our respects before skipping town." Cisco had his hands in his pockets. Alex continued. "He was a hell of a man. He's gonna be missed, even by us."

I put my arm around Riley and shook his hand. "Look me up when you want to go hunting again."

"Sure thing, Kid," Cisco said.

I closed the door when they walked away.

Riley stayed with me for a few hours, which helped keep dark thoughts from my mind. Tony, Travis, Bixby, even Urchin came by to show support. When the last of them left, it was dark. Despite all the love and support, it was by far my hardest birthday.

The doorbell rang. This time it was my Uncles and Frank. Tony Two still wore the bandages he'd received at the hospital and Tony One still had his arm in a sling. It seemed clear to me that they hadn't bothered to ask to be discharged.

Doctor Burrows cleared his throat. "Scott, Johanna, I only have a moment, but may I say..." He took off his hat and turned it in his hands. "This is much harder the second time." He took a long breath and looked me in the eyes. "We've confirmed that the coalesced energy is dissipating. Your plan worked. I hope one day, you can forgive me for putting it all on your shoulders. For now..." He held out his hand, and I shook it. "Thank you." He replaced his hat and, with a nod to my uncles, walked away.

The Tonys stepped in and Tony Two shut the door. The large box in his hands was shaking. He took a long, raspy breath. "Look, I'm not good at sentimental crap, and you know it. They cleared out the mine and found some of Scott's... personal items." He handed me the box.

I set it down and opened it. There was a folded mass of red leather, and a pair of mirrored wraparound sunglasses. I looked up, slightly puzzled. "His shades and coat?"

He nodded. "Scott would..." He cleared is throat. "Uh, he'd want them to go to you. I swiped them from the pile they were making."

I pulled the sunglasses out and placed them on the table carefully. Then, I pulled out the oxblood red leather duster. As I held it up, my eyes began to burn.

"Go on then, bon ami," Tony One said. "Try it on."

I looked up at him, then back at the coat. Part of me didn't want to wear it. Instead, I should hang it in the hall as part of a monument to a great man. But I couldn't resist the urge to have one last connection to him. I swung it around and slipped my arms in. The leather fell heavily on my shoulders.

"How's it feel?"

"Heavy. And it's a little big on me," I admitted.

"Don't worry, kid," Tony Two said with a confident smile. "You'll grow into it."

THE

END

www.ingramcontent.com/pod-product-compliance
Lightning Source LLC
Chambersburg PA
CBHW051450050726
47593CB00005B/2014